D0881299

AN
EVIL
HEART

Center Point
Large Print

Also by Linda Castillo and available from
Center Point Large Print:

Shamed
Outsider
Fallen
The Hidden One

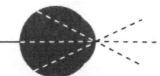

**This Large Print Book carries the
Seal of Approval of N.A.V.H.**

AN EVIL HEART

A KATE BURKHOLDER NOVEL

Linda Castillo

CENTER POINT LARGE PRINT
THORNDIKE, MAINE

AN
EVIL
HEART

This book is dedicated to my readers.
Thank you for all of your support over the years
and over the course of fourteen books.
Thank you for your emails and letters.
Thank you for your comments on social media.
Thank you for coming to my events (and
listening to my sometimes not-so-fascinating
presentations). Most importantly, thank you
for reminding me what's really important.
I very much appreciate each and every one of you.

Let the wickedness of the wicked
come to an end.

—HOLY BIBLE, PSALM 7:9

PROLOGUE

The sky above the treetops blazed in hues of fluorescent orange and Easter-egg pink when Aden Karn backed his bicycle from the shed. Dropping his lunch box in the handlebar basket, he wheeled it to the road, threw his leg over the seat, and set off at a brisk pace. The ride to the pickup point where he met his English coworkers usually took about twenty minutes. For once he was early and he was glad for it. Autumn had settled over this part of Ohio in gentle increments this year, bringing a burst of color to the maples and walnut trees that grew alongside the road. Another week and the countryside would be aflame. According to his *mamm*, they were God's colors. This morning, he had to agree.

Sweat dampened his shirt as he flew past the old bank barn at the curve, tires humming against the asphalt. His English coworkers gave him flak for riding the bike, but it was a good-natured kind of ribbing; Aden didn't mind. It wasn't like he could leave a buggy horse tied all day while he worked. Sure, he'd gotten wet a time or two, a problem easily solved by the slicker tucked away in his lunch box. Some of the Amish were using scooters now in Holmes County, but Aden wasn't interested. He liked the quiet of the bike, the physical labor, the speed and freedom of it. Somehow, he felt closer to the earth—closer to God—when he was astride the bike, drinking in the bounty He had bestowed on His children.

Aden took his time as he pedaled along the township road. He passed by the mossy pond in Mr. Yount's pasture where the ducks skimmed across the water's surface, dipping their heads to nibble on pondweed, and flapping their wings. As he passed over the bridge, he came upon the sheep that grazed the orchard grass that grew thick in the low area. He'd watched the lambs grow over the summer. Farther, he whisked past the field of "cow corn" Mr. Dunlop had left to dry. He stood on the pedals and pumped hard as he climbed the hill at County Line Road. He cruised the downhill side a little too fast, enjoying the breeze, and he leaned in as he made the turn onto Hansbarger Road.

He was so embroiled in his thoughts he didn't notice the figure in the ditch until he'd sped past. Having caught a glimpse out of the corner of his eye, Aden braked hard, surprised, wondering if there was a problem. He stuck out his foot and stopped so abruptly the back tire skidded sideways.

Both feet on the ground, he turned and looked over his shoulder. Oddly, there was no vehicle in sight. Just the figure standing in the ditch, looking at him.

"Is everything all right?" he called out.

Only then did he notice the weapon. At first, he thought it was a rifle, but that was strange; it wasn't deer season. Then he noticed the shape— the spread of the limbs, the cam on the left, the cocking stirrup in front—and he realized it was a crossbow. He watched uneasily as the weapon came up. An instant of disbelief as the figure's head tilted, eye lowered to the sight.

He felt a pang of alarm and released the handlebars, raising his hands. "Hey! What are you—"

Thwank!

An invisible fist punched the air from his lungs. A shock of pain in his chest. A burning streak shot down his back. His knees buckled. The bike went sideways, the handlebars twisting, and clattered to the asphalt. Aden glanced down in disbelief as he caught sight of the bolt sticking out. Then his shoulder hit the ground. His temple banged against the asphalt. Around him, the world went silent. He lay still, blinking and confused, the roadway warm against his cheek, pain thumping from chest to pelvis.

He moved his leg and rolled onto his back, trying to make sense of what happened. The movement brought a riot of pain to his spine. Darkness crowded his vision. Groaning, he looked down at the bolt, realized it had gone clean through and was sticking out the back.

Dear God in heaven . . .

His bladder let go. He felt the warm spread of urine on his thigh, soaking his trousers. Too much pain to care. Too much fear. The knowledge that he was badly injured hit home. Panic swept over him. He opened his mouth, tried to suck in a breath. A horrible sound poured out of him.

The crunch of shoes against gravel drew his attention. He looked up, tried to speak. He raised his hand, fingers spread. "Help."

Dead eyes stared down at him, cold as iron, dark with intent. Not seeing. Gloved hands reached down. Face set. An impersonal task, unpleasant but necessary. Both hands gripped his shoulder.

He whimpered. "Don't."

An electric current of pain tore through him as the bolt was pushed deeper. Another, as he was rolled onto his belly. The groan that followed came out as a gurgle. Breaths tearing in and out, each one an agony.

Another explosion of pain as the bolt was yanked from his body. His arms and legs convulsed. Once. Twice. Darkness encroached, stealing the light. Night pressing down. Aden felt the hands on his shoulder again. Fingers digging into his arm as he was rolled onto his back.

He lay there, helpless and terrified, listening to his own ragged breaths, pain pulsing with every beat of his heart. Vaguely, he was aware of the crossbow being lowered to the ground. The toe of a boot jammed into the stirrup. The squeak of the bowstring as it was drawn tight. The click of the string engaging with the nock.

Please don't . . .

The crossbow was lowered. Emotionless eyes burrowed into his. "I can't abide you doing what you're doing," the shooter told him.

He knew what came next and the horror of it was too much to process. Terror infused his every muscle. He tried to move, to run or crawl away, felt his leg shift and flop, useless. He raised his hands, grabbed the shooter's ankle, his fingers clasping the fabric.

"Don't," he pleaded.

The head of the bolt was placed against his mouth with excruciating gentleness. The sharp tip cut his lip as it was worked between his teeth. Steel clicking against the enamel. The salty tang of blood. The bolt invaded his mouth, depressed his tongue, and went deep. He gagged. Once. Twice. Horror and disbelief overtook him.

He tried to speak and retched.

He felt a boot on his shoulder, pressing him down, trapping him. The shooter's finger on the trigger. The bolt cutting the back of his throat. His mouth filled with blood. He coughed and gagged, his throat spasming. His hand yanked at the fabric of the trousers, twisted.

Please.

Thwank!

He looked up at the sky, but he could no longer see the sun.

CHAPTER 1

My *mamm* had a saying about life's small discomforts.

Vann es shmatza, hayva da shmatz un bayda es dutt naett letsht zu lang. If it hurts, embrace the pain and pray it doesn't last too long. This morning, the memory of my *mamm* dances in the forefront of my mind, and for the first time in a long time, I miss her.

I'm in my sister's upstairs bedroom, standing on an old wooden alteration platform. My police uniform is draped across the foot of the bed, my boots on the floor next to it. My utility belt and service revolver look obscenely out of place against the gray-and-white wedding-ring quilt.

"Katie, my goodness, you're fidgeting again," Sarah tells me. "Hold still so I can finish pinning without sticking you."

"Sorry," I mutter.

I can't recall the last time I wore a dress. This particular dress has a history. My sister wore it eleven years ago for her wedding. Our *mamm* wore it, too. Our grandmother made it. And so when my sister asked me to come over to look at it with my own wedding in mind, I had no qualms about trying it on. Now that I'm here, I realize it wasn't a very good idea.

I haven't been Amish for eighteen years. To wear a plain dress with the traditional *halsduch*, its closures fastened with straight pins instead of buttons or snaps, feels hypocritical. As if I'm trying to be something I'm not in order to please a community that will not be pleased.

Of course, my sister doesn't see it that way. She's a traditionalist, a peacekeeper, and an optimist rolled into one. Worse, she knows her way around a needle and thread and has no doubt she can make this dress work despite my reluctance and somehow please everyone in the process.

"This dress is a piece of our family history, Katie," she tells me. "Mamm would have loved for you to wear it, even if you're not Amish."

"At this point in my life, I think she would have been happy just to get me married off."

Her mouth twitches. "That, too."

I look down at the front of the dress, smooth my hands over the slightly wrinkled fabric, and I try not to sigh. It's sky blue in color with a skirt that's a tad too full and falls to midcalf. "Do you think it's a little too long?" I ask.

"I can shorten the hem," she says. "That's an easy fix."

"Bodice isn't quite right."

Always the diplomat, Sarah slides a straight pin between her lips, lifts the hem, and pins. "I'll take in the waist a bit, too. Bring the shoulders out."

The real issue, of course, has nothing to do with

the hem or bodice. For twenty minutes, we've been skirting the elephant in the room. Sarah is too kind to broach the subject.

"It's okay if you don't like the dress," she murmurs. "I can make another one if you like. Or you can just buy one."

"It's not the dress . . . exactly," I tell her.

Cocking her head, she meets my gaze. "What then?"

Drawing a breath, I take the plunge. "The problem is the dress is Amish. I'm not. There's no getting around that."

My sister lowers her hands, looks at me over the top of her reading glasses, and sighs. She's looked at me that way a hundred times in the years since I returned to Painters Mill. Times when I've exasperated or disappointed her, both of which happen too often.

"You're Anabaptist. That matters." She gives a decisive nod, turns her attention back to the dress. "We can do away with the *halsduch*."

She's referring to the triangularly shaped "cape" or "breast cloth" that goes over the head, the point side at the back, the front gathered and secured with pins. My wearing one of the most symbolic of female Amish garments would be perceived as insincere.

"That'll help." Trying to be diplomatic, I look down at the front of the dress. "Maybe add a sash or belt?"

"Hmmm." She makes a noncommittal sound, then plucks a pin from her mouth and puts it to use. "I've seen rosettes on belts, for the English wedding dresses. Mennonite, too."

For the first time since I arrived, I feel a quiver of enthusiasm in my chest. Like the dress might just work after all. "I like the idea of a rosette belt."

She nods, not quite smiling, but I can tell she's warming to the idea. "Have you decided about a head covering?" she asks.

"I thought I might go with a simple veil," I tell her.

She makes eye contact with me and raises her brows. Amish women do not wear a veil. Just a head covering or *kapp*.

"Like the Mennonites," I clarify, which means the veil will be small and round, just ten or twelve inches wide, made of lace, and worn at the back of my head.

"I think that's a good compromise," she says after a moment. "Not Amish, but . . ."

"Anabaptist," I finish.

We grin at each other, a rare moment of sisterly solidarity, and something warm shifts just behind my ribs. Progress, I think.

Sarah and I were close as kids. We worked and played together; we weathered the storms of growing up. She was there for me when I was fourteen and an act of violence altered the course of my life. The summer when a neighbor boy caught me alone in the house and turned everyone's lives upside down. Our relationship wasn't the same after that. Not because of her, but because of me. Because of what happened—and what I did about it. We grew apart, and the chasm between us only widened when I left the fold four years later. I ran as far away from my family and my Amish roots as I could—to Columbus and an unlikely career in law enforcement. Despite my best efforts to sabotage everything I'd once held dear, I couldn't eradicate those ties—or continue to deny my love for my family. Some twelve years later, when my *mamm* passed away, I returned to Painters Mill, not as the rebellious and awkward Amish girl I'd been, but as a grown woman who was offered the position of police chief. I reached out to both of my siblings, and after an uncertain start—and a few bumps along the way—we set to work rekindling our relationships.

We're still a work in progress, but we've come a long way. We've gotten reacquainted, shared a few laughs, a lot of disagreements, and a few tears. This morning's fitting is a big step in a different direction and a new closeness that's not quite comfortable, but hopeful and good.

Sarah slides a straight pin into the fabric gathered at my waist. "If it's any consolation, Katie, I like your man. William likes him, too," she says, referring to her husband. "That's no small thing."

"His name's Tomasetti, by the way." I smile at her. "And I like him, too."

A giggle escapes her and she shakes her head.

The chirp of my cell phone interrupts. Sarah raises a finger. "Wait. One more." She stabs the final pin into the fabric at the hem. "Got it. Go."

I smooth the dress, then step down off the platform and reach for the phone, answering with "Burkholder."

"Chief." It's Lois, my first-shift dispatcher. "I just took a call from a motorist out on Hansbarger Road. Says there's a DB in the middle of the road." DB is copspeak for "dead body"; we use it in case someone is listening to their police scanner.

"Who's the RP?" I ask, using the term for "reporting party."

"Julie Falknor. Local. I got her on the other line. Chief, she's still at the scene and screaming her head off. Says there's a lot of blood and she has her kids with her."

Lois has been with the department since before I became chief. She's experienced and cool under fire. This morning, she's speaking a little too fast, her words running together.

"Get an ambulance out there." I ease the dress off my shoulders, let it drop to the floor, yank my uniform shirt off the bed. "Who's on duty?"

"Glock's en route," she tells me, referring to Rupert "Glock" Maddox. He's one of my most experienced officers. If anyone can keep the situation in hand, it's him.

"Get County out there, too." Hansbarger Road is a quiet stretch a couple of miles outside of Painters Mill proper; it's my patrol beat. Even so, depending on the situation and manpower, my jurisdiction sometimes overlaps the sheriff's department's.

"Tell the RP to stay put," I tell her. "I'm on my way."

I grab my trousers off the bed, step into them, reach for my equipment belt, buckle it. I face my sister as I snatch up my boots. "I'm going to have to take a rain check on coffee."

"Of course." She cocks her head. "Something's wrong?"

"Traffic accident, probably." I don't know if that's the case, but since I have no idea what I'll be walking into, I keep it vague. "Thanks for putting up with all my squirming."

"You're entitled." She grins. "I bet your man is sweating, too."

"Literally and figuratively." Smiling, I lean into her for a quick hug, grab my service weapon off the bed, and head for the door.

Hansbarger Road is a lesser-used back road that runs between a pasture and a cornfield before meandering north toward Millersburg. I make the turn, the Explorer's tires bumping over rippled asphalt and potholes, loose gravel pinging against the undercarriage. Ahead, I see the flashing lights of Glock's cruiser. A silver SUV is parked at a haphazard angle, nose down in the shallow road-side ditch with the driver's-side door standing open. The ambulance isn't yet on scene. There's no sign of the sheriff's department.

Flipping on my overheads, I park behind Glock's vehicle and hit my shoulder mike as I get out. "Ten-twenty-three," I say, letting Dispatch know I've arrived on scene.

I notice several things at once as I approach. Glock is standing between the SUV and his cruiser, making a notation in his notebook. There's a person lying on the ground a few feet away from him—likely the victim. A bicycle with the handlebars twisted lies on its side a couple of yards away. A woman I don't recognize is standing in the grass off the shoulder, her hands on her knees. Through the window of the SUV, I see the silhouettes of children in the back seat.

"What happened?" I ask Glock as I stride toward him.

He motions toward the victim. "He's DOA." He jabs a thumb at the woman. "She says she found him like that. Maybe a hit-skip. Not sure."

Something in his voice gives me pause. Glock

may be a small-town cop, but he possesses the sagacity of a veteran homicide detective.

"You check the victim?" I ask.

"Just enough to know he's gone."

I make eye contact with him and nod, keep moving, my eyes on the victim. It's an adult male, lying supine, his head twisted to one side. The victim's mouth is open. A copious amount of blood is puddled on the asphalt beneath it. *Internal injuries,* I think. He's wearing dark trousers with suspenders. More blood on the front of a blue work shirt. The brim of a summer straw hat sticks out from beneath him. Amish, I realize.

"She see anything?" I ask, referring to the woman.

"No."

I reach the victim. Something unpleasant unfurls in my gut when I get my first up-close look. The face is suffused with the telltale white-blue hue of death. One eye open and unseeing. Not yet cloudy. The other eye is half closed. Tongue is blood-covered and protruding.

For the span of several seconds, I stand there, taking in details, trying to figure out what might've happened. An old-fashioned metal lunch box lies on the ground twenty feet away, open, a sandwich wrapped in wax paper next to it. From all appearances, it looks as if he was struck by a vehicle. Evidently, the driver fled the scene without rendering aid or calling police.

I force my gaze back to the victim. The platter-size pool of blood near the mouth. The bloodstain on the front of his shirt isn't quite high enough to be from a bloody nose or mouth. Something not quite right.

I look at Glock. "Is there some kind of injury on the abdomen?"

He moves closer, his brows furrowing. "Hole in the fabric there," he says in a low voice.

The hairs at my nape prickle, and I find my eyes scanning the woods a hundred yards away. Glock is a former marine with two tours in Afghanistan under his belt. Both of us are EMTs. Judging from the look on his face, he has the same prickly feeling as me.

I motion with my eyes to the SUV driver. She's still bent at the hip, a spill of vomit on the gravel in front of her. I've seen her around town. Grocery or coffee shop or gas station.

I look at Glock. "You talk to her?"

"Just preliminaries. Name's Julie Falknor. Says she was taking her kids to school. Running late. Victim was already on the ground. Says she almost ran over him. She's pretty shaken up, so I didn't get much out of her."

It's never wise to make assumptions when you're a cop, especially when you've just arrived at a potential crime scene in which a dozen scenarios could have played out. Situations aren't always as they appear. Freak accidents happen more often than we think.

I hit my shoulder mike and hail Dispatch. "Ten-seven-nine," I say, requesting the coroner.

I scan the field, the woods, and I feel that creeping sensation on the back of my neck. I look at Glock. "That hole in the fabric," I say. "Gunshot wound?"

"I was thinking the same thing," he says. "Sure doesn't look like the kind of injury caused by being struck by a vehicle."

The last thing I want to do is risk contaminating evidence. That said, if there's been a shooting or if there's an active shooter at large, I can't wait for the coroner or crime scene unit to arrive.

"Let's check him." I dig into a compartment on my utility belt and tug out latex gloves. Glock does the same.

"Stay cognizant of evidence." I don't have to tell him that, but I do, anyway.

Side by side, we walk to the victim. Despite the breeze, I smell the blood. The other stenches of death add a uniquely unpleasant pall. The victim is lying on his back, head twisted severely. Right leg slung out and bent at the knee. Both arms above his head.

I kneel, feel that familiar rise of revulsion that comes with the sight of violent death. This man was young, late teens or early twenties. I see the red-black blood pooled in his mouth and, again, I wonder about internal injuries.

"Broken front tooth." Squinting, Glock motions. "Split lip."

"You think this was the result of some kind of altercation?" I ask.

"Mouth injuries could have happened in the fall off the bike," he says. "Not so sure about the hole in the shirt."

The victim doesn't have a beard, which tells me he was unmarried. In the back of my mind, I think of his family, his parents, and the knot in my stomach tightens a little more.

With a gloved hand, I tug the victim's shirt out of the waistband of his trousers and pull it up so the abdomen is visible. I see white flesh interspersed with dark hair coated with a thin layer of blood where the fabric had lain against the skin. An oddly shaped wound a few inches above the navel snags my attention.

"Wound there," I hear myself say. "Strange shape."

"Knife?" Glock wonders aloud.

"Maybe." But even that's a stretch. The only thing I know for certain at this point is that this is no simple hit-and-run. I let go of the shirt, let it fall back into place.

One of the most pressing tasks for law enforcement in the aftermath of any fatal accident or crime is the identification of the victim so next of kin can be notified. Normally, I'd wait for the coroner, but since I'm already here, I make the decision to check now.

"Let's check for ID." Shifting position, I reach into the front pocket of his trousers. I find a folding pocketknife. A few coins. I check the other front pocket, find a handkerchief.

I make eye contact with Glock. "Help me roll him so I can check the back pockets."

"Yep."

As gently as possible, we roll the victim just enough for me to dig into the back pocket of his trousers. I tug out a beat-up leather wallet, spot the ID behind the plastic window. It's a non-photo ID issued by the Ohio Bureau of Motor Vehicles. This type of ID is used by many Amish who have a religious objection to having their photo taken.

"Aden Karn." I say the name slowly, the familiarity of it reverberating in my head. "Twenty-one years old."

"Damn. He's young." Glock shakes his head, slants me a look. "You know him? The family?"

"I know his parents." I get to my feet, unexpectedly shaken, hoping it doesn't show. "Not well, but I worked for them when I was a teenager."

"This kid live at home?" he asks.

I look down at the ID and shake my head. "The Karns live in town a few blocks from their shop.

According to his ID, this young man lived a couple of miles from here."

I take a moment to collect myself, scan the field, the flock of crows cawing in the trees. I feel Glock's eyes on me. We've worked together nearly every day since I became chief. We're not friends in the conventional sense, but we're close in a way that goes deeper than friendship. We share a kinship, the tie of a brotherhood to which both of us are bound. We don't talk about it, but it's there nonetheless, and in this moment I'm thankful because his very presence has lessened some of the burden I feel pressing down on my shoulders.

Cautiously, we back away from the victim, doing our best to retrace our steps.

"Call County and get some deputies out here," I tell him as I snap off the gloves. "We're going to need to tape off the area. Get the road blocked."

"You got it."

Sirens wail in the distance. I glance at the SUV, see the children moving around inside. They look young. Growing restless, probably. The body is visible to them, but I can't cover it without the risk of contaminating the scene.

"I'm going to talk to the witness," I tell him.

Touching the brim of his hat, Glock starts toward his cruiser.

I approach the woman. She's straightened to her full height, but her face is the color of paste.

"Ma'am?" I say to her. "You all right?"

"Oh my God," she says in a quavering voice. "Sorry I'm such a basket case. That poor guy. Is he dead?"

"I'm afraid so," I tell her.

I guess her to be in her mid-thirties. Judging by the bulge of her belly, she's pregnant. Brown hair pulled into a ponytail. No makeup. She's wearing a pink sweatshirt, yoga pants, and flip-flops.

"Can you tell me what happened?" I ask.

Her eyes flick to the dead man, then back to me. A fresh round of tears spill over her lashes. "I was taking the kids to school, like always. Been taking this route because it's so pretty. Kids like the ducks in the pond over there. Named all of them." She uses the tissue in her hand to wipe tears from her cheeks. "We're driving along and my seven-year-old spots him. She's like: 'Look, Mommy, that man had a bike wreck!'

"For God's sake, I almost ran over him." A breath shudders out of her. "I stopped just in time, pulled over, and . . . there he was. All that blood."

She's getting herself worked up, so I press forward. "Did you see anyone else in the area? Any other vehicles? Or buggies?"

"No." She shakes her head. "There's hardly ever anyone on this road. That's why I take it. No traffic."

I look past her to see the ambulance pull up

behind my Explorer along with a cruiser from the Holmes County Sheriff's Department. I spend another ten minutes with her, asking the same questions in different ways, giving her a chance to tell me more, but her account remains the same and she's unable to give any new details.

I pluck a card from a compartment on my belt, add my personal cell phone number to the back, and hand it to her. "If you remember anything else, even if it doesn't seem important, give me a call."

"I will," she assures me.

Two paramedics and a sheriff's deputy are standing a couple of yards from the body when I approach. I've met the deputy several times over the years. He's a rookie with a cocky personality, but generally a pretty solid cop. We volunteered for a fundraiser last summer to raise money for the local library, spent an afternoon flipping bratwursts and burgers for kids.

"Chief Burkholder."

"Hi, Matt." We exchange a handshake. Behind me, I'm aware of the woman pulling away and Glock approaching.

"That guy's deader than a doornail," the deputy says. "What the hell happened? Hit-skip? Where'd all that blood come from?"

"Not confirmed, but I think he may have been shot," I tell him. "Or stabbed."

"Holy shit." He sends a look in Glock's direction, as if my assessment isn't quite trustworthy.

Glock stares back at him, his expression dead-pan.

I address the deputy. "Would you mind blocking off the intersections for me? No one comes in or out except the coroner and law enforcement."

"Uh . . . sure." Looking put out that he's been relegated to a rookie task, he strides toward his cruiser.

Glock hands me a nicely-done smile.

"There aren't many houses out this way, but I think we need to canvass. Give Pickles a call to help you," I say, referring to my only part-time officer, Roland "Pickles" Shumaker. "Hit every farm. Stop all vehicles. Pedestrians. Anyone working out in the field. See if they heard or saw anything. Get names and contact info."

"I'm on it." Glock starts for his cruiser.

I pull out my cell phone and, without getting too close to the victim, snap a dozen photos of the body from different angles. I zoom in to get a close-up of the bloodstain on the front of the shirt, especially the hole in the fabric, and I work my way around the body. I notice a few details I missed earlier. Leather work gloves peek out from the back pocket of typical Amish trousers, telling me he may have been on his way to work. A straw hat is crumpled beneath him, as if he fell on top of it.

As I take in the particulars of the scene, questions begin to boil. Was this random? Or was he targeted? Was he riding his bike to work and someone drove by and shot him? Did a vehicle stop and an altercation ensued? Or was this some kind of freak accident? The only thing I know for certain at this point is that the person responsible is a danger to the community and it's my job to find him before he hurts anyone else.

CHAPTER 2

While waiting for the coroner to arrive, I document every aspect of the victim and scene. I take photos of everything within a fifty-foot radius: the bicycle, the lunch box, the hat, the tire imprints in the gravel shoulder, even the beer bottle in the ditch, the scrap of paper in the grass. Relief settles over me when I see the coroner's Escalade roll up to the caution tape.

I've known Doc Coblentz since I became chief. He's a Painters Mill icon of sorts, one of five doctors in town with an upstanding reputation. He's a pediatrician with a busy practice and a big personality, and the children he treats adore him as much as their parents. Doc is a regular at LaDonna's Diner. He's a weekend warrior at the farmers' market, where he's been known to set up a booth and give cooking lessons. He and his wife are socially active around town; they're generous donors to the library and animal shelter. Despite his duties as coroner, he's one of the most optimistic individuals I know.

"Morning, Chief." Hefting his medical bag, he ducks beneath the crime scene tape and approaches.

"Glad you're here, Doc."

"Saved me from devouring that plate of pan-

35

cakes I'd just ordered at the diner." He pats his protruding abdomen. "I'd appreciate it if you didn't tell my wife I was there."

"My lips are sealed."

He's a corpulent man wearing his trademark khakis, a button-down shirt—said buttons stretched taut over a Volkswagen-size belly—and one of the ugliest ties I've ever laid eyes on.

He reaches me and we shake hands. "Hit-and-run?" he asks.

Even as he asks the question, I see his eyes moving to the victim, taking in details, the position of the body, the amount of blood. I tell him what little I know. "There's a strange wound on his abdomen. I'd say it looks like a stab or even a bullet wound, but it's oddly shaped."

His eyebrows shoot up, not in surprise, but curiosity. Both of us have been around long enough to expect the unexpected. "Let's see what the victim has to tell us."

Setting down his medical case, he opens it and pulls out prewrapped biohazard protection for both of us. Though this is an outdoor scene and we're at the mercy of the elements, it's protocol to protect as much of the scene as possible. He passes me a disposable Tyvek suit, hair and shoe covers, and fresh examination gloves. We take a minute to don all of it. Then he picks up the medical case and we approach the victim.

"Copious amount of blood from the mouth," he murmurs.

I tell him about the broken tooth Glock noticed. "Internal injuries?"

"Possibly. Trauma from being struck. Could have bitten his tongue when he fell. Or a broken rib puncturing the lung. Something like that."

We reach the dead man. Doc sets down the case and kneels. "I don't have to tell you that none of what I'm about to say is an official ruling." He gives me a stern look over the top of his glasses. "The only reason I'm going to say anything at this point is because I know that if this is a result of foul play, whatever I *can* tell you will help you get started with your investigation. So, I'm going to call it as I see it and do the best I can. Final assessment will come post-autopsy."

"I understand."

He turns his attention back to the victim. With a gloved hand, he lifts the hem of the shirt and pulls it up. The wound I saw earlier looms into view. Simultaneously, we lean closer. This time, I take in the details. The injury isn't round like a bullet wound, but in the shape of a cross— two one-inch lines crossed at their centers—and about the diameter of a quarter.

"Any idea what that is?" I ask quietly.

The doc leans even closer, squinting. "Some type of penetrating wound."

I stare at the injury, trying to imagine a traffic

scenario that could've caused it. A T-post sticking out of the bed of a pickup truck? The victim traveling fast and running into something and impaling himself? The driver panicking and fleeing the scene?

I take in the broken tooth and cut lip. "Maybe he got into a scuffle or fight and was stabbed?"

Grimacing, the doc meets my gaze, his expression sober. "I've seen an injury similar to this just one time in all the years I've been practicing medicine. It was a hunting accident. Eight or nine years ago. A young man shot himself in the foot with a crossbow." He nods toward the wound. "The wound he sustained looked exactly like that one."

I stare at him, shocked, the thought making me shudder with such force that I feel gooseflesh on my arms. I look down at the dead man, a slew of dark possibilities crowding my mind. "So he was killed with an arrow?"

"It's called a bolt, actually," the doc tells me. "It looks like this particular bolt was tipped with what's referred to as a broadhead with four blades." He indicates the wound. "They're razor-sharp and do a tremendous amount of damage."

"Is it possible this was an accident?" I ask.

"I suppose it's possible." He shrugs, but his expression is skeptical. "If someone was out practicing or shooting targets. I have no idea what kind of range a crossbow has."

I've never used a crossbow, never been around them, but I know of hunters who use them, the Amish included. It's an incredibly powerful weapon, easy to use, accurate, and extremely deadly. I almost can't get my head around the idea of a man being killed with one.

I look around. "So, if this man was shot with a crossbow, where's the bolt?"

"I'm no expert, Kate, but I do happen to know the bolt fired from a powerful crossbow can travel with so much velocity that it can go completely through a body and continue traveling."

Despite the warmth of the sun, a chill slides between my shoulder blades and down my back. Carefully, I work my cell from my pocket and snap four close-up photos of the wound, my mind churning with the implications of what I've been told.

"Doc," I say slowly, "if the bolt went through, there would be an exit wound, correct?"

He nods. "Yes."

"Can we check?"

"Let's roll him over. Gently. I'll take the shoulders. You take the hip. Once we've got him on his side, I'll lift the shirttail, and we'll have a quick look."

Setting his gloved hands on the decedent's shoulder, Doc gives me a nod. Discomfort quivers in my gut when I set my hands on the victim's hip. The body is still warm to the touch, and I'm reminded that a short time ago, this young man was alive with hopes and dreams and people who loved him. At the doctor's nod, we roll. The shirt coming off the asphalt makes a wet peeling sound. Keeping one hand on the shoulder, Doc Coblentz uses the other to pull the shirttail upward toward the victim's shoulders.

Sure enough, a slightly smaller four-point wound is located just to the left of the spine.

"I'd say that's an exit wound," the doc says.

"So, if the bolt went clean through," I say slowly, "it should be somewhere in the area."

"I believe that is a logical assumption."

Which might be our first important piece of physical evidence.

I hail Dispatch. "Call Skid at home," I say, referring to my second-shift officer, Chuck "Skid" Skidmore. "Tell him we need him out on Hansbarger."

"Roger that."

I look around, spot the deputy who set up cones for the roadblock. "Hold on, Doc," I say, and stride to the deputy.

"Matt?"

"Yeah, Chief."

"Doc Coblentz thinks this victim may have been killed with a crossbow," I tell him.

"Holy shit."

"Not confirmed, but we've got entry and exit wounds, so the bolt may have gone clean through."

He nods. "You want me to look around? See what I can find?"

I look at the bicycle and try to ascertain which direction the victim may have been traveling. "Hard to tell which direction he was going, but might be a good idea to start with the woods there on the east side of the road."

"I'm on it."

"I've got another officer on the way to help."

"Got it."

I thank him and walk back to the victim, turn my attention to Doc. "Any idea how long he's been dead?"

"Not long," the doc tells me. "There's no livor present. There's no rigor, both of which begin at around the two-hour mark, give or take."

"So it just happened," I murmur.

The doc studies the platter-size pool of blood. Gently, he pulls open one of the eyelids and sighs. "My best guess is one to two hours, Kate. Of course, there are a lot of variables, so that time frame is not set in stone. I'll be able to tell you more once I get a core body temp."

I get to my feet, and I'm aware of the dull throb of anxiety in my gut. I look down at the victim. The position of the body. The bicycle. The lunch box. I take in the amount of blood that's leaked from his mouth. That's when I notice the quarter-size spot of blood on the asphalt beneath the back of his head.

"Doc?" I motion toward the blood. "Is there some kind of wound on the back of his head?"

The doc leans closer to the victim and shifts the head slightly. Sure enough, a tuft of hair is matted with blood. Using his fingertips, he separates the hair so that the scalp is visible. "Looks like a laceration."

"Something that happened in the fall, maybe?" Even as I ask the question, I realize it's not in a place that would be injured in the course of a fall.

"This looks like a penetrating wound," he says.

I stare at him, flummoxed. In the back of my mind, I recall a suicide I investigated a couple of years ago. A man put the muzzle of a revolver in his mouth and pulled the trigger. I think of the damage done. The angle of the bullet. Most importantly, *the location of the exit wound.*

"Doc, is it possible there's another wound . . . inside the mouth?"

"It would explain the heavy bleeding." Grimacing, as if he knows where my mind has taken me, he looks down at the victim. "Kate, if this man *was* killed with a bolt from a crossbow as we suspect, I think it's safe to say it was not self-inflicted."

"Even if it was some kind of bizarre accident, someone would have had to take the crossbow."

"It appears we have a puzzle on our hands." The doc sits back on his heels, his expression perplexed. "I'm not going to be able to explain any of this until I get him on the table."

"We're going to need to bag his hands," I say.

"You got it."

While the doc works, I look around, taking in the logistics of the scene. A second deputy has arrived and is tapping a length of rebar into the ground so he can finish taping off the area. I spot Skid in the woods with another deputy, ostensibly looking for a bolt from the crossbow. I look across the open field. The pond where a family of ducks flaps their wings. The smattering of trees growing alongside the fence. Such a peaceful, bucolic stretch of road. Who saw fit to shoot a young Amish man with a crossbow, possibly twice? Someone who then had the wherewithal to remove the bolts and take them.

Pulling out my cell, I dial Dispatch.

Lois picks up on the first ring. "Hey, Chief. Any news on that DB?"

"I need you to run Aden Karn through LEADS," I say, referring to the Law Enforcement Automated Data System. I spell both the first and last names. "Check for warrants. If he's been in trouble. If there have been any calls to his home." I recite the address from his ID. "Find out who owns the property. Find out if anyone else lives there."

"You got it."

I end the call, shove the phone back into its

compartment, and glance over at the doc. "Any idea when you can do the autopsy?" I ask.

"Tomorrow." Taking his time, the doc heaves himself to his feet, sets his gaze on mine. "You'll be doing the notification?"

"Yeah."

We stare at each other for a too-long moment. A silent communication passes between us, uncomfortable, and yet it bolsters me, and I realize Doc has been in my shoes. He's a doctor, after all. A pediatrician. And there have been times when all the medical know-how in the world wasn't enough. He, too, has had to rip out a parent's heart. He knows that the pain that comes with that obligation is nothing compared to the agony that's been doled out by fate.

After a moment, Doc crosses to me. He sets his hand on my shoulder and squeezes. "I'll call you as soon as I know something."

CHAPTER 3

Angela and Lester Karn live in Painters Mill proper two blocks from the boot and shoe shop they own and operate, The Gentle Cobbler. I worked for them for a short while when I was a teenager, the last summer I lived in Painters Mill. I was seventeen at the time, discontent and getting into trouble, and my parents thought the added responsibility would be good for me. The Gentle Cobbler was an Amish-owned business, after all. I wasn't a very good employee and spent most of my time screwing up. In the end, I got caught wearing a pair of shoes I'd pilfered from the shop and planned to put back on the shelf the next day. I wore those strappy sandals with three-inch heels to an outdoor rager and ended up snapping off a heel. Lester fired me, putting me out of my misery and effectively ending my career in retail sales.

As an adult, I've frequented their shop a dozen times. Tomasetti bought a pair of work boots last winter and we spent a few minutes chatting. Lester and Angela are a nice couple. They're at the shop every day except Sunday. I happen to know they open their doors at ten A.M., which is just twenty minutes from now, so I head that way.

I'm so focused on the task ahead that I barely

notice the old-fashioned streetlamps and parking meters as I turn onto Main Street. I pull nose-in to the spot in front of the shop and sit there a moment wishing with every cell in my body that Aden Karn wasn't dead and I didn't have to walk through that door and destroy the lives of the two people inside. Though there's a CLOSED sign in the window, I see the lights on inside, and the silhouette of someone moving around.

Dread keeps pace with me as I cross the sidewalk to the door. Through the window, I see Angela Karn behind the counter, working on the cash register. Lester is standing on a footstool, adding shoeboxes to a shelf. I tap on the glass.

The Amish man turns and does a double take upon seeing me. He smiles as if pleased, and the ache that follows feels like a boulder in my gut. I wait while Lester climbs down from the step stool and strides to the door, his gait jaunty. He's in his mid-fifties now with a round belly and the full salt-and-pepper beard of a married Amish man. He's wearing a white shirt and gray trousers with suspenders. Because he works with the public, he's traded the typical straw flat-brimmed hat for a black felt one.

I shore up with a deep breath and the door swings open. Vaguely, I'm aware of the bell jingling. The smells of leather and shoe polish and eucalyptus wafting out.

"*Guder mariye*, Katie," he says, offering his

46

hand. Good morning. *"Kumma inseid."* Come inside.

"Hi, Lester." We shake hands and I follow him into the shop.

"We still have those boots you tried on." He's moving back toward the footstool. It's a busy morning and he's got things to do in the minutes before they open. "Sale starts tomorrow if you're interested. Twenty percent off and a free stretch if you need it."

The words hang, unanswered. I look past him at his wife, who's standing behind the counter, looking at me as if she's realized this isn't a social call.

"I'm afraid I have bad news," I hear myself say.

Lester stops just as he reaches the stool, then turns to me, his eyes probing mine.

"There was an incident this morning," I tell them. "Aden is dead. I'm sorry."

Lester chokes out a sound that's part gasp, part laugh. Not sure if I'm kidding, but he cuts it short, and then blinks at me. "What? Aden? But . . . how can that be?"

I'm aware of Angela coming around the counter, rushing to her husband, her face a mosaic of horror and disbelief. "What are you talking about? My goodness, how could you say such a crazy thing? We just saw him a couple days ago. He was fine."

Before I even realize I'm going to do it, I reach

for the woman's hands, take hers in mine, and I squeeze gently. "It happened earlier this morning. On Hansbarger Road. I think he was on his way to work."

"He takes that way," Lester interjects. "He works over to Buckeye Construction. Rides his bike to the ice shack out there by the Lutheran church and they pick him up."

I see desperation on their faces, denial, burgeoning grief, the hope that I'm wrong. Lester actually looks toward the door, hoping someone will burst in and tell them that all of this is a mistake.

"What kind of incident?" Angela asks.

"We're still investigating." Since I'm short on facts, I keep it simple. "It looks like he was riding his bicycle. There may have been some kind of altercation or accident and Aden was killed. We're trying to figure out what happened. I just . . ." I run out of breath. I stare at them, unable to finish, my breaths coming a little too fast, and for a second I'm afraid I'm going to fail them because I can't speak.

I turn away, fight for composure. Blow out a slow breath. Take another. Angry with myself because this isn't about me. It's about them. And their son.

I turn back to them, take in the ravaged faces. The faltering hope. That first, brutal punch of grief.

"I'm sorry," I say again. An understatement.

"Someone hit him?" Lester asks, his voice high and tight. "With a car? An *Englischer*? Ran him over?"

"Oh, dear Lord." Angela's face crumples.

"We're still trying to figure out what happened," I tell them.

The Amish woman slides her hands from mine, covers her mouth as if to smother the cry that's trying to escape. "I can't believe it."

"Where is he?" Lester asks.

"Doc Coblentz is at the scene," I say. "They're going to take him to Pomerene Hospital." Not for treatment, of course, but because the morgue is located in the basement.

"Can we see him?" The Amish woman looks at her husband. "I want to see him."

Lester sets his hand on his wife's shoulder and shakes his head. *"Deahra is naett di zeit."* This is not the time.

I make eye contact with Lester. "Is there someone I can get for you?" I ask. "A family member? Bishop Troyer?"

The Amish man shakes his head, looks down at the floor. I see him blinking, fighting tears.

The Amish are generally stoic in the face of grief. Death is part of life's cycle and heaven is the reward for a life well lived. They believe the departed are in a better place—in heaven with God. Even so, they are human beings first and there is no comfort that comes with the loss of a child.

"Mr. and Mrs. Karn," I begin. "I know this is an awful time. I know you're in shock. In pain. But I need to ask you a few questions."

They stare at me as if I'm speaking a language they don't understand. Still trying to absorb what they've been told. Cling to the last vestiges of denial. Their minds seeking a way to reject the reality of the tragedy I've dropped at their feet.

After a moment, Angela turns away, lowers her face into her hands. She doesn't make a sound, but I see her shoulders begin to shake.

I turn my attention to Lester, ease my spiral-bound notebook from my pocket. "When's the last time you saw Aden?" I ask quietly.

He looks down at the floor, his mouth working. "Like we said. Two days ago. He came over for supper."

"Was everything all right with him?" I ask. "Did he mention any problems? Any difficulties in his life?"

He gives an adamant shake of his head. "No."

"Did Aden have any enemies? Was he having any problems with anyone?"

He raises his gaze to mine and for the first time, I see questions. The burgeoning realization that his son's death may not have been an accident.

"Are you saying someone did this thing on purpose?" he asks. "Ran over him?"

"We're not exactly sure what happened." It's the only honest answer I have. "I know that's not enough information, but all I can tell you at this point is I promise you I'm going to do everything in my power to find out what happened."

Shaking his head, the Amish man looks down at the floor.

I give him a moment before continuing. "Lester, was Aden having any disputes or arguments with anyone? With his neighbors? Or a girlfriend? Any issues at work? Anything like that?"

"No," he says gruffly.

"Did he live alone?"

"He lives with Wayne Graber."

"They're friends?" I ask.

"More like brothers. They've known each other since they were boys."

"Do they have a good relationship?"

"Practically grew up together," he replies. "I've known Wayne since he was a wee thing. I know the whole family." He raises his head, his eyes going wide. "Is Wayne okay? Is he—"

"As far as I know, he's fine," I say quickly. "I'll be speaking to him as soon as I can." I glance down at my notebook. "Do you know where Wayne works?"

The couple exchange looks. Lester answers.

"Last I heard he was working out at Mast Tiny Homes."

I write it down. "Did Aden have a girlfriend?" I ask. "Was he seeing anyone?"

Lester looks at me as if I've asked an inappropriate question. Angela turns slowly toward us. Her face is blotchy and red, her cheeks wet. "He's courting Emily Byler," she says.

I recognize the last name. "Andy and Clara's girl?"

"*Ja.*"

I jot the names in my notebook. "Are Emily and Aden close?" I ask. "Is it a serious relationship?"

"Serious enough," the Amish woman murmurs. "I reckon they were going to get married in a year or so. Em's a sweet thing. We like her a lot."

"Course Aden's on *rumspringa*," Lester puts in, referring to the "running around" time most Amish teens indulge in before their baptism. "Been running around, you know. Hard to keep up with the youngsters when they don't live at home."

"Poor Em's going to be torn up over this." The Amish woman's face crumples again, and she swipes at the tears with her fingertips.

Steeling myself against the other woman's agony, I tug my card from my pocket, jot my cell number on the back, and pass it to Lester. "If you remember something that might be important, call me," I tell them.

Without answering, Lester looks down at the card, but it's as if he doesn't see it.

The grief filling the room is suffocating. Again, I feel that breathless sensation in my chest. I reach out and touch Angela's hand, but she pulls it away, doesn't look at me.

I leave them like that. Silent and staring. Their lives shattered. Their hearts broken.

I sit in the Explorer with my hands on the wheel for a full minute before starting the engine. That's the thing about being a cop in a small town. Policing is a hell of a lot more personal. You know the people you've sworn to serve and protect. Whether it's to write a speeding ticket, round up escaped livestock, pull someone's dog from a frozen pond, or tell parents their teenage son has wrapped his Mustang around a tree and didn't survive, you know them. You know the families. You know their strengths and weaknesses. You know their secrets. Sometimes that personal connection hurts because you have a job to do and there's no one else.

Shaking off the remnants of their grief, I mentally shift gears and I think about where I am in terms of the investigation. This is the stage when a cop needs to be in a dozen places at once. Information is the name of the game and I need all of it yesterday. Homicides are rarely random; the victim usually knows his killer. I think about

53

Aden Karn's life and relationships. His family dynamics. The people he loved. Who did he spend time with? Who were his coworkers? His neighbors? Business associates?

Someone always knows something, a little voice whispers in my ear.

I pick up my cell as I back from the parking space and hail Dispatch. Lois picks up on the first ring. "Anything come back on Aden Karn?" I ask.

"Squeaky clean, Chief. Not even a speeding ticket."

"Run Angela and Lester Karn, will you?" I've no doubt the couple have clean records. Even so, it's always wise to check. "Run Wayne Graber, too. Emily Byler. And her parents."

"I'll call you as soon as I get all this."

I thank her and drop the cell into the console as I pull away.

Andy and Clara Byler live nearly to the Coshocton County line just off of County Road 19. It's a well-kept farm with a white farm-house, a grain silo, and two low-slung hog barns in the back. I follow the driveway around to the rear of the house and park next to a wooden wagon piled high with cut hay. The stench of hog manure hits me like a brick when I get out.

Midway to the house, I notice the Amish

woman on her knees, weeding a flower bed off the back porch. She's wearing a mauve dress, a white *kapp*, and a pair of sneakers that have seen plenty of miles. There's a pile of pulled weeds the size of a Thanksgiving turkey on the ground beside her.

"Mums are pretty," I say to her as I approach.

She glances at me over her shoulder and frowns. "Chickens sure do like 'em. The stupid things. Rooster leads the hens over here every morning and they go to town, scratching up everything in sight. I might just fry him up one of these days."

I smile. "Clara Byler?"

"That's me." Tossing a handful of weeds onto the pile, she heaves herself to her feet and brushes her hands against the skirt of her dress. I see her eyes taking in my uniform, and she cocks her head. "You're a ways from Painters Mill."

I have my shield at the ready. "I'm afraid I've got some bad news."

She goes still and I see her mentally brace, telling me she's no stranger to tragedy.

"Aden Karn was killed earlier this morning," I say. "I'm sorry."

The woman steps backward as if shoved by some invisible force. "Aden. Gone? Oh good Lord. He's so young. How?"

I lay out the fundamentals without getting into too much detail.

"Was it an accident?" the woman asks.

"That's yet to be determined. We're looking into a few things." Not wanting to get into the specifics when I have so little solid information confirmed, I press on. "I understand he was seeing your daughter, Emily."

Shaking her head, she looks down at the ground. "My goodness, this is going to be a shock for her."

"They were close?" I ask.

She nods. "She's only seventeen, but we figured they'd get married. Next year, maybe."

"Did they get along well?"

"Of course they get along," she says a little irritably. "He's the first boy that's paid her any heed and she's just bloomed. He brought her out of her shell, I reckon. She's a shy thing. They've been seeing each other for six months now and it's been a match made in heaven. He's good to her. Kind and attentive and she's been like a whole new girl."

"How well did you know Aden?"

"I've known that boy since he was yea high." She holds out a steady hand to indicate a height of about three feet. "Always was a charmer, that one. Funny. He could make you laugh even if you were having a bad day. Had a smile for everyone. Didn't need to ask him for help; the boy would just show up and take on the hardest job you've got. Liked to get his hands dirty, never complained, and he didn't leave until the work was done."

"He was your daughter's first beau?" I ask, using the Amish term for "boyfriend."

"She might've gone to a singing or two before. A frolic down to Coshocton." Her eyes flick away from mine just long enough to give me pause.

"None of the other boys had their eye on her?" I ask.

"They might've looked, but she wouldn't have it. That girl only had eyes for Aden."

I make a mental note of all of it, tuck it away for later. "When's the last time you saw him?"

"Three days ago. We've had him over for supper every weekend since he started seeing Emily. Ate like a horse. Liked my chicken and dumplings just fine." Lowering her head, she presses her fingertips to her eyes as if to keep the tears from falling. "My goodness, I can't believe he's gone."

"I'm sorry for your loss, ma'am."

"God musta wanted him for something important. Sometimes when He takes 'em young, that's the way it is. The Lord got a good one this time, that's for sure."

"Mrs. Byler, I know this is a bad time, but it would be helpful if I could speak to Emily for a few minutes. Is she home?"

"Oh, Lord, this is going to be hard on her." The tears she's been holding back spring free. She

57

wipes them away without acknowledging them. A mother who has no patience with her own grief because she knows she must be strong for her daughter. "Em's in the kitchen, peeling apples for pies." She grimaces at me. "Come on in."

I follow her into the house and through a small mudroom. The kitchen is uncomfortably warm and smells of cinnamon. The windows are open, the curtains billowing, but the breeze isn't enough to dispel the heat. A young Amish woman stands at the counter next to the sink, rolling dough with a wooden pin, her hands covered with flour. She's a scant five feet tall with a pretty face, a porcelain complexion, and full lips the color of a peach. She's wearing a wine-colored dress with an apron. Intent on the dough in front of her. Perspiration beaded on her cheeks. I can tell by the amount of flour on the counter that she's a messy baker.

"Something smells good," I say by way of greeting.

Her smile reveals dimpled cheeks. "A little too good if you ask me."

She glances at us over her shoulder. The smile falters as she takes in my uniform. Her eyes go to her mother, then back at me. "Mamm?"

Blond hair is tucked messily into a gauzy *kapp*, a single strand sticking out the side. She's got bright blue eyes. Freckles on her nose. Cheeks that still have the roundness of youth.

The kind of mouth a model would pay thousands for.

"This is Kate Burkholder," her mother says. "She's the police up to Painters Mill."

"Police?" Dough forgotten, the girl picks up a raggedy kitchen towel and wipes her hands. "What happened? Why are the police here?" She looks at her *mamm*. "Why is she looking at me that way?" she asks in *Deitsch*.

"She's got some bad news, honey," her mom tells her.

"Bad news?" The girl chokes out a laugh, but the sound is an uneasy mix of annoyance and fear. "What on earth do you mean?"

"Aden was killed this morning," the woman tells her. "Had some kind of accident on his way to work."

"*Killed?* Aden?" Another sound escapes her, disbelief with an argument on deck. "No. That's just not true. He's at work. I'm going to see him later."

Clara tightens her mouth, looks down at the floor. "God took him, baby," she whispers. "He's gone home."

"I'm sorry for your loss," I tell her.

The girl gives me a look of derision before turning away. Snatching up the rolling pin, she goes back to work on the dough. But her entire body is shaking now. She rolls with so much force that the dough sticks to the pin and tears.

59

She ignores it, keeps rolling, putting too much muscle into it.

I look at Clara.

Clara goes to her daughter. "Let's just put that crust away for now." Gently, she usurps the rolling pin. "You sit yourself down. I'll get us some tea. Chief Burkholder needs to ask you some questions."

"He's not dead!" The girl spins, points at me, a wildness in her eyes. A burst of anger in her voice. All of it laced with the desperation of a trapped, injured animal. A mind that simply cannot absorb the news. "She made it up!"

She tries to take the rolling pin from her mother. I don't know if she wants to continue with the pie crust or if she plans to hit me with it. The two women grapple with the pin and the thing falls to the floor.

"*Sitz dich anne*," the older woman says firmly. Sit yourself there.

Emily looks at her, gives herself a visible mental shake, then walks over to the kitchen table, pulls out a chair, and sinks into it. Without speaking or looking at me, she folds her arms on the table, lowers her head, and begins to sob.

"I don't believe it," she cries. "Someone's mixed up is all."

I hold my place at the doorway until Clara pours the tea. Making eye contact with me, she sets a plastic glass in front of her daughter.

"You just sip this and get yourself settled down."

After a moment, the girl straightens, tears streaming, and picks up the glass. "What happened to him?" she asks, finally turning her attention to me.

I take the chair across from her, debating how much to reveal. The last thing any cop wants to do in the course of an investigation, particularly a homicide, is relay unconfirmed information. I don't know the official manner or cause of death. I'm not certain what type of weapon was used. Even so, the more specific my questions, the more likely the answers I receive will be helpful.

"All I can tell you is that a motorist found him this morning out on Hansbarger Road," I tell her. "Evidently, that's the route he takes to work. Nothing is confirmed at this point and we're still basically trying to figure out what happened."

"He was hit by a car?" Clara asks.

I look from Emily to her mother. "Preliminarily, it looks as if Aden may have been shot with some kind of projectile. I don't know what kind of weapon was used—"

"Shot?" The girl sets down the glass so abruptly some of the tea sloshes over the side. "Are you saying someone . . . *shot* him? With a gun?" Tears streaming, she tosses a helpless look at her mother. "I don't understand how that could happen. Why would someone do that?"

"Was it an accident?" Clara asks.

"I don't think this was an accident," I tell them.

"*Mein Gott.*" My God. The girl's face screws up. "I can't bear to think of it."

"I know this is difficult," I say. "But I have a few questions—"

"I can't . . . Aden. *Aden.*" The girl puts her hands over her face, her shoulders shaking. Struggling for control that simply won't manifest. "If I could only talk to him."

Knowing she's holding on to her composure by a thread and I may not have much time, I press on. "When's the last time you saw him?"

She doesn't respond for so long that I think I'm going to have to repeat the question, when she finally lowers her hands. "Saturday." Her expression softens. "He drove all the way down here in his buggy. Helped Datt put a new roof on the chicken house and stayed for supper."

"Did he seem all right?" I ask. "Was there anything bothering him?"

"He was fine. Same as always."

"Has he had any disagreements or arguments with anyone recently?" I ask.

The girl blinks back tears and shakes her head. "Aden never argues with anyone. He'll agree with you just to keep the peace. He was kind that way."

The older woman removes a tissue from her pocket and hands it to her daughter. "What about the business with that old truck?"

My police antenna cranks up.

"Oh." Emily takes the tissue, uses it to wipe her eyes. "I almost forgot. Such a stupid thing."

"What truck?" I ask.

"Aden and Wayne bought this beat-up truck."

"Wayne Graber," Clara puts in.

The roommate, I recall.

Emily nods. "They bought it from an *Englischer* in Millersburg," she tells me. "Aden and Wayne are good with mechanical stuff; they can fix anything. So, they figured they could make repairs and sell it. Make some money, you know. They went to work on it, like guys do. Got the thing all fancy-looking and sold it for two thousand dollars to Vernon Fisher." Her brows knit. "But after Vernon had it for a few weeks, the truck stopped running. Vern got mad and stopped paying. So Wayne and Aden went over to his house in the middle of the night and repossessed it."

I pull out my notebook. "Vernon Fisher?"

"Lives up in Painters Mill," Clara says.

The name is familiar. I'm pretty sure I've pulled Fisher over for speeding at least once. If memory serves me, he's from a well-thought-of Amish family and recently purchased a defunct gas station off the highway.

"Vernon fell in with a bad crowd." Clara huffs. "Been on *rumspringa* for over a year now. Drinks and smokes like a fiend. Lives out by that trashy old gas station. Hangs out with a bunch of no-gooders. Don't think his parents will ever get him baptized or married."

"How much money are we talking about?" I ask Emily.

"I think Vernon paid six hundred dollars. Still owes fourteen hundred. Aden said Vernon wants his six hundred back."

It's exactly the kind of dispute that could escalate into something ugly.

I write all of it down. "Emily, did Vernon and Aden argue or have words about the truck?"

"I don't know."

"Did Vernon ever threaten Aden?" I ask. "Or Wayne?"

The girl stares at me, her mouth quivering as her mind tries to make sense of my questions. The meaning behind them. After a moment, her face crumples. She lowers her face into her hands and breaks into sobs.

I wait and try a few more questions, but she's inconsolable. I leave her sobbing, her arms on the table, her face buried.

CHAPTER 4

I hail Dispatch as I pull out of the Bylers' lane, make the turn onto the county road, and head north. "Ten-twenty-nine." It's the ten code for "check for wanted." "Vernon Fisher." I spell out the name.

"Stand by," comes Lois's voice.

Keys clatter and then she comes back. "Speeding citation two years ago. OVI in Holmes County," she says, using the acronym for the "operation of a motor vehicle while intoxicated."

"Do you have an address for him?"

"Got it right here, Chief." A couple more clicks and then she recites a Painters Mill address.

"I'm ten-seventy-six," I respond, letting her know I'm en route. "Who's on this afternoon?"

"Pickles."

Roland "Pickles" Shumaker is semiretired now. He's north of eighty years old and spends most of his time working the school crosswalk—and occasionally confiscating cigarettes from students who think they're going to cop a smoke on his watch. The people who know him—and those of us who work with him—do not underestimate Pickles. He may be in his golden years; he may be moving a little more slowly; he may lie about his age. But beneath the grizzled exterior are fifty years of law enforcement experience, a commendation for undercover narcotics work, and the instincts of a man who'll lay down his life to save your ass.

"Tell Pickles to ten-twenty-five." Which is the code for "meet me there."

"Ten-four."

I rack the mike, then pick up my cell and speed-dial Glock. He picks up instantly. "Did anyone find a bolt or arrow?" I ask.

"Negative," he says. "We set up a grid and checked every tree and field and ditch within two hundred yards of the scene, Chief. We got nothing."

I tell him about my conversation with Doc Coblentz. "If there were entry and exit wounds, how is it that there's no bolt on scene?"

"Maybe the shooter took it."

"From what I hear, it's not easy to extract a bolt."

"That's true," he says. "I went crossbow hunting a few years ago with a friend of mine. He got a buck. When he retrieved his bolt, he didn't pull it out. He pushed it *through*. And it took some doing."

I suppress a shiver before it can take hold. "Is Doc Coblentz still there?"

"Left ten minutes ago. Released the scene to us. Crime scene techs are still processing. I don't think they're getting much."

"According to Doc, Karn was shot at least twice," I say, thinking aloud. "Did the killer know Karn and target him? Or was it a random killing?"

"Not many people on that stretch of road," Glock says. "Of course, if you're up to no good and looking to kill someone, you'd have no way of knowing when someone might happen by, and you'd likely have a lengthy wait on your hands."

I consider that a moment. "If I were to guess, I'd say this was targeted. The killer knew Karn's routine. Knew his route. Waited for him to show."

"And ambushed him."

For the span of several seconds, neither of us speaks, our minds working through the repercussions of that.

"Karn worked for Buckeye Construction," I tell him. "When you finish up at the scene, run up there and find out who was supposed to pick him up this morning. Find out where they meet and who else rides with them."

"You got it."

"Find out where the crew was working, too. See if there were any problems on the job. With coworkers. Or the client."

"Will do."

I relay the story about the truck. "I'm on my way to talk to Vernon Fisher."

"Watch your back."

"Just so you know, I have a profound fear of

sharp projectiles that travel at three hundred feet per second."

He laughs. "You and me both."

Red's Gas Station has been a scar on the landscape as long as I can remember. When I was a kid, my *mamm* once took me in for a red pop. I don't recall why we were there, but even then it had been a ramshackle business that smelled of rubber and oil and spilled gas. A dozen FOR SALE signs have come and gone over the years, but no one wanted to buy the place. Until Vernon Fisher came along, anyway.

The establishment sits on a lesser-used county road a stone's throw from State Highway 83. It's a cinder-block structure, the kind that was popular in the 1960s, with a low-slope roof and a mullioned front. The old Sohio sign mounted on a pole is shot through with holes from shotgun pellets. Most of the window glass is gone and has been replaced with plywood upon which someone has written *Wanted: Used cars* and below that scrawled a phone number. A double auto bay takes up the left side of the building. One of the overhead doors stands open. Inside, a muscle car straddles a lift, two tires missing, a rusty chain hanging down. As I pull into the weed-riddled parking lot, I see the silhouettes of two men beneath the car. Two more men occupy lawn chairs against the wall.

I park next to the concrete island where three gas pumps used to be. Two are gone. The remaining pump is rust covered and lies on its side, its glass face crushed.

There's no sign of Pickles's vehicle. I pick up my mike. "Ten-twenty-three," I say, letting Dispatch know I've reached my destination.

"Roger that."

I rack the mike and start toward the service bay. The four men inside are young, in their early twenties. At least two are Amish. They're not dressed in Amish garb, but the "Dutch boy" haircuts give them away. An old Pink Floyd number blares from a speaker set up on the workbench at the rear. The two men standing beneath the car are wearing grease-stained coveralls. One is twisting a ratchet wrench, right arm pumping. The other man is holding something in place with a gloved hand.

All eyes turn to me as I approach. I notice a couple of double takes. They're not expecting a visit from the chief of police. I recognize Vernon Fisher immediately. He's sitting in a steel folding chair, smoking a cigarette, looking at me as if he finds my presence amusing. The fourth man has gotten to his feet and stands next to a big rollaway toolbox, watching me. A bottle of tequila, uncapped, sits on the sill of a window that looks into the office.

I enter the garage, aware that everyone's

attention is fastened to me. Expressions more curious than put off, telling me they're bored and open to some unseemly entertainment, at my expense if they can manage. The car on the lift is a Mustang with wide tires and blue metal-flake paint.

"Vernon Fisher?" I say as I approach.

"Yes, ma'am." Tossing a hold-my-beer-and-watch-this grin at his cohorts, he rises and crosses to me. Fisher is tall and lanky with angular limbs and well-defined muscle. Wearing jeans and a raggedy work shirt, he looks as if he's settled into the English life with ease.

"How can I help you?" he asks.

Though he knows exactly who I am, I show him my shield. "Is there a place where we can speak privately? I have a few questions for you."

"What'd he do now?" one of the other men mutters beneath his breath, and a round of laughter follows.

"Uh . . . well, I don't exactly have an office yet," he says. "How about we talk right here?"

"I understand you bought a truck from Aden Karn," I begin.

"I wondered when he was going to sic the cops on me." Sighing, he shakes his head. "Look, I gave that dude a six-hundred-dollar down payment. I took the truck home and two weeks later the damn thing stopped running. I said I'd give

70

him back the truck and asked him for my down payment back and he frickin' refused. I told him I wasn't going to pay the rest. Who would? Two days later, him and his buddy sneak over here in the middle of the night and steal my truck. I'm out six hundred bucks. I'm the one who should be calling the cops."

"Did you confront him?" I ask.

"I gave him some shit about it. I mean, the dude ripped me off."

"Did you file a complaint?"

He shrugs. "Figured it wouldn't do any good."

"Do you have a bill of sale or contract?"

"We done it on a handshake." He blows out a sound of regret. "Guess there's a lesson in there somewhere, huh?"

A pornographic calendar hangs on the wall behind him, a nude woman, legs spread, baring it all. I tamp down a rise of disgust as I tug out my spiral notebook.

"When's the last time you saw Karn?" I ask.

"Three or four days ago? I went to his house and told him I want my money back and we can call it even. He told me to hit the road." He looks at his counterparts and sighs. "What the hell is the world coming to when you can't even trust the fuckin' Amish?"

A round of hearty laughter ensues.

"Where were you this morning between three and eight A.M.?" I ask.

He cocks his head and for the first time he looks at me as if he's taking our conversation seriously. "What kind of question is that?"

"The kind you have to answer," I return evenly. "You can do it here, or we can do it at the police station. It's your call."

He swallows what was probably a nasty response. "At three A.M., I was in bed, sleeping." He smirks. "At eight, I was . . . having sex with my girlfriend."

"What's her name?" I ask.

A raucous round of laughter erupts. I look around, see one of the men point to the grimy window that looks into the small office. I follow his point. At first glance, I think there's a nude woman sitting at the desk. But I quickly realize it's a full-size sex doll replete with exaggerated breasts and bright pink genitalia.

The men fall into riotous laughter.

"Her name's Leandra," one of them blurts, wiping his eyes.

"He's in love!" someone else says.

"I think he's gonna pop the question!"

I look at Fisher, keep my annoyance at bay. "Do you have a valid hunting license?"

He sobers, gives me a puzzled look, wondering about the change of topic. "Do I hunt? Sure. During the season. Deer mostly. Coyote."

"The only thing he hunts is pussy," one of the men mumbles.

More laughter, but I ignore it. "Is your hunting license valid?"

"Yeah."

"Do you own a crossbow or combination bow?"

"If you don't mind my asking, Chief Burkholder, what does that have to do with the truck?"

"I'd appreciate it if you'd just answer the question."

Out of the corner of my eye, I see the man standing next to the rollaway pick up the bottle of tequila and take a long swig. Making a face, he passes it to one of the men standing beneath the car, who does the same. They're a tight-knit group. Like-minded. Troublemakers. Agitators looking for fun and games.

"I don't use a crossbow or combo," Fisher tells me. "Never have. I prefer a rifle. Like the feel of it. The accuracy."

The crunch of tires on gravel alerts me to the arrival of someone else. I glance over my shoulder to see Pickles park his cruiser next to my Explorer and get out. A couple of the other men notice, too, and exchange looks, wondering why a second officer has arrived.

"Why are you asking me all these questions?" Fisher asks. "What the hell's going on?"

"Sounds like she's trying to pin something on you." The man next to the rollaway stares at me; his expression has gone cold and deadpan.

I maintain my focus on Fisher. "Have you ever borrowed a crossbow?"

"No, ma'am."

Eyeing me with unconcealed disdain, the man beneath the car takes another swig of tequila. He offers it to me, but I ignore him. Smiling, he passes it to the man next to him.

"Fuckin' cops," one of the men hisses beneath his breath.

Pickles comes up beside me. He's in full uniform, his trousers creased, uniform shirt stiff with starch. He's wearing his trademark Lucchese boots, which are buffed to a high sheen, and he smells of Old Spice aftershave and the cigarette he sneaked on the drive over. I can tell by his expression that he knows exactly what's going on here—and that he's not the least bit fazed.

"Afternoon, gentlemen." He looks around, taking in his surroundings, sizing up the men. "Nice Mustang. Sixty-six?"

"Sixty-eight," Fisher replies.

"Good year." Pickles spots the calendar. "Three-oh-two engine?"

"Three-ninety," Fisher says. "Four-barrel."

"Damn." Whistling appreciatively, Pickles strides past the men, so close to Fisher he has to step back. Pickles goes to the workbench, plucks the calendar off the wall, and rips it in half.

"Hey, old man, that ain't yours to fuck with," says the man next to the rollaway.

Taking his time, Pickles tosses it into the trash bin, then turns to face the man next to the rollaway. "Just saving you some trouble."

"Yeah? How's that?"

"Some ten-year-old kid walks in here to air up his bike tire and sees your classy calendar, and you geniuses are going to find yourselves in hot water."

"I call bullshit," one of the men says.

"You can call all the bullshit you want, Einstein," Pickles drawls. "In the state of Ohio, if you expose a minor child to pornography, even if it's inadvertent, you'd better have a damn good lawyer." He smiles, his eyes cutting like ice. "You can thank me later."

A round of laughter, subdued this time, and then Fisher asks me, "So what's going on with Karn? Why all the questions?"

"Karn was killed this morning on his way to work," I tell him.

Fisher blinks, starts to laugh, but thinks better of it. "Holy shit. Seriously?" He gives his head a little shake. "You think I had something to do with it?"

"I think you had an argument with him about a truck," I say.

"That doesn't mean I *killed* him. What the hell kind of crap is this? You come here to my place of business and accuse me of killing some freakin' dude I barely know? In front of my employees?"

I don't bother pointing out that I gave him the option of speaking to me in private. "We're talking to everyone who knew or had a relationship with or came in contact with Mr. Karn."

"It wasn't me."

"So you say." This from Pickles.

Fisher ignores him, his mind plowing ahead. "Someone offed him with a fucking *crossbow?*"

"Watch your mouth," Pickles growls.

I pass my card to Fisher, my cell phone number jotted on the back. "If you think of anything that might be important, give me a call."

He takes the card, shoves it into his pocket without looking at it.

As I turn to leave, one of the other men walks to the trash can and pulls out the calendar. Eyes on me, he sticks out his tongue and runs the tip over the most offensive part of the image, then hangs that half of it back on the wall.

Pickles walks with me to my Explorer.

"That was a pretty badass move," I say to him as I open the driver's-side door.

His mouth twitches, but he manages to maintain his curmudgeon persona. "I don't like those cocky little shits, Chief. They got too much time on their hands and they're out here every day looking for trouble."

"I know." I slide behind the wheel. "You and Glock have any luck with the canvass?"

He shakes his head. "Talked to the Amish couple who own the farm half a mile down the road from where Karn was found. They see him ride his bike past just about every morning. They don't recall seeing anyone else."

I nod, look toward the garage, see Fisher standing beneath the overhead door, smoking a cigarette, watching us.

"Doc Coblentz says the bolt either went through or was pulled through," I say.

"Damn, that's brutal."

"Be nice to find the bolts."

"If they're there." He narrows his eyes. "You want me to go back to the scene?"

"Skid has already looked around, but a second pair of eyes wouldn't hurt." I sigh, frustrated because I know every officer in my small department will be working around the clock until this thing is solved.

"Before you do that," I tell him, "I'd like you to check with area sporting goods stores. Take T.J. with you. Dispatch can get you the names of the retailers and contact info. I want the names of anyone who purchased a crossbow or combination bow in the last six months."

"You got it."

"In the interim, I'm going to talk to the roommate."

He touches the brim of his hat and starts toward his cruiser.

I take a final look at the garage, my eyes seeking Vernon Fisher, but he's gone.

CHAPTER 5

In the early phase of a homicide investigation, there are a hundred things that need to be done simultaneously. Every potential witness needs to be interviewed, a dozen leads need to be followed up on, evidence collected, protected, and assessed. Speed is the name of the game, and there are no shortcuts. All of that is especially true if the killer is still at large.

According to his driver's license, Aden Karn lived on Rockridge Road south of Painters Mill. I've just turned onto the highway when my Bluetooth announces a call. I glance down to see HOLMES COUNTY CORONER pop up on the display.

"Hi, Doc."

"I know you're anxious for information," Doc Coblentz begins. "I wanted to let you know, I got our victim cleaned up and on the table." He pauses, sighs. "Kate, let me preface by telling you I put a call in to a forensic pathologist with BCI to assist. That's going to slow things down, but I suspect this may turn out to be a complicated case."

"Doc, did anyone ever tell you that you have a gift for being cryptic?"

He makes a sound that isn't quite a laugh.

"If you've got the time, and you'd like some preliminary information, you might want to come in and see this."

The ticking clock inside my head reminds me that a trip to the morgue pre-autopsy probably isn't the most efficient use of my time. On the other hand, I know Doc wouldn't have called if it wasn't important.

"I'll be there in ten minutes," I tell him.

Pomerene Hospital is located north of Millersburg. I park in the lot off the portico outside the Emergency entrance and push through the double glass doors. The elderly gentleman at the visitor desk waves as I pass. I give him a nod as I cross to the elevator and hit the Down button.

I mentally shore up on the ride to the basement. Two deep breaths, slowly released. I reach for the inner quiet I need to get through what comes next, but it eludes me. I remind myself I'm no rookie; I've done this before. I should know by now that facing the dead never gets any easier no matter how many times you do it.

Suck it up, Kate.

The doors swoosh open, ushering in a mix of smells that brings a sharp rise of dread. Recirculated air that's a few degrees too cool for comfort. A medicinal pong that makes me want to hold my breath. The eucalyptus from the dried plant in the vase. Something unpleasant hovering just beneath the surface . . .

"Hi, Chief Burkholder!"

I glance left to see Doc Coblentz's assistant, Carmen Anderson, sitting at a desk stacked high with legal-size hanging files. She's wearing black-and-white pinstripe today. Pencil skirt. Low-heeled pumps. Silver hoops at her ears. Dressed to the hilt, as always.

I cross to the desk and we shake. "You're working late this afternoon."

"I'm trying to usher our filing system into the twenty-first century." She gestures at the stacks of files. "Doc is under the impression technology is overrated."

"He might have a point."

"Can you believe he still uses a Rolodex?"

"Aren't those from 2000 BC?"

She tosses me a conspiratorial grin. "He's not going to like it when that thing goes missing."

"I don't think you'll be able to blame it on your coworkers down here."

She throws her head back and laughs, and I wonder how she maintains a sunny persona when she works in such close proximity to the dead.

"He's expecting you." She motions toward the corridor that will take me to Doc Coblentz's office. "Go right in."

I start down the hall, passing by the yellow-and-black biohazard sign and a plaque that reads

MORGUE AUTHORIZED PERSONNEL. At the end of the corridor, I go through a set of double doors and enter the medical sector of the facility. The autopsy room is straight ahead. To my right is the alcove where the biohazard protection is stored. Doc's glassed-in office on the left, the door open, an old Van Morrison tune pouring out.

Another quick inner pep talk, and I step into the doorway of his office, knock quietly on the jamb. "I hear your Rolodex is in grave danger," I say by way of greeting.

Doc Coblentz is wearing his usual white lab coat over blue scrubs. Tie-dyed graphic Crocs stick out from beneath his desk. He looks past me as if expecting the threat to be standing there in all of her pin-striped glory. "She's been after it for a year now. I've got twenty years of contacts in that thing."

He grumbles the words good-naturedly, but he's looking at me with scrutiny, and I know he's wondering if I'm up to the task ahead.

Resolved to let him know I am, I get down to business. "Do you have a time of death for me?"

"I do." He picks up the clipboard on his desk and flips a page, his eyes skimming. "Victim was logged in here at twelve thirteen P.M. Rectal body temp taken at twelve twenty-seven. Temp recorded at ninety-one point one degrees Fahrenheit." He looks at me over the top of his glasses. "The body loses approximately one point five degrees per hour. Keep in mind that ambient temperature can affect that number. In this case, there were no extreme temps, so I went with the median."

I start to do the math in my head, but he beats me to it. "In my estimation, this young man died around seven thirty this morning. That is not an exact time. It may change once I complete the autopsy and run a tox. But that is my most accurate number at this time. In terms of your investigation, I suggest a one-hour window in either direction. That puts the time of death between six thirty and eight thirty A.M."

I pull out my notebook and write it down. "The 911 call came in at eight oh nine A.M., so that narrows the window down to sometime between six thirty and eight oh nine."

"Do you have any idea who did it?" he asks.

"Not yet," I tell him. "So far, I'm chasing my tail."

"Well, I won't hold you up." Doc Coblentz rises and rounds his desk. "I wouldn't have called you if this wasn't important, Kate. I think you'll want to see this."

I feel a weird flutter in my gut as we go through the door. In the hall, Doc motions toward the alcove where Carmen has laid out individually wrapped protective garments. Mechanically, I tear open the packages and slip into a disposable gown. I pull the cap over my head, tuck my hair beneath the elastic band. I pull shoe covers over my boots, don a mask, and, finally, slip my hands into gloves.

Doc is waiting for me in the hall when I emerge, his eyes lingering on mine an instant longer than I'm comfortable with. "I'll make this as quick as I can," he tells me.

I hit him with a question so he'll knock it off. "You're still confident this is a homicide?"

"Now that I've taken a better look, I've no doubt." He pushes open the swinging doors. "You'll see."

The autopsy room is large and unnaturally bright. Floor-to-ceiling gray subway tile covers the walls. The air is uncomfortably cool. Despite the high-tech ventilation system, the smells of formalin and the sickly-sweet stench of decaying flesh hang in the air. A young man clad in scrubs, surgical cap, and gown stands at the counter, his back to us, working on something unseen.

The body of Aden Karn lies atop a stainless-steel gurney, draped with a sheet. A disposable paper cover has been placed over the head and shoulders. Doc Coblentz walks directly to the gurney, reaches for the pull-down work light, and switches it on.

I stand midway between the door and the gurney, taking in the scene, cognizant that I need to put on my cop face and walk over there and do my job. I remind myself that the clock is ticking and there's a killer on the loose in Painters Mill.

The doc is patient. Saying nothing, he busies himself with the light and the positioning of the disposable cover, touching the unspeakable instruments laid out on the tray. When I reach the gurney, he gives me a sagacious look. "Remember, Kate, everything we discuss prior to autopsy is preliminary. But I felt what I'm about to show you may be important in terms of your investigation."

"I appreciate it," I hear myself say, and I'm surprised because my voice sounds perfectly normal.

The young man standing at the counter turns to us. The mask prevents me from seeing his mouth, but I discern the smile in his eyes. "Hi, Chief Burkholder."

"This is Jared," the doctor tells me. "He's with BCI and he's going to assist today."

The young man looks like he's fresh out of college, and is as undisturbed by the body before us as I am disturbed.

I give him a nod and I'm glad for my own mask because I can't muster a smile.

"Here we go." The doc peels away the paper cover. A quiver runs the length of me at the sight of Aden Karn's head and shoulders. Waxy flesh. Dark hair contrasting sharply with the death pallor of the skin. One eye closed, one lid half open. Some type of stainless-steel device protrudes from the mouth, holding the cavity open. Lips drawn tight. Teeth exposed. The tongue swollen-looking and pale.

"I'm going to show you two incised wounds. Entries and exits, so there are four wounds total." The doc peels down the sheet to the victim's hips, exposing a skinny white chest. A sprinkling of hair. A flat belly. Protruding hip bones.

It's my first unobstructed look at the wound. The hair has been shaven, the blood washed away. The wound is the shape of an X or cross mark. The cut gapes slightly, the tissue beneath deep red and wet looking.

"I stand by my original assessment that this incised wound was likely caused by a crossbow bolt or arrow," the doc tells me. "What's even more interesting are the exit wounds."

He nods to his assistant. I resist the urge to step back while the two men shift the body onto its side. The exit wound is mid-back just to the left of the spine, and similar in shape, but slightly smaller than the entrance wound.

"Looks like the bolt went through the body," I hear myself say. "We searched the area for the bolt, but didn't find anything."

"I'm not surprised." The doc makes eye contact with me. "I don't believe this is a through-and-through, Kate." He looks down at the wound. "I believe the bolt lodged and was then *pushed* through the body in order for it to be removed."

Glock's words ring hard in my ears . . . *went crossbow hunting a few years ago with a friend of mine. He got a buck. When he retrieved his bolt, he didn't pull it out. He pushed it* through. *And it took some doing.*

I stare at Doc, and I grapple to find my voice. "How can you tell?"

"It's only a theory at this point. I may or may not be able to confirm it during autopsy, but I've two points to make. First, if you look at the cross marks, front and back, they do not align. Keep in mind that pushing a bolt through a human body is not an easy task and would require some degree of strength. In this case, preliminarily, it looks as if when the bolt was pushed through, it was twisted slightly. The kind of thing someone might do to force it. My second point is that the flesh around the secondary exit wound exhibits a small degree of tearing. As if the bolt head was moving in a fashion that did not have enough momentum to incise. And so the flesh was stretched and torn."

"As if someone pushed it through," I murmur.

"Exactly."

"Was the victim dead when that happened?"

"I don't know. I may or may not be able to answer that post-autopsy. But I'll try."

I think about that a moment. "You said there were two incised wounds."

The doc grimaces, then nods at his assistant.

The two men gently roll the victim back into a supine position. The doc sidles to the head. "Let's position him," he says to his assistant.

I watch as the two men slide a body block beneath the victim's neck so that the head is angled back. When they've finished, the doc looks at me. "I was curious about the amount of blood that had leaked from the mouth when we were at the scene."

"I remember," I tell him. "I assumed it was from internal injuries. Stomach or lungs."

"That was my thought initially, too." He nods to the assistant.

Jared sets a gloved hand on the deceased's forehead, then cranks the jaw-opening medical device wider, the rapid-fire clicks seeming obscene in the silence of the room. He picks up what looks like forceps, grasps the tongue, and gently pulls it outside the mouth and to one side.

Doc Coblentz adjusts the light so that the interior of the mouth is illuminated. He removes the wrapping from a long, disposable swab and indicates a point inside the mouth.

"There is a wound at the back of the throat, just behind the uvula," he tells me. "I nearly missed it during this preliminary stage."

I don't want to look, but I shift right and lean closer. I see the white-pink flesh of the dead man's gums. The pale bulge of the tongue. Teeth in good shape. A single cavity on an upper molar . . .

Jesus.

Using the swab, the doc depresses the uvula. That's when I spot the dark red wound at the back of the throat. The same cross-mark shape as the wound on the abdomen.

Puzzled, I look at the doc. "He was also shot in the mouth?" I ask. "With a bolt or arrow from the crossbow?"

"I believe so."

A hundred horrific images fly at me. But none of them quite explain how such a wound occurred. "How is it that a bolt could reach the back of the throat like that without first hitting the face? The teeth or lips?"

"That was my question, too, initially." The doc's gaze flicks to his assistant, who removes the block and repositions the victim's head, so that the back of it is visible.

The scalp has been shaved. I spot the bloodred cross mark immediately. "So the bolt entered the mouth and exited the back of the head," I murmur.

"I believe it did."

I turn my gaze back to the doc. "Unless this was some sort of freak occurrence—unless the bolt was fired when the victim's mouth was open— there's no way it could have entered the mouth without hitting the lips or teeth."

"That's certainly a logical train of thought." He nods at his assistant. "I wondered the same thing, so I shot an X-ray before you arrived."

Jared crosses to the counter against the wall and flicks a switch on the wall-mounted X-ray illuminator. The monochrome image of a skull materializes.

Doc crosses to it and uses the swab to point. "We can't see the soft-tissue injury," he says. "Only bone. But even from this perspective, you can see the teeth and jaw here." He indicates each, then runs the swab to the rear of the skull. "Here, you can see the secondary injury where the bolt went through the occipital bone, very close to where it joins the parietal. The important thing here, I believe, is the trajectory of the projectile and the angle of the injury."

"It looks like the bolt was slanted slightly upward," I say.

"But not too much," he says. "As you well know, in most homicides the injury trajectory is generally horizontal."

"But this can't possibly be self-inflicted." Even as I say the words, I hear the uncertainty in my voice. "Assisted suicide?"

"This is not a suicide. Not with two wounds, both possibly fatal. I'll know more once I do the internal exam, Kate. But I believe the initial shot was the one to the abdomen. Once the victim was down and likely immobile, I believe the shooter went to him, inserted the tip of the bolt into his mouth, and fired the crossbow a second time."

He returns to the gurney and with the swab

indicates the entry and exit wounds, which signify the trajectory of the bolt. "The bolt penetrated the soft tissue at the oropharynx. There are lacerations present at the soft palate and left tonsil. Vomitus present. All of which indicate force. Once the weapon was fired, the projectile penetrated the brain and exited through the occipital bone at the back of the skull."

I almost can't get my head around the brutality of such an act. It was a close-range killing done with cold deliberation. "Whether it was personal or random," I say, "whoever did this was intent on killing his victim."

The doc nods. "I've called in a forensic pathologist to assist with this one, Kate. This will likely be an extraordinarily complex case."

"How soon can you—"

"As soon as he arrives," the doc cuts in. "I'm waiting for a call back now."

We fall silent for a moment. As if sensing the tension, Jared clears his throat and goes to the counter to rearrange some of the items laid out on the tray.

"There's one other detail I think you should know about." Using the swab, the doc indicates the wound on the abdomen. "While we were preparing the body for autopsy, taking X-rays and photographs, Jared noticed a small amount of a . . . foreign substance at the opening of the abdominal wound."

"What kind of substance?"

He shrugs. "All I can tell you is that it is not biological."

"Poison?" I ask.

"No idea."

"Liquid? Powder?"

"Liquid and slightly oily in nature." He motions toward the victim's head. "Curious, I checked the wound inside the mouth for any foreign substance. Sure enough, we found the same."

"Do you think the substance is from the bolt?" I ask.

"I do." He shrugs. "We took samples of both and sent them to the lab in London, Ohio, for analysis."

In the back of my mind, I make a mental note to ask Tomasetti to expedite.

Doc Coblentz looks at me over the top of his glasses. He's got a doctor's eyes, innately kind and keenly adept at discerning all those feelings you work so hard to keep tucked away, out of sight.

"Whoever did this took his time," he tells me. "He stayed calm. Had the wherewithal and physical strength to push those bolts through a human body. With that second shot, he made damn sure that when he walked away, Aden Karn would be dead."

CHAPTER 6

I sit in the Explorer for several minutes with the window down, trying to make sense of every-thing I learned from the coroner. Early on, I'd hoped the death of Aden Karn was some kind of freak accident. Someone taking a blind shot or mishandling their weapon. Or even a prank gone awry, the perpetrator panicking and fleeing the scene. Now, it's obvious none of those scenarios are practicable. Aden Karn was shot as he rode his bicycle on an isolated road. Once he was injured and on the ground, the killer approached him, inserted the bolt head into his mouth, and fired the weapon a second time. It was an up-close-and-personal execution. Cold-blooded and violent. What kind of person commits such a heinous act and why?

Someone intent on killing. A psychopath. A sadist.

All of the above . . .

The possibilities taunt me as I pull onto the highway and head south toward Painters Mill. According to Angela and Lester Karn, their son lived with his longtime friend Wayne Graber. According to Emily Byler, Wayne was also involved with the sale of the truck.

I hail Dispatch as I idle through Millersburg. "Anything come back on Graber?" I ask.

My second-shift dispatcher, Jodie, answers. "He's clean, Chief."

"I'm on my way to his residence, Jodie. Who's on?"

"Skid," she says.

"Tell him to ten-twenty-five," I say, requesting that he meet me there.

"Roger that."

I'm not expecting any problems with Graber, but since I don't know him—and the individual who murdered Karn is as of yet unidentified and still at large—I err on the side of caution.

Aden Karn rented a house on Rockridge Road a few miles from where his body was discovered. It's a quiet gravel stretch that cuts a path between two large cornfields and dead-ends at the south fork of Painters Creek. I've just passed a DEAD END sign peppered with holes from shotgun pellets when I spot the mailbox. The number finger-painted on the side matches the address, so I make the turn. The driveway takes me up an incline and through a grove of pine trees, and then a split-level house looms into view. The lower part is brick, the upper story constructed of board-and-batten siding. A big deck bisects the two levels, and beneath it is a portico-type garage.

To my right, a gravel two-track leads to a workshop with dual overhead doors, both of which are closed. Beyond is the greenbelt that runs along the creek. Closer, there's a well-used burn pit. A couple of lawn chairs. A rusty fifty-gallon drum shot full of holes. There are no vehicles in sight.

It's after six P.M.; Graber could still be at work or on his way home. I'd considered calling him, but I want to catch him unprepared. I park in front of the house and get out. A cacophony of birdsong greets me. The caws of crows in the cornfield behind the house. It's so quiet I can hear the rattle of the stalks as a breeze eases through.

I hit my radio as I start toward the house. "Ten-twenty-three," I say, letting Dispatch know I've arrived on scene.

"Copy that."

I take a shoddily constructed flagstone path to the portico garage. A charcoal grill lies on its side to my right. A welcome mat is caked with mud. The door is a nine-light that offers an unobscured view of a small living room. Secondhand furniture inside. Worn carpet that isn't quite clean. Big-screen TV on the wall.

Standing slightly to one side, I knock, listening for Skid, taking in as many details as I can. Inside, a black cat skulks past the door. A couple of spindly plants beneath a window on the other side of the room. Through an interior doorway, I can see a galley-style kitchen with off-white linoleum and pine cabinets.

I tug out my cell and call Dispatch.

"Hey, Chief."

"No one here at the residence. Can you get me a number and address for Mast Tiny Homes?" I ask, thinking he might still be at work.

"Call you right back."

Dropping my cell into my pocket, I backtrack to the flagstone path and look around. That's when I spot the souped-up Nova behind my Explorer. Uneasy surprise quivers through me when I see the driver's-side door fly open. A male jumps out, moving fast, pauses to look at my vehicle. He's tall with an athletic build. Fair-haired. Wearing dark trousers and a work shirt. He's got his cell phone pressed to his ear, talking to someone, gesturing wildly.

I call out to him. "Hello?"

He startles at the sound of my voice, swings around to face me. "What's going on?" he asks. "What happened?" He drops the cell into his pocket and breaks into a run, coming toward me at a fast clip.

Caution whispers a warning in my ear, reminding me there's a shooter on the loose. I don't know this man; I don't know his intent or frame of mind.

Aware of my radio mike at my lapel, my .38 strapped to my hip, I raise my hand. "Stop right there," I tell him. "Don't get any closer, okay?"

His stride falters and he halts. He cocks his head and looks at me quizzically. "Someone just told me . . ." His voice breaks as if he's run out of breath. "I just heard Aden Karn was killed."

I don't see any weapons on him, but I don't like the way he's looking at me. Too intense. Too much emotion. Distressed.

I identify myself. "What's your name?"

"I'm Wayne Graber," he says. "I live here."

The description I have for Graber fits. Twenty-two years old. Fair-haired. Blue-eyed. He's wearing a Caterpillar cap. Too-long hair sticking out the back and curling at the ends. He's nice-looking, with a runner's build. His clothes are dirty as if he spent his day partaking in some form of manual labor.

"You just get off work?" Pulling out my shield, I close the distance between us, cautious, not getting too close.

"What the hell happened to Aden?" he demands. "Is it true?"

"Who told you that?" I ask.

He chokes back a sound of frustration. "His old man called. He could barely speak. Told me Aden was killed this morning. Is it true?"

Most Amish don't have phones for personal use; the *Ordnung*, or unwritten rules of the church district, prohibit it unless it's used for business purposes. I happen to know Lester Karn keeps a cell phone beneath the counter at his shop.

"I'm afraid so," I say. "It happened this morning."

"Oh my God." He raises his hand to his forehead, presses his fingers against the bridge of his nose. "For God's sake. He's *dead?* What the hell happened to him?"

"We're still trying to put all of it together." I pause. "What's your relationship to Aden?" I've been told the two men are best friends and roommates, but I ask anyway, feeling him out. Always a good idea to confirm hearsay.

"He's my best friend." He gestures to the house, looking helpless, lets his hand fall to his side. "We live here. I just saw him this morning."

"I'm sorry for your loss," I tell him.

"Yeah. Shit." He looks past me toward the house as if expecting his friend to appear and prove all of this is just some perverse joke.

I give him a moment to regain his composure, then motion toward the Nova. "Where are you coming from?"

He looks down at the ground and shakes his head, as if still trying to absorb what he's been told. "Work. I get off at five. I stopped by the Brass Rail for a beer. Then I get that frickin' phone call from Lester and I rushed over here thinking it was some kind of mistake."

The sound of a vehicle pulling into the driveway draws my attention. I look up to see Skid's cruiser pull up behind the Nova.

"When did you last see Aden?" I ask.

He slants a glance toward the cruiser, then

turns his attention back to me. "Like I said. This morning. Before work." His voice breaks, and he falls silent.

I pull out my notebook. "What time was that?"

"Six thirty or so. We were both rushing around, getting dressed." He closes his eyes a moment, chokes out a one-syllable laugh. "Hungover."

"Where did Aden work?"

"Buckeye Construction," he says. "Been with them about a year now. He's good with his hands. Likes to build stuff."

"Did he drive at all?"

"He rides his bike just about everywhere. Some dude he works with picks him up every morning." His face goes taut as if he's struggling with another round of emotion. He gestures toward the workshop. "Aden just bought his first car. A couple of weeks ago. It's a junker, but it's got a big engine. He was excited, you know? We've been working on it." He motions toward the workshop. "Gonna be badass when we're finished."

He closes his eyes as if trying to stanch tears. "Shit."

"Do you know the name of the guy who picks him up?" I ask.

"Jeez, Aden mentioned him a couple times. Works at Buckeye, too. Kevin . . . something." His brows knit. "Waddell. Kevin Waddell. That's it."

I write it down. "Where do they meet?"

"Jesus." Turning away, he walks over to the Nova, sets his hands on the hood, and shakes his head as if he's trying to wake from a bad dream. "A few miles north of here. They meet in the parking lot of that old Lutheran church off Township Road 34."

I know the church and the area. It's not terribly far from the property owned by Vernon Fisher. . . .

I look at Graber. He seems genuinely upset. I've got pretty good instincts when it comes to people. If someone is lying or being disingenuous, I can usually spot it. Shock is particularly difficult to fake. Grief even more so. That said, I've seen killers genuinely mourn the person they murdered.

"What happened to him?" Graber asks the question without looking at me. "Someone hit him or what?"

"The coroner hasn't made an official ruling yet, but from all indications it looks as if he was shot."

"*Shot?* With a gun?" Straightening, he turns to face me. "You mean like an accident?"

"We believe he may have been shot with a bolt from a crossbow or combination bow. We're still trying to figure things out, but it was likely deliberate."

"Oh my God. That's . . . crazy. Why would—"

100

Mouth pulled into a grimace, he slaps a hand down on the hood, angry and overcome. When he raises his eyes to mine, tears shimmer. "Who the hell did it?"

I hold his gaze, but he doesn't blink, doesn't look away. "We don't know yet."

I'm aware of Skid getting out of his cruiser, hanging back a few feet, watching the exchange.

"Mr. Graber, did Aden have any enemies that you know of?" I ask. "Was he involved in any disputes or have problems with anyone?"

"No, ma'am. He was a laid-back dude. Funny. Everyone liked him. They really did. They—" He stops talking and swings his gaze to mine. "Wait a minute. Vernon Fisher and his clan of losers. Aden and me . . . we sold him a truck. Fisher ran the shit out of it and blew the engine. Then he accused us of selling him a lemon and refused to pay. So Aden and I went over there one night and we repossessed it." He relays a story similar to the one I heard from Vernon Fisher except from a contrasting perspective.

"If the truck wasn't running, how did you get it home?" I ask.

"Tug strap and a big V-8."

"Did Fisher threaten Aden?"

"Threatened to beat his ass. I mean, Fisher was pretty hot about the truck. You know, after we repoed it. Dude wanted his down payment back."

101

I wait, but he doesn't continue, so I press. "What else?"

He looks away and shakes his head. "Look, I'm not going to say anything bad about Aden. He was a good guy. Period. But to tell you the truth, Chief Burkholder, I think he should have considered giving Fisher his money back. I mean, we had the truck. We rebuilt the engine. Got it running. And we had it resold to someone else in a week."

"How upset was Fisher?"

"He was pretty pissed off."

"Do you think Fisher is capable of violence?" I ask.

He tightens his mouth as if reluctant to say. "He's an asshole. He's a mean drunk. Saw him get into it a few times over the years."

"With who?"

"Just those clowns he hangs out with. I saw him get in a fight once at the Brass Rail, too. He's a dirty fighter."

I write all of it down. "Can you tell me how you spent your morning this morning?"

"Me?" His face darkens. "You think I . . ." He cuts the words short, looks down, shakes his head. "Maybe you ought to be asking Vernon Fisher that," he snaps.

"Everyone gets asked," I tell him. "Including you."

He raises his head, looks from me to Skid and

back to me. "I went to work, like always. You can check with anyone there. Left the house around six thirty or so and drove straight there. Clocked in at seven."

"Did Aden have a cell phone?" I ask.

"No, but he was going to get one," he tells me.

"How long had he been on *rumspringa*?" I ask.

He recognizes my pronunciation and looks at me a little more closely. "You're the cop used to be Amish."

I nod.

After a moment, he shrugs. "Aden started running around three or four months ago. I mean, he was twenty-one. Past time to have a little fun if you ask me. But talk about a fish out of water. Early on, the guy didn't even know how to drink. You know how it is when you're Amish. You go from living a godly life to hanging with the devil. I reckon I corrupted him." He laughs, but there's a shudder in his voice, as if his emotions are still too close to the surface. "He liked the freedom and all, but I figured he was going to get baptized pretty quick. He was seeing that Byler girl."

"Emily Byler?"

He nods. "Aden was pretty smitten with her."

"Do they get along?" I ask.

"They were tight. Everyone figured they were going to get married."

"Did Aden see any other women?"

103

He looks away, shoves his hands into his pockets, and shrugs.

"Wayne?"

He sighs. "He might've . . . you know, seen one or two over the last few months. English girls, you know." A ruddy hue climbs into his cheeks. "Look, he's a guy. He'd just discovered his freedom. He liked women, if you know what I mean."

"Any angry boyfriends?" I ask. "Or husbands?"

"No, ma'am, nothing like that. I mean, he's pretty discreet about stuff like that. Especially since he was Amish and . . . you know, seeing Emily and all."

"Do you have any of their names?" I ask. "The women he was with?"

"No, ma'am."

I shove the notebook into my pocket. "Do you mind if we take a quick look around?"

His eyes skate from mine to Skid and back to me. "If you think it'll help . . ."

He seems surprised by the request, so I add, "With your permission to search, I can forgo getting a warrant. That'll save us some time. The sooner we can find the person responsible and get him off the street, the better for everyone involved."

"Sure, just . . . do whatever you need to do. I'll let you in."

I make eye contact with Skid, then gesture

104

toward the workshop. He nods and starts that way.

I follow Graber to the house, wait in the garage portico while he unlocks the door. "Sorry about the mess," he mutters as we go inside. "Neither one of us is a very good housekeeper."

The house is the epitome of a bachelor pad. There's a ratty sofa, the arm damaged from cat scratching. A thin layer of dust on a 1980s coffee table. A pair of sneakers tossed on the floor.

"Did Aden have a desk or office?" I ask.

"Naw . . . just a bedroom." Graber motions. "Room at the end of the hall."

I catch a glimpse of another cat darting out of the bathroom on my left as I start down the hall. The door to my right is closed. I continue to the door at the end and push it open. The room is small and dark and smells faintly of dirty socks. A navy bedsheet secured with nails covers the single window. I flick the switch, but the light doesn't come on, so I pull out my mini Maglite, shine it around the room. There's a closet to my left, the door standing ajar. Twin-size bed, unmade. Next to it, a night table with three drawers. A rickety-looking chest against the wall.

I start with the night table, slide open the top drawer. Not much inside. A disposable lighter. A roll of masking tape. Deck of cards. Methodically, I go through each drawer. A rubber-banded stack of paid bills—electric and cable TV. A receipt from the Walmart in Millersburg. A corncob pipe that smells vaguely of marijuana. An old Polaroid camera, no film. Nothing of interest.

I go to the bed, kneel, and look beneath it. A wadded-up T-shirt. Box of tissues. I lift the mattress just enough to see beneath. A brown envelope stares back at me. I pull it out. Nothing written on the outside. I peer inside, pluck out six photos. I try to suppress a feeling of shock at the sight of female genitalia, close-up and raw. Quickly, I shuffle through. There's nothing written on the back. No face and no way to identify the woman who was photographed or the photographer.

There's no law against viewing or possessing pornography in the state of Ohio as long as it doesn't involve a minor child and the person being photographed consented. Adults are free to do as they please. With a young man having been murdered, these photos may or may not be relevant. As far as I know, Karn could have been killed for posting revenge porn. While I don't have an official warrant, I do have permission to search. If I feel the need to take a piece of evidence that may or may not be related to the case, I can do so and follow up with an official warrant later.

Using my lapel mike, I hail Skid. "What's your twenty?"

"Just finished up the workshop."

"Anything?"

"Just a bunch of damn wasps."

"I'm inside the house. Back bedroom. Bring your ECK, will you?" I say, referring to the evidence collection kit all my officers keep in their vehicles.

"Roger that."

I put the photos back in the envelope and set it on the bed. Then I move on to the closet, open the door, and shine my beam around. Karn was neat for a twenty-one-year-old bachelor. Work clothes on one side. A couple of nice shirts and trousers on the other. A pair of sneakers toe-in against the baseboard. There's a shelf a foot or so higher than my head. I can't see if there's anything on it, so I run my hands over the surface. My fingertips brush against what feels like a cardboard box that's just out of sight.

"Chief?"

I glance over my shoulder to see Skid enter the room. "Good timing," I say. "Something back there I can't reach."

"I got it." He crosses to the closet, stands on his tiptoes, and pulls a shoebox off the shelf. "There you go." He hands me the box.

I open it, feel a rush of heat in my cheeks at the sight of the purple dildo. "Well . . ."

"Uh." Skid laughs, but it's an embarrassed sound.

Glad I'm wearing gloves, I set my beam in the

box. I see several packaged condoms. A tube of lubricant. A vibrator.

Skid clears his throat. "All righty then."

"Yep." I motion to the envelope on the bed. "There are some . . . pornographic photos, too."

"Polaroid?"

I nod. "No idea if it's important or relevant."

"Seems like a little much for an Amish kid."

"I think so, too."

He nods, not quite looking at me. "Are we going to take it?"

I can't tell if he's kidding, so I don't smile. "I'll just take a few pics in case this turns out to be some kind of revenge-porn thing. We can always come back later if we need to."

We spend another twenty minutes in the house looking through the kitchen drawers, the desk off the living room, even the bathroom and garage, but there's nothing of interest, certainly nothing remotely connected to the murder of Aden Karn. The one scenario that rises above everything else is the disagreement about the truck. Six hundred dollars isn't exactly killing money. It's a sad fact, but I've seen people killed for less.

CHAPTER 7

The early stages of a homicide investigation are a frenetic mix of interviewing witnesses, false starts, hard stops, and sleep deprivation. It's been nearly twelve hours since Aden Karn's body was discovered and all I have to show for my efforts is a half-baked theory and a headache the size of Lake Erie.

I've put multiple calls in to Mike Rasmussen, the sheriff of Holmes County. I've also called John Tomasetti, who is an agent with the Ohio Bureau of Criminal Investigation—not to mention the man I'll be marrying in a few days. Unfortunately for me, neither man has returned my calls.

I'm in my cubbyhole office at the police station, trying to jump-start a brain that's running on caffeine and frustration, when my second-shift dispatcher, Jodie, peeks in.

"Everyone's here, Chief," she says, referring to my small team of officers. "Including the pizza."

Frazzled as I am, I smile. "You have no idea how happy I am to hear that."

Snapping up my legal pad and the file I've amassed in the last hours, I follow her to the meeting room. It's an impossibly small space jammed with a beat-up table, six mismatched chairs, and my entire team of officers—all five of them. The aroma of pepperoni and yeasty crust wafts from the pizza box on the tabletop. I go to the half lectern at the head of the table.

"Sorry for the late meeting, but I think all of you have heard about the murder this morning." I look down at the two squares of pizza on a paper plate someone has set out for me. "I think we can eat and talk at the same time."

"We'll see," Pickles mutters from his place across from me.

Since everyone has already put in a full day and then some, I get right to it, outlining everything I learned from my visit to the morgue.

"I'm leaning toward the scenario that Karn was targeted," I tell them. "The killer knew his route. Knew his routine. Evidently, he felt he could get away without being seen."

"He picked the right spot." Mona Kurtz is a rookie and my only female officer, but she never hesitates to jump in with her thoughts when we're brainstorming, a trait I appreciate very much. "Hansbarger Road is pretty secluded."

"A lot of trees out that way, too," Skid adds.

I look at Pickles. "What did you and T.J. find out about crossbow and/or bolt sales in the area?"

He straightens, flips open his notebook. "I checked with Larry Peterson over at Nussbaum Sports first thing. They do not sell crossbows or combination bows. I also spoke with Pat Donlevy over at Donlevy Sporting Goods." He glances down at his notes. "In the last six months, they sold three crossbows, one combination bow, and half a dozen boxes of bolts."

He rattles off the names of four individuals, two of whom I'm familiar with in a nod-on-the-street kind of way. "Any of them have a criminal record?" I ask.

"They're clean," Pickles puts in.

Which doesn't automatically rule them out, but always good to check. "Go talk to them. Find out if they have any connection to Karn. See if they have alibis. Find out if they've let anyone borrow their bow."

"Yes, ma'am."

"If nothing pans out, let's expand our six-month time frame to one year and include sporting goods stores in Millersburg." I look at Pickles. "Speaking of, I want you to run up to the Walmart there and see if anything pops."

"I'm on it," the old man says.

I glance down at my notes. "Glock, tell me about the canvass."

"I checked every farm on the block, Chief." He denotes the roads that intersect Hansbarger. "I hit two more farms off the township road. Some of the folks mentioned seeing Karn riding his bike, mornings and evening. No one recalled seeing him this morning. No one saw any other individuals. No one on foot. No vehicles. No buggies or bikes. Nothing unusual."

"Do any of them have a security camera or game cam?"

"One game cam." He grimaces. "Battery was dead."

"Did you contact Buckeye Construction?" I ask, referring to Aden Karn's employer.

"Talked to his boss, Herb Schollenberger. He says Karn was well-liked. Easy to get along with. Reliable. Never missed a day. No problems with coworkers or clients."

"Someone didn't like him," Pickles mutters.

"Roommate, Wayne Graber, told me he rides with a guy by the name of Kevin Waddell," I say.

"He lives in Painters Mill." Glock glances at his phone, scrolls to his notes, and rattles off an address.

I add it to my notes. "Anyone else ride with them?" I ask.

"A couple of Amish guys." He recites their names, both of which are familiar. "They all meet at the Lutheran church."

"Go talk to them, will you?"

"Yes, ma'am."

I look at Jodie, who's standing in the doorway, listening for the switchboard. "Run Waddell through LEADS. I also want a tip line set up. Five-hundred-dollar reward for information leading to an arrest. Callers can remain anonymous. Get that info out on social media. Call Steve Ressler at *The Advocate*, too. I think some people still read newspapers. If you need help, draft Lois and Margaret."

Flashing me a thumbs-up, she backs from the room.

I look out at my officers. "I don't have to tell you we're on mandatory OT until we figure out who did this," I tell them. "Keep on it. My cell is on twenty-four seven."

The brutality of Aden Karn's murder occupies my thoughts as I drive to the mobile home park where Kevin Waddell lives. I've never owned or fired a crossbow, but I've seen them used. They seem heavy and unwieldy, slow to load, and they cannot be concealed. Only someone comfortable with that kind of weapon would use it for such a high-risk endeavor as murder. Hansbarger Road isn't well traveled; there are only a handful of farms out that way. Whoever ambushed Karn didn't happen upon him and commit an impulse kill. No, this was planned. The killer knew Karn would be there. He knew the area. And he was confident enough in his skill as a crossbowman to know he could make the shot and get away without being seen.

Kevin Waddell lives in a newish double-wide in a pretty area shaded by mature elm and oak trees. A dozen mobile homes are generously spaced with concrete driveways and well-maintained yards. I park curbside and take the sidewalk to the deck. I know even before I knock there's no one home. There's no car in the driveway. No sound of a TV or stereo coming from inside.

"You're striking out, Burkholder," I mutter.

I walk back to the Explorer and slide behind the wheel, sit there for a moment. It's getting late and I'm tired and cranky. One of the most difficult things for a cop to do when working on a homicide case is go home. That's especially true if the murderer is at large. How can you walk away when the people you've sworn to serve and protect are in danger? Some cops can turn off that nagging, agitated voice. They can curb the urge to keep pushing. I'm the cop that keeps going, past my endurance, sometimes to my own detriment. Good or bad or somewhere in between, that's the way I roll.

Sighing, I tug out my cell and pull up a map of the area. Buckeye Construction is just south of Millersburg. I shrink the map, isolate the place where the murder occurred. I find the pickup point at the Lutheran church. I measure the distance to my current location. If I were to draw a line from point to point to point, the triangle would include the address of the one place that might call out to a man after a long day. The Brass Rail Saloon.

I pick up my cell and call Dispatch. "Anything come back on Waddell?" I ask.

"No outstanding warrants. Simple assault conviction six years ago. Happened in Wooster. Sixty days in jail. Paid a fine. He's also had a couple of OVIs. First offense four years ago. Second offense, three years ago. License suspended for a year. Thirty days in jail. Paid a fine."

"I'm at his place now, but he's not here," I tell her. "I'm going to swing by the Brass Rail before I head back to the station."

"Be careful out there, Chief. I hear that place gets pretty sketchy Thursday nights."

"Not that you know that from experience."

She snickers. "I'll take the fifth on that."

The final vestiges of daylight hover on the horizon when I pull into the parking lot of the Brass Rail Saloon. The gravel lot is so jam-packed full of vehicles some of the trucks have parked in the grass. I idle through the lot to see if I can spot Waddell's white Ford van, and I find it a couple of rows from the front, telling me he's been here awhile. I'm not sure if that's good or bad.

I score a parking spot next to a Ford dually hooked up to a stock trailer—sans livestock—and head inside. A gaggle of young women smoking cigarettes, long necks in hand, line either side of the steps as I take them to the front door.

"Evening," I say.

The woman sitting on the rail gives me an eye roll. I hear a whispered "bitch cop" as I push open the door, but I ignore the comment. This isn't exactly the kind of establishment that welcomes cops.

The screech of steel guitar chafes my eardrums when I enter. The place teems with Thursday-night partygoers, getting a jump on the weekend. From the stage, a band belts out a chain-saw rendition of Lou Reed's "Sweet Jane." Someone has brought in dry ice, which brings a rise of fog to the light show and makes for a nice effect. Fifteen years ago, a younger me would have been duly impressed. Tonight, the gaudiness of it makes me sigh.

My uniform draws stares as I make my way to the bar. I make eye contact with a couple of people I recognize, but no one greets me. I spot the bartender as I approach and he gives me a nod. Jimmie has served up alcohol and smart-assed commentary for as long as I've been chief. He's fortysomething going on twenty-two and looks snazzy in his white button-down shirt, gold chain, and jeans. His goatee almost hides the scar that splits his chin. He told me he got the scar in a car accident. Rumor has it a biker hit him with a Louisville Slugger. While he may be a touch disreputable, if there's something shady going on, Jimmie is the man in the know. I make it a point to stay on his good side because, surly as he is, he usually comes through.

"Hey, Jimmie," I say as I sidle up to the bar. "You staying out of trouble?"

He frowns at me over the tap as he fills two mugs. Hard eyes on mine and laced with something akin to disdain, but I know it's not personal. "Get you something?"

"Ice water."

Grabbing a glass from beneath the bar, he jams it into the ice box, fills it from the tap, then expertly slides it over to me. "Heard about that murder over to Hansbarger Road. You guys figure out who did it?"

"Working on it." Aware that the man sitting next to me is paying attention to our exchange, I lower my voice. "I'm looking for Kevin Waddell."

"He's here." Lifting the two beer mugs he just filled, he takes them to two men a few patrons down.

The place is too loud to hear much but the music. Definitely too loud to carry on a conversation, especially if you want it to remain private. Propping my elbow on the bar, I watch a couple stumble onto the dance floor and break into a raucous hip-grinding lambada.

"What do you want with Waddell?" Jimmie lines up four shot glasses and dribbles a generous amount of Patron into each.

"Just a quick chat."

His eyes burn into mine. "He's tipping good tonight."

I pick up the glass and drink. "I'll try not to screw up his mojo."

He gives me a halfhearted smile. "Last I seen, he was in the booth over there at the back, by the men's room."

I lay a ten-dollar bill on the bar and start that way. I spot Waddell as I weave through the crowd. He's sitting with three men, talking animatedly. A pitcher of beer and four mugs on the table in front of him. According to his driver's license, he's thirty-two years old. But he looks older. Long blond hair. Scruffy beard. Light blue eyes. A wiry build covered with the sinew of a man who works with his hands.

I reach the booth. "Kevin Waddell?"

Four pairs of eyes sweep to me. I see varying degrees of surprise and drunkenness. Uneasiness interlaced with curiosity. A little scorn thrown in for good measure.

Waddell sets down his mug. "Can I help you?"

I can tell by the thickness of his tongue, the glassiness of his eyes that this isn't his first beer. Probably not his second. Certainly not an ideal situation for gleaning information, but I don't want to wait until morning.

"I'm sorry to intrude on your evening," I tell him. "I'd like to ask you a few questions if you have a minute."

The four men exchange looks, telling me they've likely heard about the murder. The man next to him breaks into a grin, elbows him. "Told you they were going to come for you."

"At least she's polite about it," one of the other men says.

"She don't look too bad, either." He snickers. "And it ain't even midnight."

I don't acknowledge any of it.

Waddell doesn't so much as break a smile. "This about Karn?"

I nod. "It's a little loud in here," I say. "Would you mind stepping outside with me?"

I'm aware of eyes on us as I lead him to the exit at the rear. I push open the door. Two men smoking to my right. I go left, stop next to a dumpster.

"What's this about?" Waddell says as he approaches me. He's trying to look sober. Back straight. Walking with the meticulousness of a man being given a sobriety test.

"You're not in any trouble," I begin, hoping to put him at ease.

"That's good because I didn't do anything wrong."

"I understand you drive Aden Karn to work every day."

"Ain't no law against that, is there?"

I give him the fundamentals of what happened. "He was found on Hansbarger Road around eight o'clock this morning."

"Dang. Hated hearing about that. He was a nice kid." He shakes his head. "Hansbarger is just a couple miles from where we meet. That old Lutheran church out there by the ice shanty."

I nod. "How well did you know Karn?"

"Aw, we worked together a few months. Kid was Amish, you know. Didn't drive. I told him I practically drove by his place every day and offered to give him a ride."

"Were you friends?"

"Well, we didn't run in the same circles or anything. But I drank a beer or two with him. You know, after work. Right here at the Brass Rail." As if remembering, he laughs. "Good-looking kid. Let me tell you, he was a chick magnet."

I touch on the same questions I covered with Wayne Graber and the others, but he doesn't give me anything I haven't already heard.

"Everyone seemed to like Aden," he tells me. "He was always on time. You could tell this kid was Amish. I mean, he had a good work ethic, you know? Believe me, a lot of them young ones don't these days."

"Was Aden having any problems with anyone?"

Waddell scratches his head. "Come to think of it, he wasn't too happy with that buddy of his."

"Which buddy is that?"

"The dude bought the truck from him."

"Vernon Fisher?"

He snaps his fingers. "That's the guy."

No one had mentioned that Fisher and Karn were friends. I'd assumed their only connection was the truck. "They were friends?" I ask.

"Good friends. In fact, I had a beer with the two of them a couple times right here at the Brass Rail. Mostly, they hung out at that old gas station. Worked on cars. Drinkin' and listening to music and shit. Then that whole truck thing happened and I think their friendship went down the toilet." He takes me through the same story I heard from Vernon and Wayne.

"Did Vernon Fisher or anyone else make any threats against Aden?" I ask.

"All's I know is that Fisher wasn't happy with Aden or Graber when they repossessed that truck. He wanted his money back. Ruined their friendship, and I think they'd known each other since they were little kids. That's all I know."

CHAPTER 8

There's a quiet inner joy that comes with arriving home. That moment when the rest of the world melts away and for a small snatch of time, you're exactly where you want to be. It's nearly ten P.M. when I park the Explorer next to Tomasetti's Tahoe and shut down the engine. I called him twice over the course of the day. Usually, even if he's in the midst of a case or caught up in meetings, he'll at least text. Today, though I'm sure by now he's heard about Karn's murder, he didn't respond. I try not to let that niggle at me as I grab my laptop case and start for the door.

The kitchen smells of cooked pasta and garlic. On the stove, a covered pot quietly burbles. Two place settings on the table. A wine bottle and opener on the counter next to the sink. Hefting my laptop case, I cross through the kitchen and living room toward the small bedroom we've transformed into a home office. I've case-related work to do this evening—mainly to catch up on all the things I didn't have time to do today. First, I want to see Tomasetti. Share some conversation and a glass of wine. A quick dinner.

The office door stands open. The light is off. I'm midway to the desk and reaching for the lamp when I spot Tomasetti. He's sitting at the desk, looking down at his laptop. A tumbler containing two fingers of whiskey sits comfortably on the blotter next to him. The blue glow of the monitor illuminates his face enough for me to see that whatever he's doing isn't pleasant. The clenched jaw. Tight mouth. The eyes I know so well and tell me so much, even when he doesn't want me to know. He looks up, surprised, and makes an attempt to conceal the darkness I see in his features.

"I didn't hear you come in," he says, his voice rough.

"Didn't mean to surprise you." I set my laptop case on the floor at the side of the desk. "Working late?" I ask.

"Thinking mostly," he says.

"Is everything okay?"

He hits me with a pointed frown, knowing he's busted despite his halfhearted attempt to mislead me. "Everything's fine."

"Fine, huh?" I go to him. "Well, that's good."

Grimacing, he rises. I fall against him, put my arms around his neck.

"I'm glad you're home," he says after a moment.

"Me, too." I close my eyes when his arms go around me. For the span of several seconds, we don't speak. We soak each other in. Give what we can. Take what we need.

When he releases me, I switch on the banker's

lamp. He squints at the sudden light. "I'm sorry I didn't return your call," he says. "I heard about the murder."

"A crossbow, of all things," I say. "He was Amish. Just twenty-one years old."

"You know him?" he asks. "The family?"

"The family," I say. "Not well."

But I can tell his mind isn't on the murder of Aden Karn and for the first time since seeing the young Amish man lying in the road dead, it's not the case that's hammering on my brain, but Tomasetti.

"So are you going to tell me what's bothering you?" I ask.

"I guess you're not going to let me hang out in my cave and sulk."

"Not a chance."

His mouth curves, but it's a tired and resigned facsimile of a smile that's for my benefit. "You and I have been cops for a long time," he says. "It's what we do. Who we are. It's what we know. Sometimes, I think it's *all* we know."

"A few individuals might even say we're good at it," I tell him.

He pauses, pensive, studying me. I stare back, saying nothing because I want him to continue. Because whether he realizes it or not, he needs to.

"Back when we were rookies," he says, "experience was everything. Training was king and knowledge was the key to the universe. While those things are still true, with age comes the realization that sometimes you can know *too* much. All of the knowledge and training and experience we've amassed becomes baggage. And sometimes we know how a case is going to play out before it actually plays out."

John Tomasetti is the strongest person I know. I watched him overcome the kind of tragedy that would have destroyed most of us. The murders of his wife and two children left a wound on his heart and disfiguring scars on his soul. And came within a breath of killing him. The injustice sent him hurtling into a black hole so deep no one thought he'd ever be able to climb out, least of all him. Somehow, he did.

"This is about a case?" I ask.

He nods. "I'm assisting on the Johnson kidnapping."

I know the story. Even from the outside looking in, it's a heartbreaker. I've not followed the investigation closely; I haven't had time. But it's dominated the news cycle. Two little girls, about the same ages as Tomasetti's when they died, went missing in Cleveland four days ago.

"Two kids," he says. "Walking home from school. They never made it. Parents called Cleveland PD in less than an hour of them being late. Cops found their books. Little pink backpack. Homework still inside. No sign of the kids." He sighs. "I drew the short stick."

I try to read him, but he's good at keeping his emotions in check, keeping them buried. "That's the toughest kind of case," I say.

"Especially for the parents."

"Any leads?" I ask.

"We got nothing." He shakes his head. "From all indications, it was a stranger kidnapping." An abduction by an unknown individual is the most dangerous kind. He knows it. I know it.

. . . sometimes you know too much . . .

Tomasetti is the kind of cop who pours everything he's got into a case. He's obsessive and intense; he's to the point. Sometimes he's not very nice. He's driven, but he doesn't get caught up in the drama. Not in an emotional way. It's something both of us struggled with early in our careers, finally achieving the safe-distance state of mind only recently. That said, some cases hit harder than others. Parallels, I think, and I feel the pain of the connection spread in my chest.

"This case isn't going to end well," he says after a moment. "Not a stranger abduction. Not after four days."

"You don't know that."

"I wish I didn't. But I do, Kate. I've seen it happen too many times." He scrubs a hand over his head, mussing his hair. "Maybe I've been doing this too goddamn long."

"You know that's cynical."

He leans against the desk, picks up the tumbler

of whiskey and sips, gives me the whiskey grimace. "That's the thing about baggage and age, especially when you're a cop. You see too much too many times. You see the family suffering. You see their hope. Their desperation. And you lie to them because you know bad things happen to good people far more often than we'd like." He offers me a grim smile. "More about my mindset than you ever wanted to know, but there you go."

I discern the pain in the depths of his eyes, and my love for him fills my heart. "Is there anything I can do?"

He looks down at me and I see him come back to himself. To that place I know. "Just . . . keep coming home."

Saying his name, I turn to him, take the tumbler from his hand, sip, and set it down. "If it's any consolation, to you or the family or anyone who needs to hear it, you are the best man for the job. If anyone can bring them home, it's you. It's going to hurt, but you're going to do it anyway. That's got to count for something."

"I hope so," he says quietly.

"That's the thing about pouring your life into a case like that. Even if there's a bad outcome, life goes on. With or without us. Hard as it is, we pick ourselves up. We focus on the good. And we put one foot in front of the other."

A smile whispers across his features. Small,

but genuine. "Well, I'm glad I've got you here to point that out."

Smiling back, I reach up and set my hand against his cheek. "What do you say we focus on the good for a little while?"

"Does that include wine and dinner?"

I take his hand and lead him from the room.

CHAPTER 9

When an individual lies to me in the course of an investigation—even if the lie is by omission—it automatically puts him on my "person of interest" roll. When more than one individual fails to mention the same detail, I know there's something there. According to Kevin Waddell, Vernon Fisher and Aden Karn were friends. And yet neither Graber nor Fisher mentioned it. Coincidental omission? Or are they hiding something?

As I pull out of the lane and head south toward Painters Mill, I call Glock. "I want you to pick up Vernon Fisher."

"My pleasure, Chief. Charge?"

I tell him about my conversation with Waddell. "He failed to mention his friendship with Karn, so I think we need to get his attention. Let him know we're serious."

"You think he's involved?"

"I think he knows more than he claims." I think about that a moment. "Let's pick him up for questioning. Take him to the police station. Put him in an interview room and let him stew until I get there."

"My morning just keeps getting better," he tells me.

Not for the first time, I'm reminded why I like Glock so much. "I'm going to talk to Wayne Graber," I tell him. "I'll be at the station as soon as I can."

Mast Tiny Homes is located south of Millersburg on a busy highway across from a farm store. A dozen or so wood structures, everything from modern chic to farmhouse to chicken coop, welcome shoppers to the notion of a simpler life and a little piece of heaven in the country. A large metal building with twin overhead doors, both of which are closed, is set back from the road and nestled among the trees. There's a smaller man door with an OFFICE sign at the side, so I head that way.

The whine of saws and the punch-punch-punch of a nail gun sound from the interior. I enter to the smells of fresh-cut wood and the oily tang of stain. A man wearing blue coveralls works the blade of a miter saw through a massive chunk of oak. A red-bearded older man with a bandanna tied around his head makes use of a nail gun to put the finishing touches on a structure not much bigger than an outhouse. Two more men wheel a good-size tiny house toward a rear overhead door.

"Help you?"

I turn to see a middle-aged man approach. Amish-type beard. Work shirt, dark trousers, and suspenders. "I'm looking for the manager or owner," I tell him.

"I'm the owner." He gives me a curious once-over. "Someone do something wrong?"

"No, I just need to have a quick chat with Wayne Graber."

His eyes narrow. "This about that crossbow murder happened down to Painters Mill? I know he was friendly with the guy got shot." He whistles. "Heck of a thing."

I nod noncommittally. "I won't keep him long."

"You guys figure out who did it?"

"We're working on it."

More questions show in his eyes. I'm thankful he's too busy to voice them. He jabs a thumb at a man door at the rear of the shop. "Wayne's staining in the back. You take your time, Chief Burkholder. Hope you get the bad guy."

Giving him a nod, I head that way.

I make my exit and spot Graber on the front porch of a gorgeous log cabin, brushing stain onto a door, a five-gallon bucket on the deck floor next to him.

I start toward him. "That's a nice color," I say when I reach the steps.

He looks at me over his shoulder and does a double take. "Usually, we paint the doors. You know, to break up all that wood. Guy that bought this one wants it stained. I prefer paint myself."

"What kind of wood is that?"

"Knotty pine. I like the movement of the knots. And it takes stain real nice."

I ascend the steps and cross to where he's working. "Why didn't you tell me Aden and Vernon Fisher were friends?"

He stops brushing and turns to me. "Well, I'm not sure I'd classify them as friends exactly."

"How exactly *would* you classify their relationship?"

"They're more like . . . acquaintances."

"Who just happen to have the occasional beer together."

He stares at me, saying nothing.

I let the silence work a moment, then start back in. "How long have they known each other?"

"Since they were kids, but—"

"Since they were kids? And yet they're nothing more than acquaintances?"

"Look, Chief Burkholder, maybe 'acquaintance' isn't quite the right word. Sure, they hung out sometimes, but they didn't exactly get along."

"Why didn't you tell me that?"

He shrugs. "I guess I didn't realize it was important."

"Wayne." I add some steel to my voice. "I have a twenty-one-year-old dead man who had an ongoing dispute with another man days before he was murdered, and you somehow didn't think it was important to tell me those two men were friends?"

"I figured you knew. I mean, come on. Painters Mill is a small town. They were Amish."

"Which is it?" I ask. "That you didn't think it was important? Or that I should have already known?"

"Both."

"Is there anything else you didn't mention?"

He looks at me as though he can't believe I'm asking. "Look, I'm not trying to hide anything. I have nothing to hide."

"Tell me about their relationship."

He frowns, shakes his head. "Look, they were close when they were younger. Played together when they were kids. You know how it is when you're Amish. Everyone knows everyone. You go to singings and stuff. As they got older, Vernon started getting on his nerves."

"Why is that?"

He looks down at the ground and sighs. "Look, I gotta be honest with you, Chief Burkholder. All these questions . . ." He lets his voice trail; then he raises his eyes to mine. "I'd rather not get anyone in trouble."

"If you want to keep yourself out of trouble, I suggest you start talking."

He looks away, tightens his mouth.

"Who don't you want to get into trouble?" I ask.

"Look, Vernon Fisher might be an asshole, but he's not a killer." Shaking his head, he looks down at the floor, then back at me. "If I tell you what I think, you're going to be all over his shit, and he's going to know where you got it. And I'm going to get called a damn stool pigeon."

I stare at him. In the periphery of my thoughts, I see Karn on the gurney at the coroner's office. The wound in his abdomen. The knowledge that he'd also been shot in the mouth, likely when he'd been alive and unable to protect himself. That the killer had the wherewithal to push the bolts through his body to remove them. The cold-bloodedness of it outrages me.

Taking my time, I go to Wayne, invade his space, close enough that he backs up a step. "Answer my question, Wayne, or you're going to find yourself in a place you don't want to be."

He stares back at me. "Vernon had a thing for Emily Byler. Always has. He was jealous of Aden. Jealous that the two of them were so tight."

"How did Emily feel about that?"

"I doubt she even realized it."

"What about Aden?"

"He knew. Vernon wasn't exactly subtle. He made some pretty uncool comments. I mean, about Emily."

"What kind of comments?"

"Crude stuff." I'm surprised when color rises in his cheeks. "He'd say she was hot. Said Aden was getting it every weekend. Stupid stuff like that."

"Did they ever have words?"

134

"Not that I know of. Aden was a cool guy. Didn't get bent out of shape about things."

"How is it that you know about it?"

"I'm not blind. Everyone saw the way Vernon looked at her. Everyone heard what he said."

"Do you think Fisher was in love with Emily?"

"In lust, maybe."

"Do you think Fisher is capable of—"

"No." He cuts in. "I don't. Yeah, he's an idiot about women and a crude asshole to boot, but he's no killer. That's why I didn't say anything, Chief Burkholder. Now, you're going to go stir up trouble."

"You let me worry about that," I say.

He frowns at me. "Yeah. Right."

"Is there anything else you haven't told me that I should know about?" I ask.

"I think I've said enough."

I close my notebook and tuck it back into my pocket. "If I find out you've lied to me about any of this, I'll be back for you, Wayne. Do you understand me?"

"I told you everything I know."

"If you have to leave town for any reason, let me know."

"I'm not going anywhere."

At that, I turn and walk away.

One of the fundamental truths I've learned from my years in law enforcement is that people usually don't lie without a reason. I don't believe Wayne Graber murdered Aden Karn. I checked his alibi, after all; he was at work and clocked in the morning it happened. His supervisor at Mast Tiny Homes substantiated it. However, because he's playing it loose with the truth, Graber stays on my suspect list. At least for now.

I enter the police station to find my first-shift dispatcher, Lois, sitting at the switchboard, fielding calls and burning up the keyboard.

"I'm surprised that computer isn't smoking," I say by way of greeting.

"It was a minute ago." Grinning, she waves a stack of pink message slips at me. "Everyone you know has called at least twice in the last hour."

"Thanks for the warning." I pluck the messages from her hand.

She places her caller on hold. "Vernon Fisher is in the interview room, Chief. Been in there for nearly an hour and he's mad as a hornet. Every ten minutes or so he starts pounding on the door and calling his mother the most awful names."

Having overheard our exchange, Glock stands, looks at me over the top of his cubicle, and grins. "Morning, Chief."

"You got a few minutes?" I ask.

"You bet."

"Let me grab some coffee," I tell him. "I have a feeling I'm going to need it."

Ten minutes later, Glock and I walk into the

interview room. It's a small, windowless space that was once used to store office supplies. Vernon Fisher slouches in a chair at the table, looking like an unhappy kid who's been sent to detention. He's trying to look calm, as if he's taking all of this in stride. But he can't hide the anger radiating off him.

I set my file on the table and pull up a chair so that I'm sitting across from him. Glock closes the door behind us and takes his place against the wall, folding his arms in front of him.

"I appreciate your agreeing to come in and talk to us," I begin.

Fisher makes a sound of irritation. "Like I had a choice. I've been sitting here for an hour, Chief Burkholder." His eyes flick to Glock. "Your goon over there picked me up and here I am. No one bothered to come in and talk to me."

"I'm here now." To keep all of this on the up-and-up, I recite the Miranda rights to him from memory. "Do you understand those rights?"

He chokes out a sound of disbelief. "I don't need to know my rights because I didn't do anything wrong!"

Ignoring his outburst, I open the folder. "Why didn't you tell me you and Aden Karn were friends?"

"What?" He blinks as if Aden Karn is the last topic I'd raise. "You didn't ask."

"Let me refresh your memory." I look down

at my notes from the last time I spoke to him. "When I asked you about the truck, this was your answer. And I quote: 'You come here to my place of business and accuse me of killing some freakin' dude I barely know?' "

"I don't remember saying that."

"You did. Verbatim. Which means you lied to me." I make eye contact with him. "You know lying to the police is against the law, right?"

He sits up straighter. "Look, Karn wasn't exactly my best bud. I didn't know him that well. I didn't—"

I slap my palms down on the table hard enough to make him jump. "You lie to me one more time and there will be consequences. Do you understand?"

"I didn't do anything wrong."

"Were you friends with Karn?"

"We hung out sometimes. Drank beer. That's it."

"How long have you known him?"

"Just . . . since we were little kids."

"And yet you weren't friends? Didn't know him well?"

"We were frickin' Amish. When you're Amish, everyone knows everyone."

"When's the last time you talked to him?"

"Shit." He lowers his head, sets his fingertips against his temple as if trying to remember. "Three or four days before he was killed. I told you that."

"Can anyone substantiate that?"

"I think Wayne was there. I mean, I went to Aden's house to tell him I wanted my money back."

"Did you argue?"

"Well . . . yeah. I mean, I wasn't happy with him and I let him know it. For God's sake, I gave him six hundred bucks and the truck turns out to be a piece of crap. Then he goes and repossesses the truck. So, yeah, I was a little hot. But, for God's sake, I didn't fuckin' kill him!"

"Check the language," Glock snaps from his place by the door.

Fisher glares at him.

I stare at Fisher, let the silence work. He can't hold my gaze, and looks down at the table in front of him.

"What about Emily Byler?" I ask, keeping the question open ended.

"What about her?"

"You had a thing for her."

Groaning, he slouches in the chair. "This is such a crock of shit."

"Just answer the question."

"Yeah, she's cute. But I don't have a thing for her. I was just . . . being a jerk. Messing with Karn."

"Were you jealous?"

"No."

"You sure?"

His expression tightens and he doesn't answer.

"First you lie to me about your relationship about Karn. Then I hear you had a thing for his girlfriend." I let the statement ride a moment and add, "That's pretty close to motive."

Fisher stands so abruptly, he nearly knocks over the chair. "I didn't kill him!"

Glock comes off the wall. "Sit down." He points at the chair. "Now."

Looking defeated, Fisher sinks back into the chair.

I wait a beat. "Who else had a problem with Karn?" I ask.

"No one." He shakes his head. "That's why all of this is so crazy. Aden was a solid guy. People liked him. Hell, *I* liked him."

"Except for when he repossessed the truck."

Then he adds, "You want to know what else is crazy? I think eventually he would have given me my money back."

"Vernon, did you kill him?"

He raises his gaze to mine. "No, ma'am."

"Do you know who did?"

"No."

We lock gazes and for the span of a full minute neither of us speaks. "You're free to go."

Behind me, I hear Glock go to the door and open it.

Fisher scoots back the chair and rises, looks from me to Glock. "I need a ride home."

"Officer Maddox will take you."

When he brushes past me, I reach out and stop him, lock eyes again. "If I find out you've lied to me about anything we discussed, I'll come for you. You got that?"

"I got it," he mutters, and goes through the door.

CHAPTER 10

Every case has its own unique personality. Some are orderly from the get-go; not quite cooperative, but the puzzle pieces come together with some degree of congruity. Other cases are a study in chaos. Every move is a misstep. Every lead is a dead end. Every break, a false flag. The murder of Aden Karn falls into the latter category. It's like trying to put together a puzzle in which the pieces simply do not fit.

The thing that bothers me most about the case is that I still don't have a motive. Usually, if I can figure out the why, I can find the who. From all indications, Karn was well-liked. He was a people magnet, popular with the Amish and English alike. He worked hard, kept his nose clean, and didn't engage in high-risk behaviors. The only conflict in his life involved Vernon Fisher over the repossessed truck—and Fisher's obsession with the woman Karn planned to marry. As much as I dislike Fisher, I don't think he murdered Karn.

What have I overlooked?

Was this about money? An owed debt? A repossessed truck? Or was this about something more personal? Was it about a woman? Is there a romantic relationship I don't know about?

Was Emily Byler the only female in his life?

It's dusk by the time I leave the police station. I'm cranky and sleep-deprived, my productivity having long since played out. In the madness of the day, I managed to skip both lunch and dinner, and I taste acid from too much coffee. This is the point when a smart cop goes home to regroup. Take a shower, eat a decent meal, grab a few hours of sleep. Recharge the battery. There's no shame in admitting you've hit a wall.

I tell myself I'm going to be that smart cop. But as I back out of my parking spot, the case rides me, a vicious master that's deadweight on my shoulders, my mind, my conscience. And I know even if I go home, I won't be able to turn it off. I'll drag Tomasetti into it. I'll pace or drink too much or lie sleepless, thinking of all the things I should be doing, all the things I should have done. I'll spin my wheels and dig myself a little deeper into the hole this case has become.

Instead of heading north on Ohio 83 toward home, I make the turn onto the county road and then onto Hansbarger. I roll up to the place where Aden Karn was killed, park on the shoulder, and shut down the engine. The only indication that this spot was a crime scene is the flattened grass in the ditch, the tire ruts off the shoulder, and a single scrap of yellow caution tape discarded in the grass.

I get out, take a deep breath of evening air,

and look around. It's so quiet I can hear the buzz of insects. A mourning dove coos from the treetops in the woods. A forlorn sound that seems to echo the gravity of what transpired here. I walk to the place where Aden Karn had lain. The fire department hosed away the blood; there's nothing left. On the gravel shoulder, someone placed a small bouquet of flowers, carnations and baby's breath. A teddy bear sits next to a small book of poems. The citizens of Painters Mill paying their respects. A piece of paper protrudes from the pages of the book, so I bend to it, tug it out, and find myself looking down at a smiling image of Aden Karn that's been printed on copy paper. Oddly, someone has used a red marker to draw an arrow sticking out of his chest. At the bottom of the page someone scrawled:

Vann di meind uf flayshlichi sacha ksetzt is, sell fiaht zu'm doht.

It's a Bible passage; Romans if I'm not mistaken. In English it means: "For to be carnally minded is death." "What?" I mutter. Who would write that particular passage in *Deitsch*? What does it mean? And who would draw such a crude picture and leave it at the site of a murder? A prankster? Someone who didn't like Karn? Someone who hated him?

144

I walk to the shoulder and scan the trees at the edge of the woods, but there's no one there. Tugging a baggie from my duty belt, I slip the paper into it. Everything I know about Aden Karn churns in my brain. Not a single person I talked to had a negative thing to say about him.

So who hated him enough to ambush him on a lonely back road and end his life with a cross-bow?

I look north, the direction Karn was traveling the morning he was killed. He was on his way to meet his ride to work, the man who'd driven him to and from his construction job for the last year. Who else knew Karn's routine? Who knew he took this route? What time he met his coworker? *Someone close to him,* my cop's voice whispers. My brain scrolls through the list of names. Emily Byler. Wayne Graber. Vernon Fisher. His coworkers. His parents. Someone I don't yet know about . . .

For to be carnally minded is death.

The passage seems to refer to sex or lust. I recall the photos and sex toys I found in Karn's bedroom and I wonder: Who cared about the sex life of a twenty-one-year-old male? Emily Byler? If Vernon Fisher was interested in Emily, he may have kept an eye on Karn. I recall Wayne Graber's response when I asked him if Karn was seeing anyone else. *He might've . . . you know, seen one or two over the last few months. English*

145

girls . . . He'd just discovered his freedom. He liked women . . .

Did Karn commit some perceived transgression that, in the mind of his killer, warranted murder? According to Doc Coblentz, the second bolt had been fired at close range. The intimate nature of that second shot tells me this crime was personal. The killer knew him. Hated him. Wanted him gone at any cost and he was willing to risk his freedom to do it.

I walk to the spot where the body was found. According to Doc Coblentz, the bolt entered the abdomen from the front. Turning, I look down the road. The woods are to my left. Open field to the right. In order for the bolt to penetrate from the front while Karn was riding his bike toward the pickup point, the killer would have been standing on the road or one of the shoulders or ditches. At some point, Karn likely would have spotted him. He would have noticed the crossbow. Did the killer discharge the bolt before Karn could react? Or did Karn recognize the shooter and believe he had nothing to fear?

I look down at the asphalt where the body had lain. I walk to the shoulder where the shooter may have stood. "Why did you take the bolts?" I wonder aloud.

"Because they are evidence," I whisper.

The *swoosh!* of doves taking flight startles me. I'm swinging around, wondering what disturbed them, when I hear the *crunch! crunch! crunch!* of someone running through fallen leaves within the cover of the trees. I stand still, watch for movement, listening, but nothing else comes. There are no vehicles in sight. No place to hide a vehicle. No trailhead that I can see. No one around.

So, who's in the woods, Kate?

Aware that the light is fading fast, I traverse the ditch, and approach the barbed-wire fence. I'm midway over the top when I hear the rustle of leaves and I know without a doubt someone is there and on the move.

I swing my leg over the top of the fence and drop to the other side. "Painters Mill Police!" I call out. "Stop and identify yourself!"

No response.

The pounding of feet against the ground breaks the silence. Twenty yards away. Too many trees to get a look. I break into a run, hit my shoulder mike as I enter the trees. "Ten-eighty-eight," I say, using the ten code for "suspicious activity." "I'm ten-eighty." Giving chase. "Ten-seven-eight." Need assistance.

I release my mike and pour on the speed. "Police! Stop! *Stop!*" I hear my quarry ahead and to my left, so I veer that way. I dart around a massive walnut tree, pick up the pace as fast as I dare. In the periphery of my thoughts, I hear my radio light up. Skid is on duty and en route. ETA eight minutes. A lot can happen in eight minutes.

I hurdle deadfall, miscalculate, and get slapped in the face by a branch hard enough to open the skin on my cheek. Cursing, I stop and listen, hold my breath. Over the roar of my pulse, I hear footsteps again, the crackle of leaves. Dead ahead. Closer now. I launch into a sprint, dart around a tangle of raspberry, and catch a glimpse of movement ahead.

"Stop!" I call out. "Police!"

The trees open to a narrow deer trail. It takes me down a gulley. I splash through a shallow creek. I clamber up the steep incline, slide on loose rock, end up using my hands to claw my way up. At the top, I spot a patch of blue through the trees. Just a few yards ahead. A kid, I think. White ball cap. I'm outrunning him.

Adrenaline pumping, I sprint to him, running all out. "Stop right now!"

The trail veers left around a big rock, then right. I take the curves fast, catch sight of the runner. I'm so close I can hear his labored breaths. Ten feet away. He's small in stature. Not very fast. Six feet between us. Three . . .

I lunge, plow my shoulder into the small of his back, wrap my arms around his hips, and take him down in a flying tackle. A high-pitched scream rends the air as we fall. Only then do I realize the perpetrator isn't a kid at all, but female. Smaller than me. Young. An Amish girl.

148

She breaks her fall with her arms, but I come down on top of her. Her elbows buckle from our combined weight and she slams into the dirt. I hear the breath rush from her lungs. My forehead strikes her shoulder blade. Setting both hands against her shoulders, I scramble up, set my knee against the small of her back.

"Do not move!" I reach for the cuffs on my belt, fumble the snap. My hands are shaking from adrenaline and exertion.

"Let go of me!" the girl screams. "Help!"

"I'm not going to hurt you." I snap out the cuffs, reach for her left hand, and pull it behind her back. "I'm a police officer. Calm down."

"You're hurting me! Please! Stop it!"

She's starting to panic, so I reach for her right hand, bring it back. After a couple of attempts, I get the second cuff into place and snap it closed.

I get to my feet, too winded to speak. I leave her on the ground, facedown, her body heaving. I lean forward, set my hands on my knees, and concentrate on catching my breath. A few seconds and I straighten, speak into my shoulder mike. "Ten-ninety-five," I pant. Suspect in custody.

"You hurt my knee," the girl tells me. "Why did you do that?"

I glance down at her and cringe inwardly. Her dress is tangled around her legs, her *kapp* askew. She lost a sneaker at some point. Her head is turned to one side, a smear of dirt on her cheek, tears beneath her eyes. I guess her to be sixteen or seventeen years old. She looks pitiful and harmless and I can't help but feel a tinge of guilt.

"Why didn't you stop when I asked you to?" I ask. "Why did you run from me?"

"You scared me!" she cries. "Please, let me up."

"Just calm down," I tell her. "I'll help you."

Bending, I reach for her forearm. "Come on. Up and at 'em."

She gets her knees beneath her and rises. I can feel her shaking. Tears stream down her cheeks, but there's no sobbing. She's an inch away from hyperventilating.

"What are you doing out here?" I ask.

A too-long pause and then, "Nothing. I was . . . just . . . taking a walk."

"In the woods? In the dark? With no flashlight?"

She doesn't respond.

"What's your name?" I ask.

A brief hesitation and then she says, "Christina Weaver."

"Do you have any ID on you?"

She looks down at the ground and shakes her head.

"How old are you?" I ask.

"Sixteen."

"Where do you live?"

She motions with her eyes in the direction

we were traveling. "A couple miles thataway. Township Road 42."

"You live with your *mamm* and *datt*?"

She looks at me from beneath her lashes, curious about my Amish pronunciation. "*Ja.*"

She's small in stature. Five feet. Barely a hundred pounds. "Why did you run away from me?"

"You . . . scared me. I . . . didn't know who you were or what you wanted."

"Do you have anything you shouldn't have in your pockets?" I ask.

"No."

I check her *kapp* for anything hidden, straighten it for her, and then, as quickly and impersonally as possible, I run my hands over her dress. I squeeze the pockets of her apron and my hand stops. I reach inside and pull out a red marker. The same kind of marker that was used to draw the crude arrow on the image of Aden Karn.

I hold up the marker. "What are you doing with this?"

The girl looks down at the ground, thinks better of it, and meets my gaze. "My little brother. He . . . he must have put it in my pocket."

"You know you're not a very good liar, right?"

She shakes her head as if I've annoyed her and drops her gaze to the ground.

"That's a compliment," I add.

She doesn't respond.

I sigh. "Christina, if I take off those handcuffs, will you behave yourself?"

"Yes, ma'am."

Taking her arm, I turn her around, and then fish the key out of its compartment and unlock the cuffs. While she's rubbing her wrists, I pull the photo from my pocket and show it to her. "Did you use that marker to draw on this photo?"

She looks at it and her expression crumples. Pressing her hands against her face, she begins to cry. "Please. Don't tell."

I wait for her to expound, but she continues to cry, her shoulders shaking. After a full minute, I motion toward the deer trail in the direction from which we came. "Let's go back to my vehicle."

Hands shaking, she wipes tears from her eyes. "Please don't take me to jail."

"No one's going to jail." I motion again. "Walk."

Neither of us speaks as we retrace our steps back to Hansbarger Road. It's nearly dark now, and as we get closer to the road, I speak into my radio. "Ten-twenty-two," I say, canceling my earlier call for assistance.

"Copy that," comes my dispatcher's voice.

We reach the fence, and I wait while the girl climbs over. She stands patiently while I do the same. I spot her lost shoe just off the path, and point. I wait while she puts it on and laces up.

We reach my Explorer and I open the passenger-side door for her. "Get in."

She obeys without speaking. I go around to the driver's-side door and slide behind the wheel.

"Where are you taking me?" she asks.

"I'm taking you home," I tell her.

"I'm sorry I ran away from you." She reaches into her apron, pulls out a tissue, and hands it to me. "Your face . . . it's bleeding."

I take the tissue, then lean to look at the damage in the rearview mirror. Sure enough, a small line of blood trails down from an inch-long scratch.

Thinking of my upcoming wedding, I frown, blot it with the tissue. "I'm wondering why you marked up the photo like that."

She looks down and smooths the front of her dress. "I don't really want to talk about it."

"Did you know Aden Karn?"

She looks out the window, doesn't answer.

Sighing, I start the engine. "Were you friends?"

I hear a quick intake of breath. Her shoulders stiffen. Both are minute responses, but I notice, and they are telling.

"No."

Checking for traffic in my rearview mirror, I pull onto the road. "When's the last time you saw him?"

She interlaces her fingers, but not before I notice her hands are shaking. "I don't want to talk about him."

"Judging from what you drew on the photo, I'm assuming you didn't like him very much."

No response.

I keep my eyes on the road ahead, puzzled, trying not to be annoyed by her refusal to talk, giving her some space. But I know there's something there. Most people believe that when you're Amish, life is simple and perfect. The reality is that even the plain life isn't always so simple. Especially when you're a teenager and trying to understand the world around you, and you don't have the guidance or tools to do it.

I can't fathom why this girl would draw such a crude image on the picture of a dead man and leave it at the scene of his death. I have no idea if they were friends or enemies or simple acquaintances. The one thing I do know is that she's keeping secrets. If I want to get to those secrets, I need to play it smart.

"Do your parents know?" I ask.

She swings her gaze to me, her eyes wide and alarmed. "Know what?"

"Do they know you were friends with Aden?"

She squeezes her eyes closed. "They don't know anything. Please don't tell them I was here. I just want to forget all of it."

I pull into the lane of the farm where she lives. "What is it you want to forget about, Christina?"

When she only continues to stare down at her hands twisting in her lap, I add, "You know Aden Karn was murdered, don't you?"

"Of course I know. Everyone knows. That's all they're talking about."

I switch to *Deitsch*. "You mean the *Amisch*?"

She nods.

"What are they saying?"

"Just that no one knows what happened. They're frightened and they're sad."

I nod. "Do you have any idea why anyone would want to hurt him?"

"No."

"Do you know who killed him?"

"Of course not." She gapes at me as if I've accused her of murder. "Am I in trouble?"

"I'm going to do you a favor and let you off the hook for running from me," I say. "I know you were scared. But in the future, don't run from the police. We're here to help people, not harm them, okay?"

She hangs her head and nods. "Please don't tell my parents I drew that picture."

I park behind a manure spreader in the gravel area near the big farmhouse and shut off the engine. When it comes to any interaction between me and a juvenile, it's my policy to never withhold information from parents or a legal guardian. That said, drawing an image on a photo isn't illegal or even relevant and, therefore, is out of my realm of responsibility.

"How about if I let you tell your parents what happened?" I say. "Does that sound fair?"

She looks away, nods.

I hand her my card, which has my cell phone number on the back. "Christina, if you think of anything important that you forgot to say, or if you just want to talk about something, will you call me?"

Another nod.

"I promise I'll listen, okay?"

Without answering, she opens the door and slides from the seat. Outside, she looks at me, then slams the door and runs as fast as she can to the house.

CHAPTER 11

Criminals keep terrible hours. They work nights. Weekends. Holidays. You name it and they're out there, wreaking havoc. Shortly before I began my law enforcement career, I did a ride-along with a veteran officer in Columbus, and I'll never forget what he told me. "If you want to see action, schedule your ride-along for the graveyard shift," he'd said. "That's when the zombies come out. That's when you find out what really goes on after the sun goes down. That's when you'll know if you have what it takes."

It's nine P.M. and I'm on my way home, my heart set on a shower, food, and a few hours of sleep, when the call comes over my radio.

"Ten-ten," comes my second-shift dispatcher's voice, using the ten code for "fight in progress."

Skid is on duty until midnight, and he's more than capable of handling a fight, depending on the number of individuals involved, of course. But when the dispatcher rattles off an address I recognize—the old service station where Vernon Fisher lives—I realize I'm not going to make it home anytime soon.

I snatch up my radio. "Ten-seven-six," I say, letting her know I'm en route. "Who's the RP?" Reporting party.

"Ricky Shafter says he drove by there on his way home from work, Chief. Said there were a bunch of guys in the driveway slugging it out. He thought someone might get hurt so he called us."

"Skid, ten-twenty-five," I say, requesting he meet me there.

"On my way," he says.

It takes me four minutes to reach Fisher's place. Sure enough, when I pull into the driveway, I spot a commotion in front of the overhead door. My headlights illuminate at least two men on the ground, locked in battle. The silhouettes of half a dozen people surround them. Young men holding beers and cutting up, egging the fighters on.

"Shit," I mutter beneath my breath as I cut the engine and scramble out.

"Police Department!" I call out.

By the time I push my way through the crowd, the fighters have separated. A disheveled Vernon Fisher stands just inside the overhead door, his T-shirt wet with sweat and covered with grime. The collar hangs down, stretched to three times its normal size. Wayne Graber is just around the corner at the side of the building, bent at the hip, gulping air as if he's just run a four-minute mile.

I recognize three of the bystanders from when I was here the other day. Three others I don't know, at least two of whom are Amish. All of them are looking at me, pumped up on alcohol, adrenaline, and testosterone. One of the Amish men is leaning against the wall next to the overhead door, a bottle of tequila in his hand.

I point at him. "Who was fighting?"

He startles, looks around, not wanting to get his pals into trouble. "Uh . . . they were just . . . horsing around."

I shift my gaze to Fisher. "You." I point to the external office door. "Go stand outside by the door and do not move. Now."

Anger flashes in his eyes. For an instant I think he's going to refuse—or charge me. Despite the haze of alcohol, he shakes off the urge, steps back, and starts toward the door.

I'm about to approach Graber when the lights of Skid's cruiser flicker off the side of the building. I turn to see him tear into the parking lot, dust flying. He slides to a stop behind my Explorer. Then the door flies open and he's striding to me, his eyes taking in the scene. "Chief?"

I jab my thumb at Fisher, lower my voice. "I think he was fighting. Get his story. I'll talk to Graber."

"I wasn't fighting!" Fisher snarls.

"Be quiet." Skid approaches Fisher and motions to his vehicle. "Let's go."

Two of the bystanders move closer to me, eyes alight with the kind of disrespect that could quickly edge into hostility. Too drunk to realize any physical contact would be a very bad idea. I raise my hand and shove my finger at them. "Don't do anything stupid. Do you understand?"

I make eye contact with each of them as I stride past. I don't miss the smirks, the open expressions of glee, of insolence in their eyes, or that they're enjoying this a hell of a lot more than I am.

I keep them in the periphery of my vision as I approach Graber. He's still bent at the hip, hands on his knees. He raises his head and looks at me as I approach and mutters, "Shit."

"Why were you fighting with Fisher?" I ask.

Shaking his head, he straightens. "We were just goofing off, Chief Burkholder."

The shirt he's wearing looks as if someone tried to tear it from his body. Several buttons have popped off at the waist, revealing a belly covered with a sprinkling of dark hair. There's dribble of blood beneath his left nostril. An abrasion the size of a marble next to his eyebrow.

"Don't lie to me," I say.

"We weren't fighting."

"I saw you, Wayne. When I pulled up."

He tosses me a sheepish look. "Look, we had a few beers. A few laughs. We started talking MMA, you know, mixed martial arts, cage fighting, and one thing led to another."

I laugh. "Do you seriously expect me to believe that?"

"It's the truth." Looking uncomfortable, he shifts his weight from one foot to the other. "The tequila didn't help, I guess."

Aware that the other men are craning their necks in an effort to eavesdrop, I motion Graber to my Explorer. "Let's go," I tell him. "Put your hands against the fender."

"You're not going to arrest me, are you?"

"I haven't decided."

Throwing up his hands, Graber slogs over to the Explorer. "This is a bunch of crap."

"I couldn't agree with you more."

I follow him to the Explorer. In the back of my mind, I wonder if the fight is about the truck. If it's about Emily Byler or related in any way to the murder of Aden Karn.

We reach the Explorer. "Put your hands against the fender," I repeat. "Spread your feet."

Sighing, he obeys. "I don't have anything on me."

"We'll see." I don't expect to find any weapons; I don't expect any problems from him at all. But I go through the motions, mainly to let him know the police showing up isn't some joke to be laughed at.

"You can turn around," I tell him.

Turning to me, he leans against the fender, and folds his arms in front of him, petulant.

"You know I could haul both of you to jail right now."

"Yeah, I get that." Frowning, he looks down at the ground and shakes his head. "I don't know what else to say, Chief Burkholder. We didn't do anything wrong and we sure don't want any trouble."

"Two days ago, you and Vernon Fisher were archenemies and arguing over a truck. Now you're drinking buddies? Wrestling partners?"

"Look, he's a jerk. We had a legitimate disagreement . . . I mean, before—" He cuts off the sentence without finishing. "After what happened to Aden . . . I just didn't want to deal with it so I gave him his damn money back."

"Tonight?"

"Yeah."

I wait for him to elaborate. When he doesn't, I ask, "If you made things right, why were you fighting?"

"Just because we worked out a problem doesn't mean we like each other."

It's a plausible story. I have no way of knowing if he's telling the truth or lying through his teeth or if reality falls somewhere in between. But I've been around long enough to know I'm not getting the whole story.

"Does any of this have to do with Aden Karn?" I ask.

"This isn't about Aden."

"What about Emily Byler?" I say, fishing.

"What about her?"

"Fisher had a thing for her and now Aden's dead."

He tosses me an irritated frown. "I got nothing else to say."

"I've been talking to a lot of people about Aden. I keep hearing he was a good guy. Kept his nose clean. The only ongoing disagreement he had was about the truck. And Emily." I motion toward Fisher. "And now I catch you and Fisher in a physical altercation. What am I supposed to think?"

Temper darkens his face. "What the hell do you want from me?"

"The whole truth would be a good start."

"I loved Aden like a brother." For the first time, emotion resonates in his voice. "Not a minute goes by that I'm not thinking about him. Or wishing he was still around." Even as his voice breaks his hands clench into fists, his anger focused on me, as if I'm responsible for the pain.

He's on the edge, so I give him another push. "I'm getting the runaround and I don't like it."

"You want the truth?" His mouth pulls into a snarl. "Maybe you ought to do your damn homework."

"Why don't you get me started? Point me in the right direction?"

"If you want the truth so badly, maybe you ought to get the hell off my back and go talk to Emily Byler's ex."

My interest surges. I'd asked about the existence of an ex-boyfriend, but no one had mentioned it and not once did a name come up. "Who is he?"

"Try Gideon Troyer on for size."

I almost can't believe my ears. Gideon Troyer is the grandson of the bishop, a larger-than-life man who's presided over the church district since I was a kid. In the backwaters of my mind, I recall Clara Byler's reaction when I'd asked about a past boyfriend and for the first time her discomfiture—and her silence—makes sense.

"Emily was involved with Gideon before Aden?" I ask.

"How's that for an inconvenient truth?"

I search my memory for what I know about Gideon. He still lives in the area. I've pulled him over once or twice . . . I pin Wayne with a look. "He's quite a bit older than Emily, isn't he?"

Wayne hefts a bitter laugh. "No one wants to talk about that, either, do they?"

"Were there problems between Aden and Gideon?"

"You mean aside from Gideon being a jealous son of a bitch?" His eyes harden on mine. "And yet here you are hassling me and that dumbshit Fisher."

Ignoring the jab, I pull out my notebook and write down the name, underscore the words *jealous* and *age.* "Why didn't you mention this

164

last time we talked?" Even as I ask the question, I already know the answer.

"That's a stupid question coming from a formerly Amish woman." Another bitter smile twists his mouth. "You know as well as I do that there's not a soul in the district willing to break that Amish code of silence, especially when the guy's name is Troyer."

CHAPTER 12

When you live in a town the size of Painters Mill, especially if you're a cop, you know or know of just about everyone. I've known Gideon Troyer since I was a kid simply because I was Amish and he is Bishop Troyer's grandson. I never knew him well; he's quite a bit younger and male to boot, so our paths never crossed. As chief, I know he leads a quiet life and has never been in trouble with the law.

After arriving home last night, I spent an hour or so combing through the ever-growing file I've amassed on the murder of Aden Karn, trying to connect the dots, and failing miserably. I ran Gideon Troyer through the pertinent databases only to determine I was right about him. He doesn't have a record. Never been arrested. Not even a traffic citation. The only information I could come up with was his age and address. Striking out there, I turned to social media. Most people assume the Amish don't have online social lives. For the vast majority, that is correct. But during *rumspringa*, or if a guileful adult has access to a computer or cell phone for his business, some find a way. Keeping all of that in mind, I spend a couple of hours scrolling through page after page of more-than-I-ever-wanted-to-know brain rot.

At some point after I went to bed, Tomasetti's cell phone sounded loudly. I vaguely remember a murmured apology as he rolled out of bed, and the brush of a kiss on my cheek before he left.

It's a little after seven A.M. when I make the turn onto the road where Gideon Troyer lives. I've just pulled into the narrow lane that bisects a cornfield when I spot the elevator hood of the picker skimming the tops of the corn. I stop and get out to the clank-and-rumble of the picker. The contraption is a single-row, which means it only picks one row of corn at a time, and is being pulled by two aged Percheron horses. A wagon has been attached to the rear of the picker, where the cleaned ears of corn are thrown by the elevator belt. An Amish man stands on the platform section of the picker, leather lines in hand, and guides the horses between the rows. It's painstaking physical labor that, for a field this size, will take several dawn-to-dusk workdays to finish.

I cross through the ditch and climb over the fence at the edge of the field. I'm not sure he'll stop; honestly, I wouldn't hold it against him if he didn't. Still, I stand there at the edge of the field and wait. I know from my research that Gideon Troyer is twenty-four years old. Blond hair sticks out from a straw summer hat. Blue eyes. The description from the Ohio Bureau of Motor Vehicles fits.

I'm relieved when I hear his shouted "Whoa!" over the rattle of the machinery.

"Looks like it's going to be a good harvest," I call out to him in *Deitsch* as I traverse the distance between us.

"God gave us abundant rain in the spring and a nice, dry fall." He wraps the leather lines around a wooden knob and climbs down. "You here about Aden?" he asks in English.

I nod. "So you know what happened to him."

"All the Amish know," he says.

"I won't keep you long. Just a few questions."

He glances back at the horses. "They could use a break, anyway."

I take him through the most pressing central questions, watching his reactions, but he answers each inquiry without hesitation. He's known Karn most of his life. They went to school together, but weren't close. Last time he saw Karn was at worship a few weeks ago. They didn't speak. Troyer seems to be a straightforward guy. Serious-minded. More focused on harvesting corn than my questions—or what happened to Karn.

"I understand you were seeing Emily Byler for a time," I say.

"Ah." He cocks his head, looks at me from beneath the brim of his hat. "I reckon that's the reason you're here."

I nod. "I'm questioning everyone who knew or had contact with Karn."

168

He looks out over the field, then jerks his head. "I courted her for a bit."

"I heard it was more serious than that."

"I thought it was serious. I mean, I'm the age when a man starts thinking about a wife. A family."

"You asked her to marry you?"

"I reckon I did." He sighs, looks over at the horses, and then back at me. "Em had other plans, I guess."

"What do you mean by that?"

He frowns, letting me know the question is too personal. He's astute enough to know he has to answer. "Aden had his own ideas about courting her. Came on strong. They carried on behind my back. Kept me in the dark."

"Were you sleeping with her?"

"I ain't going to say."

"Were Aden and Emily sleeping together?"

"I reckon you'll have to ask her."

"How did you feel about that?"

"I don't know what you want me to say, Chief Burkholder. I didn't like it. The guy stole my girl right out from under me. They carried on behind my back. Made a fool of me."

"Did you confront Aden?"

He pulls a handkerchief from his pocket and wipes sweat from the back of his neck. "What do you think?"

"I think you need to answer the question."

"Yeah, I confronted him. We argued. I could have punched him or done worse, but I didn't. I'm Amish and that's not our way. You should know that, but I'm not sure you do."

"Did you threaten him?" I ask.

"I told him to stay away from my girl."

"Have you ever been to Karn's house?"

"Just that one time," he says.

"When's the last time you saw him?"

"I told you I saw him at worship three weeks ago."

"Where were you the morning of October second?" I ask.

"I was here." He motions to the corn picker. "Fixed a wheel on that thing. Took me a couple days."

"Can anyone substantiate that?"

"I reckon not. These geldings ain't much for conversation."

I nod. "Do you own a crossbow?"

He laughs. "Oh boy. I guess you *do* think I did it."

"I'd appreciate it if you'd just answer the question."

"I got a compound bow. A nice one. Killed me a dozen bucks with it over the years."

"Have you used it recently?"

"Last time I shot it was about a year ago. During the season. Got me a ten-pointer." He looks at me and sighs. "The one thing I didn't do was shoot Aden Karn with it." He looks over his shoulder at the team of horses and the corn picker. "I gotta get back to work."

I have my card at the ready. "If you think of anything else that might be important, will you get in touch with me?"

Shaking his head, he drops the card into his pocket without looking at it and walks away.

Jealousy is a powerful emotion, especially when it bears down on an immature, insecure, or violent mind. Infidelity is betrayal in its most insidious form and has been the basis for countless murders. Gideon Troyer had every reason to be angry with Karn; he had every right to be jealous. That he admitted it when asked doesn't exclude him from suspicion. Some people believe lies are somehow more convincing when they skate that razor's edge of truth. Usually, those are the individuals who excel at hiding the evil that lurks in the darkest corners of their heart.

The stink of hog manure hangs heavy in the air when I park in front of the Byler farm and shut down the engine. I'm midway to the door when someone calls my name. I turn to see Clara Byler striding toward me, a wire basket filled with brown chicken eggs at her side.

"Looks like your hens are good producers," I say as I cross to her.

"They sure eat enough." The Amish woman

171

says the words with a smile, but I can tell by her expression she's not pleased to see me. "Thought I'd make noodles for supper."

"How is Emily doing?" I ask.

"Having a hard go of it." She glances toward the house. "Funeral's in two days. She's just beside herself. Cries all day." She sighs. *"Bloosich."* Depressed.

"I know this is a bad time, but I need to ask her some questions."

She tightens her mouth, doesn't respond.

"About Gideon Troyer."

Her gaze snaps to mine. "Oh."

If I hadn't been looking for a reaction, I would have missed the quicksilver wince at the mention of Troyer's name. "You should have told me about him," I say quietly.

She looks down at the basket of eggs.

The Amish code of silence, I think.

"You talked to Gideon?" she asks after a moment.

"About an hour ago."

She puts her hand over her mouth. "Did he . . ."

"All I can tell you is that it's an open investigation. We've not made an arrest. The most important thing I need right now in order to do my job is information."

Grimacing, she nods.

I send a pointed look toward the house. "I

wouldn't ask to speak with Emily if it wasn't important."

"*Sitz dich anne.*" Sit yourself there. She motions toward a picnic table beneath a big elm tree in the side yard. "Might do her some good to be outside, I guess. Get some fresh air and sun. I'll go fetch her."

Nearly ten minutes pass before I hear the slam of the screen door. I glance over to see Emily shuffle down the steps and start toward me. There's a gauntness about her that hadn't been there before. Angry-looking patches of acne glow red on her forehead and chin. A greasy-looking strand of hair hangs from a *kapp* that isn't quite clean. She moves as if in slow motion, her eyes as dull as tarnished brass.

"Hi." I rise when she reaches me. "How are you holding up?"

"Okay." She slides onto the bench seat across from me, her shoulders sagging.

"I know this is a tough time, so I won't keep you." I reclaim my seat. "I understand you were involved with Gideon Troyer before you started seeing Aden."

Her eyes widen and she looks around as if looking for a place to run. "Oh . . . well."

"It's okay," I tell her. "You can talk to me."

"W-we went out a few times. You know, to a frolic or singing. That sort of thing."

Singings are social gatherings for Amish

173

teenagers, usually held after morning worship. Unmarried young people gather, sing songs, and socialize. During summer months, they might set up volleyball nets and both girls and boys play.

"How serious was your relationship?" I ask.

"It was . . . I mean . . . I don't think it was that serious."

It's an indeterminate answer. Is she uneasy discussing Troyer because he's the bishop's grandson? Or because she two-timed him? "I know who he is," I tell her. "Anything you and I talk about today, I'll keep confidential if I can, okay?"

Another swallow followed by a nod.

"How serious was the relationship?"

"We liked each other just fine."

"Who broke up with whom?" I ask.

"I quit him. I mean, Gideon was nice, but when I met Aden . . ." She sighs as if remembering. "I just knew he was the one. Mamm and Datt liked him better, too. They thought Gideon was too old for me."

"Was Gideon upset when you broke up with him?"

"Well, he wasn't very happy. More hurt than angry." Her brows knit. "I think he understood."

"Was there a period of time when you were seeing both boys at the same time?"

Color infuses her face, confirming what I've

already been told. "I tried not to do that, but Aden was so . . . good to me. And Gideon . . . just kept coming back . . ."

"Were there any problems between Aden and Gideon?"

She looks down at the tabletop. "Gideon might've been a little jealous. I mean, at first. But he's that way. Strong, you know. Like his *dawdi*." Grandfather.

"Were there any fights or arguments between Gideon and Aden?" I ask. "Anything like that?"

"Not that I know of."

Glancing down at my notebook, I change gears. "Emily, last time I was here, we talked about Aden and Vernon Fisher."

"*Ja.*"

"Is there a reason why you didn't mention they were friends?"

Her shoulders tense. It's a minute reaction, but I'm seeking those small tells and I don't miss it. "They weren't *that* close," she mutters.

"But they were friends?" I ask.

"I guess. They hung out together sometimes. Over at that trashy old gas station."

"Did they get along?"

"They got on okay."

"Did you spend time with them?"

This time she winces. An emotion I can't read flashes across her expression. The patch of acne seems to glow red against her pale skin. Curiosity flickers in my chest. *Something there,* a little voice whispers.

"I went over there a time or two," she says. "I mean, with Aden."

I pause, wait for her to look at me, but she doesn't. "Did you get along with Vernon?"

She raises her eyes to mine and for the first time the dull sheen is gone, replaced with the sharp edge of another emotion I can't decipher. "I never liked him much," she tells me.

"Why not?"

"He's . . . a *leshtah-diah.*" Beast that blasphemes.

It's an archaic *Deitsch* term that basically describes a person who speaks ill of God or, I'm assuming in the way Emily is using it, is an evil person.

"How so?" I ask.

Her brows knit and she seems to consider. "All of those guys who hang out over there. Always drinking and laughing and taking the Lord's name in vain. They're rough and crude. And Vernon, it's like he makes fun of you behind your back. It was always better when Aden came here, where it was quiet and we could talk." As if remembering, she bows her head, tears tracing a path down her cheeks.

"Did Aden know you didn't like Vernon?"

"I never really said," she mutters.

Something there . . .

"I understand Vernon had a crush on you. Is that true?"

"Never heard such a thing."

"Did he ever make a pass at you?" I ask. "Or behave improperly?"

She raises her eyes to mine, color climbing up her neck and into her cheeks. A thin sheen of sweat slicks her upper lip and forehead. It's not overly warm, and I don't know if the sweat is from discomfort or stress or if she's simply not feeling well.

"Never."

"Did any of the other men ever behave improperly with you?"

She starts to shake her head, but stops as if thinking better of it. "I heard the whispers. They called me names. Behind my back, you know. But I could see the mean in their eyes."

"How did Aden feel about that?" I ask.

She looks away. "I'm sure he didn't like it much."

"He didn't say?"

"We never talked about it." She shrugs. "Maybe he didn't notice."

Something there . . .

I keep fishing. "Were any of the men at the gas station ever hostile to Aden?" I ask. "Did they tease him? About his relationship with you?"

"If any of them had done anything improper, Aden would have stood up to them," she says

177

emphatically. "He was brave that way. Would have stood up for me."

"Did he ever have to do that?" I'm not exactly sure where I'm taking this. But I want her to keep talking, so I can get a handle on the relationship dynamics. Between her and Aden—but especially with Vernon Fisher and the other players.

"No." But her expression is a study of mixed messages. "All those men. Such a crude bunch. Playing with that gross doll. The fake woman, you know. Talking about it as if it was a real girl. I didn't like it."

I study her face, her expression, try to read between the lines. "How did Aden feel about all of that?"

"He didn't like their antics one bit. He was good that way. Good to me. He was always good, you see. Always."

"Why didn't you tell him you didn't like being there?"

Emily stands abruptly, then looks around as if she hadn't intended to and isn't sure what to do next. "I don't think I want to talk about this anymore," she whispers.

I stand, too. "I appreciate your opening up to me."

Before I even finish the sentence, she turns away and runs to the house.

CHAPTER 13

There is an incongruity inherent in being a cop and being formerly Amish. Those two worlds are incompatible and clash in a fundamental and profound way. One repels the other and there is no reconciliation. There's no fitting them together no matter how hard you try to pound the pieces into place.

The divergence of those two worlds is a beast that tracks me as I pull into the long gravel lane of my brother's farm. With a homicide investigation spooling and a killer on the loose, the last thing I want to deal with—despite its importance—is my wedding. For weeks, Tomasetti and I have waffled between having our wedding at our own farm and having it on my brother's farm, the place where I grew up. Today, we're meeting with Jacob and my sister-in-law, Irene, to make the final decision.

The bad news is, I'm an hour late. I'm frazzled because I've been running full bore since five A.M. and there simply aren't enough hours in the day. My brother and Tomasetti have only met a handful of times. While their interaction wasn't contentious, it was tense and kept me on edge. Both men have strong personalities, deep-seated convictions, and no qualms about speaking their minds. The notion of them spending an entire hour together without my being there to referee fills me with a low-grade anxiety.

I barely notice the apple orchard as I zip up the lane or the golden spires of pampas grass as I slide to a stop beside an old manure spreader. Tomasetti's Tahoe is nowhere in sight. I'm not sure if I'm disappointed or relieved that he's already gone. Then I'm out the door, and I'm jogging to the house when I hear my someone call out my name.

I glance over to see Irene standing at the clothesline, a wicker basket propped on her hip. "You're looking for the men?"

"Sorry I'm late." Trying not to look as frayed as I feel, I start toward her. "I got tied up with the investigation."

She looks at me from beneath her lashes. "I think they got it worked out."

"I didn't see any blood when I pulled up, so . . ." I tack on a smile, but my delivery is off.

Irene laughs anyway. "That man of yours knows what he wants, no?"

"Yes, he does."

"Jacob is the same. They have that in common." She motions toward the barn. "You've some details to work out, but I think they want to have the ceremony here. Lunch afterward."

Surprise trills in my chest. I didn't expect Jacob and Irene to host the wedding. Because I left the

Amish. Because Bishop Troyer will not officiate. Because there's an impossible amount of work to be done and just a few days in which to do it. Until this moment, I didn't fully realize how much it means to me to have the wedding here.

"Thank you," I tell her. "There's a lot of family history here."

"And more memories to be made, Katie. Don't forget that."

I look toward the barn. "I should say hello to Jacob," I say. "Thank him."

She looks down at the basket and sighs. "And I need to get back to my laundry."

I reach out and touch her hand, give it a squeeze. "*Danki.*"

I start toward the barn, noticing the sliding door is open a few feet.

"Katie?"

I turn at the sound of Irene's voice.

"If Jacob's not in the barn, check that old cottonwood tree out by the pond," she says. "He was talking about taking a saw to that old thing."

It takes all of two minutes for me to ascertain that my brother isn't in the barn. I clatter down the steps to the livestock stalls on the underside of the barn, climb over the rail, and start across the pasture. Two Jersey cows eye me as I jump the small creek and start up the hill. It is here that the beauty of the land embraces me and I feel the stress of the day begin to melt. The cool shade of the towering elm. The metallic chip of a cardinal calling for its mate. A hundred memories press into me as I crest the hill. The day I fell off our old draft horse and broke my wrist. Sarah and me picking raspberries for jam. Jacob catching his first sunfish in the pond. Sarah and me making mud pies on the bank and decorating them with morning glories.

I'm midway down the hill when I notice the pickup truck parked next to the pond and I realize Tomasetti has stayed to help Jacob cut down the cottonwood tree. My steps falter when I hear the whine of a chain saw. Irene's words about making new memories echo in the back of my head.

I crest another rise. The scene ahead stops me in my tracks. The tree is large, probably forty feet tall with a trunk as thick as a barrel. The men's backs are to me. Feet spread, Tomasetti wields the chain saw I bought him for Father's Day. Setting the blade against the trunk, he cuts a notch at a forty-five-degree angle, about three feet from the ground. The men are talking. I'm too far away to make out the words over the scream of the saw. Sawdust flies, coating Tomasetti's work shirt and jeans. He's wearing safety glasses and gloves, mouth pulled into a grimace, expression set in concentration.

Jacob stands a few feet away, leg cocked. He's tied a rope around the trunk about three feet above the notch. I'm no stranger to farmwork or do-it-yourself projects, but I feel a smidgen of uneasiness climb up my spine when the sound of splintering wood cracks the air.

Sure enough, the tree leans in the direction of the notch, and then falls away from the pond and, of course, our truck. Branches crash against the ground, bringing a rise of sawdust and dirt.

Tomasetti lowers the chain saw to his side and takes a moment to admire the felled tree. Jacob unsheathes a handsaw and sets to work sawing off the branches. It's such an unlikely sight that I stop a dozen yards away and stand there, trying to get my head around it, putting it to memory.

I need to walk over to them. Thank my brother. Collect Tomasetti and get back to work. And yet for the span of several seconds, I don't move. For some silly reason my heart is lodged in my throat and the last thing I want to do is make a fool of myself. Or, God forbid, cry in front of either of them.

Then Tomasetti spots me. His eyes grab mine and hold on. Setting the chain saw in its case, he starts toward me.

A quick check of my emotions, a swipe of my cheeks, and I start toward them. "You slayed the beast."

"With bare hands, no less."

He reaches me. I lean in to him for a peck on the cheek, but he pulls me close and presses his mouth against mine. "You missed our meeting."

"I hope there was no bloodshed."

"Not a drop."

Ever aware that my brother is standing a few yards away, that he's stopped sawing, I pull back and brush sawdust off the sleeve of his work shirt. "I heard we're getting married here," I say.

"Your brother suggested it and I concurred." He narrows his eyes. "That okay with you?"

"I can't think of a better place."

"Never thought I'd see the day."

I turn at the sound of my brother's voice. He's standing at the rear of the pickup, an insulated jug of water in his hands. Jacob and I have had our moments, good and bad and everything in between. He disapproves of large swatches of my life. He's vocal about it, and he's no pushover when it comes to debate.

I feel myself brace for the anticipated rebuff.

He grins. "My little sister all grown up and getting married."

The tension leaches from my shoulders. Generally, the Amish aren't big on displays of affection, whether it's romantic or familial. Certainly not our family. We learned early on to keep our emotions in check. Not for the first time this afternoon, I feel a mercurial snap of emotion. Without thinking, I go to him. I see him stiffen an instant before I stand on my tiptoes and kiss his cheek.

"*Dank*," I whisper.

The moment is so awkward I break a sweat beneath my uniform. Dropping my gaze, I step back. Clear my throat.

Jacob keeps his arms at his sides and handles it well. "We grew up here. You're my sister. Even though you left, you're Anabaptist. Blood aside, that alone makes you *freindschaft*."

It's the *Deitsch* word for the extended family of Pennsylvania Dutch people across the globe. He rolls his eyes toward Tomasetti. "Him, too." But he punctuates the statement with the hint of a smile.

"You know Bishop Troyer can't officiate," I point out.

"I know that."

"The Mennonite preacher from Sugarcreek is going to marry us."

Another motion toward Tomasetti. "He told me."

I stand there, staring at him, not sure what to say. It's as if my brother has suddenly realized I'm a human being.

"Need some help cutting off those branches?"

Vaguely, I'm aware of Tomasetti's voice behind me. Jacob shifting his gaze from me to Tomasetti and back to me. "I suspect I might be out here a couple days with this saw," he says slowly.

I step back, look from man to man, find them staring at me, their expressions curious and per-plexed.

"I have to get back to work," I hear myself say.

"Any breaks in the case?" Tomasetti asks.

"Working on it," I say. "You?"

For the first time his expression darkens and I realize he needed this time away as badly as I did. "They're still missing."

"So, there's hope."

"Yeah." He closes the distance between us and reaches for my hands. "Glad you could make our meeting, Chief."

"Wouldn't have missed it."

He raises his hand and brushes his knuckles across my cheek, then motions toward the tree. "Just so you know, I think we got the situation under control."

"You mean the tree?"

"Among other things."

A quick squeeze of my hands, and he looks over his shoulder at my brother. "I'll take the thickest branches," he tells him. "Since I have the chain saw. Why don't you start with the smaller ones, and we'll get this big fellow whittled down to size?"

CHAPTER 14

I'm still thinking about my exchange with Jacob and getting used to the idea that Tomasetti and I will be getting married on the farm where I grew up as I drive to the police station. I feel optimistic and somehow lighter as I pull into my parking spot. I notice the buggy parked a few spaces down and I wonder who's waiting for me inside.

I enter to find two Amish women standing at the reception desk, talking to my dispatcher. Only when the smaller of the two looks over her shoulder at me do I recognize her. A tingle of curiosity moves through me at the sight of Christina Weaver.

She actually startles at the sight of me, a deer in the headlights of a Mack truck that's about to mow her down. She turns away, her eyes seeking a route of escape.

Lois stands. "Chief Burkholder." Her eyes hold an apology, letting me know that the two women showed up without notice. Usually, that's not a problem; that's why I'm here, after all—to serve the citizens of Painters Mill. Of course, I'm in the midst of a murder investigation.

"This is Naomi Weaver and her daughter, Christina," Lois tells me. "They'd like to speak to you if you have a few minutes."

The incident at the scene where Aden Karn was killed scrolls through my brain. The defaced photo. The jaunt through the woods. The odd exchange between us once I caught up with her. I hadn't been able to get much out of her, but I'd left with the sense that she knew more than she was letting on.

"Christina and I have met." I nod at the two women. "*Guder nammidaag.*" Good afternoon. "Let's go into my office and talk."

I lead them down the hall and into my office and motion them into chairs. They decline my offer of coffee, and as I settle into the chair at my desk, I sense the tension coming off them.

I look from mother to daughter. "What can I do for you?" I begin.

Christina stares back at me as if she's an inch away from bolting. She fidgets, unable to sit still. Her hands tangle in her lap, her fingers shaking, nails bitten to the quick.

"My husband and I saw you drop her off the other night." Naomi tightens her mouth. "If you hadn't done that, I'd have never known what she did."

"Christina told you what happened?" I ask.

"She told me a few things and I still don't know if I got the whole story." She frowns at her daughter. "Chief Burkholder, Christina didn't want to come here today. Honestly, I can't blame

188

her. But I thought we should. I thought it was the right thing to do. Duty, you know."

"Is this about Aden Karn?" I ask.

"Among other things."

Beside her, the girl sinks more deeply into the chair, brings up her knees and wraps her arms around her shins as if trying to make herself smaller.

Naomi notices and reaches over to make her sit up straighter. "She's just sixteen. Still a baby in a lot of ways. Innocent for her age, you know." The Amish woman shakes her head and for the first time, she looks upset. "We haven't told a soul what happened, and we sure don't want any of this getting out. None of it. Not to anyone. Can you promise me that?"

"Are we talking about a crime that was committed?" I ask. "One that Christina was involved in?"

"She didn't do anything wrong."

"Christina is a minor child," I tell her. "If there was . . . a crime that occurred and a minor child was involved, the name of the child isn't made public." It's the best I can give her. As I rise to close the door, I hope it's enough to keep her talking.

I go back to my desk and sit, divide my attention between them. "If you have something to tell me about Aden Karn, I think you need to start talking."

"You have to understand, Chief Burkholder, Christina is a good girl. *A good girl.*"

"I understand."

"These days . . . sometimes even good girls . . . get caught up in things they shouldn't. They get talked into doing things they shouldn't do."

Across from me, the girl lowers her forehead to her knees.

I wait a beat, but no one speaks. After a moment, the Amish woman nudges her daughter. "You go on now. You tell her what you told me. They gotta know what he did."

What he did . . .

The girl raises her head and looks at me. Misery swims in her eyes. At some point, she's begun to cry, though she doesn't make a sound. Tears stream down her cheeks, but she makes no effort to wipe them away. Beneath the collar of her dress, I see stark red blotches. Hives, I realize.

It's been a long time since I was a sixteen-year-old Amish girl. God knows I'm no expert on kids. I've no clue how to get inside her head or get her to open up. I opt to wait her out.

For the span of a full minute, no one speaks, the only sound coming from the purr of my printer and the tick of the wall clock.

"He was so nice." The Amish girl's voice is so faint I have to lean forward to hear.

"Aden Karn?" I ask.

The girl nods. "He was funny, too, and made me laugh."

Her mother catches my eye. "Christina sells fishing bait on Saturdays. Down there at the bridge over Painters Creek. Worms and minnows and crawpappies, if she can catch them. She hauls everything in that old Berlin Flyer of hers. Well, she was on her way home and a wheel came off the thing." She looks at her daughter, nudges her. "Go on and tell her now. It'll be okay."

"I was on my way home and the wagon broke," the girl blurts. "The wheel fell off. I had bait left and didn't want to just leave it. The next thing I know Aden pulls up. I'd seen him around lots of times. I mean, he wasn't a stranger. He'd bought night crawlers from me the weekend before." She brings shaking hands to her face and swipes at the tears. "I told him I didn't need a ride. I was just going to walk home and get Datt. Only had a mile or two to go. But I didn't want all my worms to die in the heat, so I went with him."

"How long ago was this?" I ask.

"Last summer."

"Was he driving a car or buggy?"

"Car."

I recall being told Aden didn't have a car. "Do you know what kind of car?"

"It was green, I think."

I make a note. "What happened when you went with him?"

191

"He took me to the ice cream place and we got cones. Kept me laughing the whole time. Sweet like, you know? Then we were on our way to his house to get some tools. He said he'd fix the wheel for me.

"Only he didn't take me to his house. He drove out to Layland Road and stopped the car." She falls silent and stares at me, her mouth open, her lips quivering.

Layland Road is a desolate dirt road that parallels Painters Creek and a cornfield. It's a favorite location for lovers to park or for under-age drinkers to congregate. Pickles claims half the population of Painters Mill was conceived on Layland Road.

"He started . . . acting weird," she whispers. "It was like he turned into someone else who wasn't very nice. I didn't know what to do. So, I got out and started walking. He came after me, so I ran into the cornfield. I was going to cut through and get back to the main road. But he caught me."

Up until now, I've not heard a negative word about Aden Karn, and for a fleeting moment I wonder if this girl is fabricating a story to excuse what she did with the marker. I wonder if she's confused or has a bone to pick with Karn. But I know a liar when I see one and this girl isn't making up stories. In the back of my mind, my conversation with Emily Byler begins to churn.

He was good that way. Good to me. He was always good, you see. Always.

"And then it's like . . . he wasn't Aden anymore," the girl whispers. "He was . . . somebody else. *Something* else. Something bad."

Her face crumples and she lets out a wail. The words that follow pour out of her like poison from a festering wound, putrid and stinking. I listen, unable to move or look away, and cold sweat breaks out on the back of my neck.

When she's finished and it's my turn to ask questions and seek clarification, I can't speak. I can only stare because I don't trust my voice. I don't want these women to know I am so affected by what I've heard.

"He forced you?" I ask. "Sexually assaulted you?"

Crying, the girl looks at her mother. "Mamm . . . I can't."

The Amish woman takes her daughter's hand and holds it tightly. "She came home covered with dirt and mud. It was in her hair. All over her clothes. She was crying so hard she couldn't breathe. I didn't know what to think, and she wouldn't say. She didn't say a word to anyone for five days, Chief Burkholder. She didn't eat or leave her room. It was only when I did laundry that I found the blood on her clothes. Her underpants. And I knew."

The mother makes a sound that's part sob, part

gasp. She quickly gets her emotions back under control. "We're supposed to forgive. And I know that boy isn't here to ask for forgiveness himself. But let me tell you something, Kate Burkholder. Aden Karn didn't have a soul. Or a conscience. I had to take this poor child to the doctor. Get her fixed up. Her mind will never be the same. That's all I'm going to say. That's enough, dragging her through all of this again."

I look at the girl and I see a thousand years of misery condensed into the span of minutes, a dark mix of horror and shame and grief reflected back at me. I feel those same emotions inside me, behind the door where I keep them locked down tight.

The woman shakes her head. "He took things from her that can't be gotten back, Chief Burkholder. It's taken six months for her to be able to go outside. Can't even sell her bait anymore." Her look turns pained. "The only time I heard her laugh since that day is when she found out he was dead."

The girl turns sideways and curls into her mother and actually shields her face from me with her hand.

Naomi pats her daughter's hand. "Everyone thought Aden Karn was a good man, but did they really know him?" She scoffs. "Let me tell you about Aden Karn. The devil whispered his name and Aden Karn took his hand and he went."

. . .

I sit at my desk for a long time after Naomi and Christina leave, trying to pull the pieces of myself back together—and make sense of a case that's gone in a direction I didn't expect. Until now, I'd believed Aden Karn was a wholesome, well-adjusted, well-liked young Amish man who'd been the victim of a senseless crime. He personified everything I love about the Amish. I'd put him on a pedestal. And now, even though he's three days dead, I feel as if he's sunk a knife into my back.

Were the signs there? If so, how did I miss them? Am I so biased that I simply didn't *want* to see? Did I believe in Aden Karn so steadfastly because I was once Amish and I feel more than I should for the community as a whole? The questions sting with enough force to make me question everything I've come to believe about the case.

I think of the brutality and violence of Karn's murder, and I wonder if this is the missing link I've been looking for all along. Did someone find out what Karn had done to Christina and seek retribution? If so, who? A father? Lover? Another family member?

Is she the only one?

I pick up the phone and speed-dial Mona.

She picks up on the first ring. "Yeah, Chief?"

"I want you to get me everything you can find

on Christina Weaver. Sixteen-year-old female. Amish. See what you can find on her parents and siblings, too. Check for warrants." I give her the names I have. "Check social media, too."

"Anything in particular you're looking for?" she asks.

"Names, mostly. Father. Uncles. Brothers. Known associates." I kick myself for having not asked some of those questions when she was here, but I was so shocked by what she had to say . . .

"See if you can find out if she has a boyfriend or if she has any male friends. Find out if she's working. If she has a male boss."

"Got it."

"Keep this under your hat, Mona, but I think Aden Karn may have been a sexual predator."

"Oh shit."

"Yeah." I sigh. "You're probably not going to find much since they're Amish, but hang with it. See what's out there. I'll see what I can do on my end, too."

CHAPTER 15

Elma Glick loved her in-line skates more than anything in the world. They were her Ferrari. Her jet airplane. The rocket ship that took her to exotic places that would otherwise be out of reach. Datt didn't approve, of course, but then he didn't approve of a lot of things, especially if it was a new idea. The Amish never approved of fads. Mamm wasn't crazy about the skates, either. But when she needed groceries and didn't have time to hook up the buggy horse and run into town to get them, it was Elma and her skates to the rescue.

"Just milk and cereal and a loaf of bread if it's fresh," Mamm had told her. "Just to tide us over till I can get to the grocery day after tomorrow."

Elma didn't mind. In fact, she thanked her lucky stars because she enjoyed getting out of the house this time of day, when the sun was sinking and the air was cool. When she skated, she could fly, and she wouldn't trade these forbidden excursions for the world.

Hire's Carry Out was only two miles from their farm. The store closed at eight P.M. and Elma had made it by the skin of her teeth. Now, a grocery bag in each hand—a chocolate bar tucked into the pocket of her apron—she sped along the road at the speed of sound. The asphalt surface was so rough it vibrated her teeth, but Elma was used to it. She blew past the old Miller place, laughing when the fat corgi tore out of the gate and tried to catch her. The trees flew by in the blur as she approached the bridge at Little Paint Creek. She was almost across when something on the creek bank snagged her eye. It was half in the water, half out. She'd caught a whiff of something dead and thought maybe it was a sheep that had drowned and been swept away during the rainstorm last week. Curious, she slowed and circled around, and then skated back to the guardrail at the side of the bridge for a quick look-see.

Not a sheep, she realized. It looked like a big wad of trash, as if someone had wrapped something in plastic. From where she stood, she could see the crisscross of duct tape.

"Was der schinner is sell?" she said aloud. What in the world is that?

Setting down the grocery bags, Elma stepped over the guardrail and worked her way down the steep incline, keeping the wheels of her skates sideways to avoid a spill. Midway down she caught the smell again, a stink she knew well. One of their calves had been hit by a car last summer. Datt hauled the carcass to the back of the field and every time she'd gone there to pick raspberries, she smelled it.

Her thoughts ground to a halt when she spotted what looked like a bare foot sticking out of the plastic. She wanted to think it was a mannequin; the kind at the department store up in Millersburg. Maybe it was broken and the manager had thrown it away. But Elma knew that wasn't the case. That was no mannequin foot; she could see the toes. She'd smelled the smell. Her stomach turned a slow somersault.

Making a sound like a frightened child, she spun and clambered up the bank, moving too fast, fingers digging into mud, skates hindering her. At the top, she tripped and went down on her knees. Heart wild in her chest. Blood roaring in her ears. The sight of that pale foot flashing in her brain. On the road's shoulder, she scrambled to her feet.

"*Mamm!*"

Groceries forgotten, she set off at a too-fast pace, a scream stuck in her throat, terror nipping at her heels.

I'm in my office at the station. Around me, every smidgen of information I've amassed on the case is spread out on the desk. I've spent the last two hours going through all of it, this time with a fresh eye. I created a timeline. I watched the videos I took at the scene. Studied my sketches. I looked at the photos until every horrific image is branded on my brain like red-hot iron on flesh.

I'm so immersed in my work that I'm startled when my second-shift dispatcher rushes into my office. "I just took a call from Leroy Glick, Chief. Says his daughter found a dead body."

"What?" I get to my feet. "Does he know who it is?" In the back of my mind, I'm thinking heart attack or maybe a pedestrian-related hit-and-run.

"He doesn't know."

"Where's the body?"

"Beneath the Little Paint Bridge out on Mill Road."

"I know the area." I yank open my pencil drawer, grab my keys. "Jodie, where's Mr. Glick?"

"He called from the pay phone out on Dogleg Road. Said his daughter was the one who found the body and she was upset, so he needed to get back home."

"I know where they live." I glance at the wall clock, my mind scrolling through my officer work schedule. "Is Mona still on duty?"

"Yes, ma'am."

"Tell her to meet me at the scene." I yank my jacket off the back of my chair. "I'm on my way."

It takes me six minutes to arrive on scene. Mona is already there; I can see the lights of her cruiser blazing as I make the turn onto Mill Road. I nearly run over the orange safety cones she's set out to block traffic. I park behind her vehicle and get out. Spotting the glow of her Maglite on the bridge, I head that way.

"See anything?" I call out.

"Hey, Chief." She glances at me over her shoulder and then focuses the beam of her Maglite on the creek bank below us. "RP said the body was wrapped in plastic. Definitely something down there on the bank wrapped in plastic."

The faint smell of decaying flesh hangs in the humid night air. Not too strong, but present nonetheless. I have my Maglite at the ready and my beam joins Mona's. Sure enough, a bundle of something wrapped in plastic lies on the bank, partly in the water.

"Could be an animal," Mona says. "Livestock. Or a pet someone disposed of."

"Definitely something dead." I shift my light toward the water. Uneasiness quivers in my gut when I see what looks like a human foot. "You see that?" I ask. "There in the water?"

She cranes her neck, squints into the darkness. A gasp escapes her when her beam illuminates the foot. "Shit. Is that—"

"We need to check." I backtrack and throw my leg over the guardrail. "Watch your step," I tell Mona as I start down the steep bank. "Keep an eye out for evidence."

"Not to mention snakes," she mutters.

I wade through hip-high weeds, trying not to slide in the mud.

"I was hoping the RP was mistaken," Mona says from behind me.

"I'd settle for a hoax at this point."

I reach the base of the creek bottom and stop fifteen feet away from the object. The air is dank and still down here, the reek of decaying flesh stronger. The beam of my flashlight reveals plastic wrapped around an object about the size and shape of a human body and held in place with duct tape.

Mona comes up behind me and shines her light, and points. "I don't even want to say this, but it sure looks like a body."

"Size is about right," I say.

"Look there." I follow her point. Now that we're level with the object in question, we have a better vantage point. The foot is submerged. Pink polish on the toenails . . .

"Jesus," Mona whispers.

"Stay put." Pulse thrumming, I move closer, and I can see what looks like flesh beneath a couple of layers of plastic. "Caucasian," I hear myself say. "Female, I think."

I take another step, thrust my flashlight out in front of me. Through the transparent sheeting, I can just make out the pale flesh of a torso. The L-shaped angle of a bent arm. Blond hair. Head twisted to one side.

"I think she's probably been here awhile," I say. "Tape isn't worn or frayed."

"Looks like blood on the plastic," Mona whispers.

Sure enough, a ruddy spot the size of a quarter stands out against the lighter-colored flesh.

Though we left our headlights on, it's dark as a cave down here in the creek bottom. The body is partially submerged. The bank is steep and overgrown. The worst kind of crime scene . . .

I shine my Maglite in a 360-degree circle. I'm aware of the trickle of water now. To my left, I notice some of the weeds have been pushed over and crushed. I look up and I wonder if someone dumped the body from the bridge, pushed from a vehicle. The body struck the ground and rolled down the hill and into the water.

"Mona." I turn and look at her. "We're probably trampling evidence. Retrace your steps. Go back up. I'm going to make sure what we're dealing with here and I'll meet you up there in a minute."

"Roger that." She's already turned to make her way back up the bank.

I stand still for a moment, shine my light all around, looking hard for anything out of place, but there's nothing unusual in the vicinity. No personal items or trash. No clothing or footprints I can see. Just the human-size bundle wrapped in plastic. Vaguely, I'm aware of Mona climbing over the guardrail and walking to the bridge above me, her light shining down to help me see.

Giving her a thumbs-up, I start toward the

object, keeping an eye out for anything out of place. There's no breeze here next to the creek and the smell burgeons, damp and unpleasant. I reach the body, and I go to one knee. I'm close enough to see hair through the plastic. The pale skin of a face. The dark shadow of an eye. The mouth is open. The pink shadow of a tongue against the plastic. A smear of what looks like blood. I don't see any clothing, but I can't be sure because the plastic is bunched up in places and I'm unable to see through. I skim the beam of my flashlight lower, and I see the tips of fingers sticking out. Through the caked mud, I see that her nails are painted the same pink as the toes. Alongside the horror of confirming we are, indeed, dealing with a dead body, I feel a punch of grief because mere days ago, this woman cared about something as mundane as a manicure.

"Shit," I whisper, close my eyes, take a breath. "Shit."

"You okay down there, Chief?" comes Mona's voice.

"Yep." I shift the beam to the foot. It's submerged, water moving over it. Something has nibbled on one of the toes and I can just make out the pink protrusion of bone. . . .

I swallow hard, find my voice, look up at Mona. "Definitely a body, Mona. Get the road blocked off. I'll notify the coroner."

"Roger that."

Rising, I back away from the body, hit my shoulder mike and hail Dispatch. "Ten-seven-nine," I say, using the ten code for "notify coroner."

"Ten-four," comes Jodie's voice. "Any idea who it is, Chief?"

"No," I tell her. "Just . . . get the coroner out here. Notify County, too. We're going to need to search the area. Start a canvass."

I release the Talk button and take a moment, try to get my head around what this means. The discovery of two bodies in such a short period of time in a town the size of Painters Mill is an anomaly. It simply doesn't happen. I have no idea how this female was killed or who she is. At this point, I'm not even certain this is a homicide. She could have died from a drug overdose and whoever was with her panicked, wrapped her body in plastic, and dumped it.

In the chaos of my thoughts, one obvious question stands out. Is the death of this woman in any way related to the murder of Aden Karn?

I shine my flashlight on the victim. I can't see much of her face due to the plastic and duct tape. But she looks young. I've no idea if she's local or from out of town. Whatever the case, someone is probably missing her. Someone is worried because she didn't come home. In the coming days, the people who loved her are going to have their lives taken apart piece by piece by piece.

CHAPTER 16

When you're a cop and you need information, you can pretty much bet your ass you're not going to get it any time soon. I spent most of the night at the scene where the body was discovered. Doc Coblentz was reticent; there was simply no way he could relay any preliminary information regarding cause or manner of death because the body was wrapped in plastic and bound with tape, all of which must be handled as evidence.

I was loath to call Tomasetti when he already has a major case on his plate. But with two homicides on my hands, even with the involvement of the sheriff's department, I'm in over my head. So I called him and, of course, he came.

In an effort to preserve evidence, I limited the number of people allowed in to the scene to recover the body. That, of course, slowed down the process tremendously.

Once the body was recovered and the crime scene turned over to us by the coroner, I stayed another couple of hours, hoping the BCI techs would come up with some scrap of evidence. But there was nothing to be had. At dawn, rather than pacing the bridge and accomplishing nothing, I left the scene to interview the Amish girl who discovered the body.

All I learned was that the discovery was happenstance. A girl going to pick up groceries for her *mamm*. Instead, she discovered a scene out of a nightmare, one she and her family won't forget any time soon.

Tomasetti did his job; he gave it his all and, as always, his presence was tremendously helpful. He got the victim fingerprinted quickly, the prints scanned and sent to AFIS, the Automated Fingerprint Identification System. He gave the police lab in London, Ohio, a heads-up and asked them to expedite the evidence coming their way. I could tell he was distracted. No doubt he's preoccupied with the two missing girls, wondering if today is the day their bodies will be found. If this is the day he'll have to sit down with the parents and tell them their children won't be coming home. He had to be in Cleveland at seven A.M., so he left around two so he could grab a couple of hours of sleep and a shower. I miss him already. I know he's a strong man; he's certainly been through worse. Even so, I worry.

It's nearly eight A.M. now. I'm in the waiting area of the morgue at Pomerene Hospital, checking my phone for the hundredth time, waiting for information.

The door swishes open. I glance up to see Sheriff Mike Rasmussen enter, looking as tired and frazzled as I am. He looks at me with a frown as he strides over to me. "Anything from Coblentz?"

Shaking my head, I rise and we shake. "He's not talking and I've been here an hour."

"We should have heard back from AFIS by now." He glances at his watch and curses. "We need to get her IDed."

I've known Mike since I became chief. He's a decent man with a boatload of common sense; he's fair-minded and diplomatic, all of which make him not only a good sheriff, but a good politician.

"Anything new at the scene?" I ask.

"We got nothing, Kate. No one saw or heard anything. No vehicles or buggies. Not a footprint or tire track. Not a damn thing."

Both of us were present when the victim was placed in a body bag, lifted onto a gurney, and loaded in the coroner's van for the ride to the morgue. In order to preserve evidence, the duct tape and plastic were left in place; no one has had a good look at her face. She appeared to be nude beneath the plastic, but it was difficult to make out much detail. No ID was found at the scene. That was over four hours ago and we're still waiting to identify her.

"You think this is connected to the Karn homicide?" Rasmussen asks.

"The timing is certainly suspect," I tell him.

"Gotta be a link . . ."

"Chief Burkholder?"

At the sound of the voice, I glance over to see

a young man clad in surgical scrubs emerge from the corridor leading to Doc Coblentz's office and, farther back, the morgue.

"We're ready for you," he tells us.

Rasmussen and I cross to him, and the three of us exchange handshakes. "I'm Alan Han, the forensic investigator from Franklin County."

"Thanks for coming," I tell him.

"As you can imagine, we're anxious for anything you can tell us," Rasmussen says.

"I understand." Han motions toward the corridor. "Suit up and we'll get this done."

We don't speak as we enter the alcove and slip paper gowns over our clothing. Shoe covers over our boots. Gloves. Head covering. Masks. Han waits at the door, snaps on a fresh pair of gloves, and leads us into the morgue. Until this moment, I'd been so preoccupied by the occurrence of a second homicide that I hadn't been plagued with the customary dread that precedes my every excursion to the autopsy room.

The lights overhead buzz with maddening clarity as I cross to the stainless-steel table. The victim is covered with a paper sheet. Several quarter-size points of moisture have soaked through. The morgue is a modern facility, but not even the state-of-the-art ventilation system can sift out the stench of decaying flesh.

Doc Coblentz turns to us and nods, his expression grim. "Dr. Han took blood and urine samples.

We swabbed her. Took nail scrapings. Dental impressions."

"Everything has been couriered to the lab in London, Ohio," Han adds.

"We've cleaned her up and this is what we have." The doc glances down at the victim. "Eighteen-to-twenty-five-year-old female. Caucasian. Five feet six. A hundred and thirty pounds. She was nude. Wrapped in plastic sheeting. Sheeting was secured with common duct tape."

"Any ID?" Rasmussen asks.

"No."

"Any idea how long she's been dead?" I ask.

"Preliminarily, two days," he tells me. "Maybe three."

Doc nods at Han, giving him the floor.

"As you probably already know, I was able to get fingerprints," the investigator begins. "They were sent to AFIS for matching. DNA was sent to the lab via courier." He looks down at the victim as if trying to decide where to start. "We dusted the plastic sheeting. There were a couple of smudges, but no prints, preliminarily anyway. We sent all the sheeting as well as the duct tape to the BCI lab in London, Ohio, for further analysis."

"Time frame on the prints or DNA?" This from Rasmussen.

"Less than twenty-four hours on the prints," Han tells him. "DNA? Depending on how badly the lab is backed up." He shrugs. "Four days. Maybe a week?"

I send a silent thank-you to Tomasetti for making that call. "Tox?"

"Ten days," Han replies.

I look at the doc, meet his gaze. "Is this a homicide?"

"I think it's safe to say we're dealing with a homicide." He reaches for the paper sheet and peels it away. "Here we go."

No amount of toughness or experience or hardened heart can prepare you for the sight of a young woman who has been dead for two or three days.

Next to me, Rasmussen stiffens, takes a half step back. I don't move, stand there, shaken, staring down at what was once a young woman. The only thought I have is: *What in the name of God happened to you?*

The flesh is gray with reddish-pink marbling in areas. The abdomen is swollen. The pelvic area sports a greenish tinge. The skin of the hands is brown and dry looking. She's monstrous and I need to look away, focus on something else, anything else. I can't, of course, because it's my responsibility to see this. It's my job to find the son of a bitch that perpetrated this atrocity.

Silently, I work to calm myself. I try to see her as the person she was. Blond hair. Dark brows. She'd been pretty, I realize. Young. Physically fit.

"Jesus," Rasmussen mutters.

Doc Coblentz sighs beneath his mask. "I wish I could offer you something in the way of helpful information, but at this point I simply can't. Most of what you need will come post-autopsy. But I'll give you what I can."

I look at him and nod, swallow the spit that's pooled in my mouth.

I find my voice. "Did you find any jewelry?" I ask. "Clothing?"

"No."

I study the victim's hair. Too blond to be natural. I take in the pink paint on the toenails and fingernails. Probably not Amish, and a dark sense of relief sweeps through me even as that little voice in the back of my head whispers that she could have been on *rumspringa* . . .

"She has several piercings and a few other identifying markers," the doc tells us. "That includes a navel piercing. Nose piercing. Brow piercing. Tattoo on the ankle." He indicates the right ankle.

Due to the dark coloration of the skin, it's difficult to make out the tattoo.

"Looks like a marijuana leaf." Rasmussen leans close, narrows his eyes. "If her prints aren't on file, we might be able to check with some of the area tattoo parlors."

"Another tattoo at the small of her back," Doc Coblentz tells us. "We photographed everything and will send JPEGs to you ASAP." Turning, he plucks a swab from a stainless tray on the counter. "Her hands were bound. Behind her back."

"With duct tape," Han interjects. "Which was also sent to the lab."

"Sexual assault?" Rasmussen asks.

"I'll get to that in a minute." The doc indicates the victim's throat. "We've got marks here. Bruising. So I took an X-ray, which revealed the hyoid bone was fractured."

"She was strangled?" I ask.

"Yes, but I don't know if that's what killed her. Kate, she also had a plastic bag over her head. It was sealed with tape at the base of her neck. She also had adhesive around her mouth."

"From tape?"

"I don't know, but that is a likely scenario," he tells me. "I won't know cause of death until after I get her on the table."

The horror of that takes some of the breath from my lungs. "Any other injuries?" I ask.

"There is evidence of sexual assault. A multitude of lacerations and bruising, both vaginal and anal. Enough injury to cause hemorrhage. I suspect foreign-object rape as well. Not causal of death, but there may be additional internal injuries as well."

I stare at the victim, aware that my heart is pounding, my face hot with anger, my mouth so dry I can't swallow, can't speak. The heat of outrage almost overcomes me.

213

"Did you find the object?" Rasmussen asks.

"No."

I look at the sheriff. "We need to get someone back out to the scene to look."

He nods. "Road is still blocked. I'll get a deputy out there." His mouth tightens into a snarl. "Semen?"

"We expedited samples of everything to the lab," Han tells us.

The doc looks down at the victim and grimaces. Over the top of his mask, through the goggles, he looks tired and . . . angry. It's the first time in all the years I've worked with him that I've seen any sign of emotion. I wonder if in the past he's been better at hiding it or if something about this particular case got under his skin.

"At least one bite mark on her left breast." Using the swab, he indicates the left breast. "Possibly the buttock, too."

"Forensic odontologist will be here later this morning," Han adds.

"She went through a lot," I hear myself say.

"Yes, she did," Doc replies.

"Was this done by one person?" I ask. "More than one?"

"I don't know," Doc tells me.

"This took some time," Rasmussen says slowly. "The rape. The bag over the head. Wrapping the body in plastic with tape. It required some privacy."

I look at Rasmussen. "It didn't happen at the scene," I say. "She was raped and murdered elsewhere and dumped in that creek."

"I agree," the sheriff replies.

"When we canvassed, did we check for security or game cams?" I ask.

"We got nothing."

I look at Doc. "We need photos of everything you have."

"I'll send them as soon as humanly possible," he tells me.

"How soon can you do the autopsy?" I ask.

"I'll cancel everything on my schedule. We'll do it today. Probably this afternoon or evening." He looks down at the victim and sighs. "I figure we owe this poor young lady that much."

I don't speak to anyone as I strip off the biohazard gear and stuff everything into the receptacle. I'm vaguely aware of the sheriff speaking to Han in the corridor. Wanting only to get out, I leave the alcove, rush down the hall and into the restroom, where I scrub my hands clean with the hottest water I can tolerate. I shove open the door and nearly plow into Rasmussen, who's waiting his turn. We make eye contact for two seconds; then, without speaking, I brush past him and go directly to the door marked STAIRS and take them two at a time to the ground-level floor. I hit the security bar with both hands, punch open the door. The reception area is a blur as I rush through. I exit through the double doors, sucking in fresh air, letting it fill my lungs. I break into a run as I leave the portico. I don't stop until I reach the Explorer. Breaths rushing, I yank open the door, but I don't get in. My mouth is full of saliva, so I go to the island of grass and spit. I set my hands on my knees and gulp air, and I wait for my stomach to settle.

"Shit," I pant. "Shit. Damn it."

"Kate."

I straighten to see Rasmussen striding toward me, his expression concerned. "Hell of a damn thing to see," he growls.

Hoping I don't look as strung out as I feel, I take another breath, try to get a handle on my emotions and remind myself I have a job to do. I sure as hell don't have time to curl up in a ball and let some murderous prick get away with what was done to that girl.

For a time, neither of us speaks.

"Mike, how did that happen?" I say. "I mean, here? In Holmes County? In Painters Mill? What kind of monster does that?"

It's not a very cop-like opening question. Too much emotion. Too much anger. I grapple for composure, can't quite get my hands on it.

The sheriff clears his throat. Looks down at the ground. "I don't know."

"Two bodies inside a week."

He narrows his eyes. "Gotta be related."

"The homicides . . . are different in nature."

"Yeah."

I raise my eyes to his. "Do we have any missing females in the county?"

"We're checking now."

I try to remember if I've heard anything from the Amish and I make a mental note to get in touch with my sister, do a little poking around, even if no one has reported anything.

"We're going to need to set up a task force," I say.

"I'll get things rolling on my end."

"I'll get with BCI."

"Look, I know you're tied up with the Karn thing. I can jump right into this one, Kate. I got the manpower. Take some pressure off you and your department."

He's right, of course. The sheriff and I have worked multiple cases together and we've never had a beef about who does what. But I've never been very good at taking a back seat, even when it's the prudent thing to do.

I nod, but I feel the gravity of the case pressing down on me. "Mike, we need to get her identified."

"Yeah." He glances at his watch and frowns. "If we strike out on AFIS, I'll put out a press release."

"Painters Mill has an active social media account," I add. "A lot of citizens. It's mostly recipes and garage sales, but I'll put something out. Someone's got to be missing her."

He studies me a moment. "We probably need to keep some of this close to our chest, Kate. I mean, certain aspects of the crime."

"I agree. Let's think about what information we want to make public and what we don't."

"Sure."

For a moment, the only sound comes from the rattle of a big rig on the road. "So you okay?" Rasmussen asks.

I meet his gaze, muster a smile that feels lopsided on my face. "Pissed off mostly."

"Me, too." Another silence, and then he adds, "Once we ID her, we'll get him. Chances are she knows him. Or someone who knows her will know him. We'll get him."

Generally speaking, I would agree. Most victims know their killers. But something about this woman—maybe the tattoos and piercings—points to something else I haven't quite gotten a handle on yet, so I let it go.

"Somewhere, a parent or husband or even a kid is waiting for her to come home," I say.

"Yeah." Grimacing, Rasmussen sets his hand on my shoulder, squeezes gently, and then he turns and walks away.

I call Mona on my way to the station. "Where are you?"

"At the station."

"Find a computer. Pull up a map. Locate the nearest residences or business, churches or school, to the scene where the victim was found. Check to see if there's a dumpster or garbage can. Then I want you to get out there, go through the garbage and see if you can find a purse or ID or . . . anything that might be related to our victim."

"Duct tape or plastic, cell, stuff like that?"

"Clothing, too." I pause, my mind spinning. "I know this is a long shot. Chances are, the killer ditched everything elsewhere. I know it's dirty work—"

"Don't worry about it, Chief. I'm on it. If there's anything there, I'll find it."

"If you need help, call T.J."

"I might do that just to see him climb into a dumpster."

I feel myself smile. Not for the first time I'm thankful to have such a good team of officers working for me.

I think about other priorities. "Mona, find out who did the canvass. Check with them to see if they asked about game cams. Home security cams."

"You got it."

"I'm on my way to the station," I tell her.

"Roger that."

CHAPTER 17

I've just pulled into my parking slot at the police station when my cell phone chirps. I catch a glimpse of the display as I snatch it up. BCI LABR LONDON.

"Burkholder," I snap.

"This is the latent-print examiner at the lab in London, Chief Burkholder," she tells me. "We got a hit on those Jane Doe prints."

"ID?"

"Paige Rossberger. Twenty-six years old. Last known address: Massillon." She recites the street address and I write it down.

"She was in the system?" I ask.

"Arrested for prostitution in 2019. Two more arrests in 2020. Prostitution, second offense, and possession of a controlled substance. She was on probation."

"Next of kin?"

Keys click on the other end. "Unmarried. No minor children. One surviving parent, her mother, lives in Massillon."

"Email me everything you have," I say.

"It's on the way."

I find Lois at her desk at the dispatch station, headset clamped over her ears, the switchboard ringing off the hook. She must see something in my eyes because she puts her caller on hold, gets to her feet, and gives me her full attention.

"I got an ID on our victim." I tell her the name and spell it. "I need everything you can find on her. Known associates. Social media accounts. Get me contact info for her probation officer. I'll send the rest of the info I have in an email. NOK have not been notified, so not a word to anyone."

"You got it."

Glock had been sitting in one of the cubicles down the hall and joins us. "Is she local?" he asks.

"Last known address is in Massillon." I relay what I've learned so far.

"Since she was a working girl, she probably hung out with some sketchy individuals," he says.

"And spent time with people she didn't know."

"Need a hand with anything?" he asks.

"Give me a few minutes to call the PD up there so they can do the notification. Then I thought we might make a run up there."

I stop at the coffee station, locate the biggest mug I can find, fill it with coffee, and carry it into my office. While my laptop grinds to life, I call the Massillon PD and ask for the detective bureau.

"Davidson," comes a curt male voice on the other end.

I identify myself and get right to the point. "I just IDed a body that was dumped along a rural road here in Painters Mill. Her name's Paige Rossberger and she's from Massillon."

I literally hear him sit up straighter. "I know the name," he says. "She's been on the radar for a couple years. Mother called us this morning. Filed a missing-person report."

I tell him everything I know so far. "Any known associates? Friends? Family?"

"Let me check. Hang on."

The sound of computer keys clicking comes over the line and then he comes back on. "Paige Rossberger lived with her mother. Aside from what you already have, that's all I got."

"Anything on a boyfriend?"

"Not that we know of."

I pause, thinking. "Detective Davidson, I've got two homicides on my hands here in Painters Mill. I'm trying to figure out if they're connected, and it would be tremendously helpful if I could talk to the victim's mother."

He sighs, telling me this isn't the first time he's had to relay terrible news to a loved one. "We've got a chaplain works with the department. Let me get with him and we'll do the notification."

"Thank you."

"Look, can you send me what you have on the case? Keep me apprised?"

"Of course."

222

"Chief Burkholder, June Rossberger has had a couple of brushes with the law herself over the years. Got herself straightened out now. Losing her kid like this . . . it's going to be tough on her."

"I understand," I say. "But I don't think there's any way around my talking to her. I'll do my best to keep it as brief as possible."

"Appreciate it."

I glance at the time on my computer screen. "I've got a couple of things to tie up here, Detective Davidson, and then I'll head that way."

According to her probation officer, Paige Rossberger had kept her nose clean since her last arrest. She passed every drug test, landed a part-time job with a local grocery store, and opened a checking account to get her finances in order.

"She swore up and down she was staying away from the crowd that got her into trouble," he'd told me. "Despite her brushes with the law, Paige had a good head on her shoulders. We had a standing appointment every month and she didn't miss a one. Until yesterday, anyway."

I took him through some of the same questions I covered with Detective Davidson, but he was unable to add anything I didn't already know.

"Did she have any problems with anyone?" I asked him. "Any threats? Or disagreements or arguments? Anything like that?"

"Paige wasn't the kind of person to talk about

stuff like that," he told me. "I hate to say it, but even if she'd found herself in trouble, the last people she'd turn to would be us." Another sigh, heavy with regret. "She didn't trust the system, Chief Burkholder. Had I known she was heading for this kind of trouble, I'd have found a way to step in and help. But she didn't say a word."

It's midmorning when Glock and I arrive in Massillon. June Rossberger lives in a small house a few blocks from the public library. Usually, when tragedy strikes a family, friends and extended family rally. When I pull up to the house and park curbside, I'm surprised to find a single car in the driveway.

Glock notices, too. "Locals did the notification?" he asks.

I shut down the engine. "Detective said he would."

"Hate it that there's no one here to be with her," he says as we get out.

"Maybe they've already come and gone." It seems like an optimistic statement as I take in the aged Corolla in the driveway. "We'll make this quick."

The sidewalk and driveway are a jigsaw puzzle of broken concrete with weeds jutting from the cracks. We take the steps to the small porch and I knock.

The thump of feet sounds and the door swings open. I find myself looking at a middle-age woman with thin brown hair shorn nearly to the scalp. She's wearing sweatpants and a flannel shirt. Her face is devoid of makeup. She doesn't look happy to see us standing on her front porch.

"Haven't you people given me enough bad news for one day?" she says in a gruff voice.

Her face is ruddy, her eyes bloodshot, but I can't tell if she's been crying. I identify myself. "June Rossberger?"

"That's me."

"Have you spoken to Detective Davidson, ma'am?"

"He told me." She's got a smoker's voice, as rough and deep as a quarry. "Left an hour ago."

"I'm very sorry for your loss."

Her eyes soften a little when Glock removes his cap. She seems oddly unemotional for having just lost her daughter. Of course, people deal with loss and grief in different ways. I wonder if they were close.

"I hadn't seen her in a few days," she tells me. "Left all her stuff—what little she had—and went off on whatever kind of binge them kids go on nowadays."

"I'm trying to figure out what happened to her," I say. "Can we come in and talk for a few minutes?"

"I gotta be at work in an hour." She looks from

me to Glock and back to me. "I suppose if you make it quick. I got a long shift ahead."

I feel Glock's eyes on me as we enter. The house is uncomfortably warm and smells of burnt toast and cigarette smoke. Rossberger moves like a woman who spends too much time on her feet and leads us to a living room furnished with secondhand furniture and wall-to-wall carpet from the 1990s. She motions me to a ragtag sofa and offers a chair to Glock, but he declines and takes up his position in the doorway.

"Suit yourself." She falls into an overstuffed chair across from me and props her feet on the matching ottoman. "Detective said she was murdered. That true?"

"The coroner hasn't made the official ruling just yet," I tell her. "But, yes, we believe it was a homicide."

"You the cop going to be investigating?" Her eyes flick over my uniform and she laughs. "A woman?"

"Her body was found in Painters Mill, where I'm chief. The Ohio Bureau of Criminal Investigation and the Holmes County Sheriff's Department are involved, too. I want you to know we're going to do everything we can to find the person responsible."

"I hope you get him. Paige wasn't exactly a good girl, but she sure didn't deserve to get killed."

I pull out my notepad. "When's the last time you saw her?"

"Four days ago. She comes and goes. More going than coming, I guess."

"Did she have any ties to Painters Mill?" I ask. "Did she ever travel there or mention Holmes County?"

"Not that I recall. She wasn't exactly the Amish-country type, if you know what I mean."

I recall the probation officer telling me Paige had landed a job. "I understand she worked part-time."

The woman frowns at me. "You know she did."

It takes me a second to understand the meaning of her response. "I mean a regular job," I clarify. "Her probation officer said she was working at a grocery store. Is that correct?"

"Got fired a couple weeks ago. That girl had more jobs than I have toes. She didn't like being told what to do. Never could hold one down."

I pause, take a moment to get my words in order, get them right. "She was arrested for prostitution a couple years ago?"

She gives me a sage look. "You're wondering if she was still working the street?"

I nod. "Was she?"

"Lookit, we didn't talk about it. She knew I didn't approve. But, yeah, I think she was out there, doing what she could to make some money."

"Is there anything in particular that makes you think that?"

"She kept crazy hours. Always had cash. Got a lot of calls." Grimacing, she shakes her head, and her thoughts seem to turn inward. "I always knew something bad would come of it. I tried to tell her. She wouldn't listen to anyone, least of all me."

"Do you have a recent picture of her?"

"I think so." She pulls out her phone, scrolls, then hands the device to me. "Took this a couple of weeks ago. Her birthday. God's sake, I didn't know it would be her last."

I take the phone, look down at the photo. Paige Rossberger was blond and pretty with a toothy, born-to-laugh smile. She's looking at the camera, sticking out her tongue at the photographer. "Did you take the photo?"

"Sure did. We had dinner together that night."

I look back at the photo and realize it's her eyes that grab hold of me. They're big and green and reflect mischief and trouble. "She was pretty."

The woman laughs. "A pretty lot of trouble is what she was."

"May I send this photo to my email?" I ask.

"Sure."

I poke around, find the Share button, and send it. I hand her the phone. "Do you know where Paige's cell phone is?"

She shakes her head. "I've called her six or seven times in the last couple days. Goes right to voice mail. That's why I got worried. Even if she doesn't answer, she'll always text back."

I ask for the number and she gives it to me. I write all of it down.

"Did she have a boyfriend?" I ask. "Or was she seeing anyone regularly?"

"No one regular." She huffs. "Ain't a man alive put up with a woman screwing any loser off the street for fifty bucks. That just ain't right."

"What about enemies, Mrs. Rossberger? Did Paige have any ongoing disputes or arguments with anyone?"

"Not that I know of."

"Did she have a best friend? Was she close to anyone in particular? Someone she might've confided in?"

"Paige was different that way. Never got too close to people. Didn't do normal stuff, like go to movies or shop or go out to eat." Her brows knit as if she's thinking about it. "She was kind of a loner, I guess."

The woman takes a deep breath and presses her lips together. "I probably argued with her more than anyone. I told her: No drugs in this house. No booze. And no men." A phlegmy laugh rattles in her throat. "I guess that's why she didn't come around much. Last year or so, she'd become a stranger to me. Someone I didn't know. Someone

I didn't want to know. I never could get through to her. It's sad, really."

"Mrs. Rossberger, do you have any idea who might've done this?" I ask.

Taking her time, she reaches into the pocket of her sweatshirt, pulls out a pack of Camels, and lights up. "If I had to guess, I'd say it was one of her men. These are some hard times and there are some rough men out there." She cocks her head. "She didn't put up with any crap, but a lot can go wrong when you lead that kind of life."

"Did she have problems with any man in particular?" I ask.

"She never brought them here. I couldn't handle it. Wouldn't have it." She sucks hard on the cigarette. "She told me she only dates safe guys." She hefts a bitter laugh. "What else are you going to tell your mother, though, right?"

I nod, tuck my notebook into my pocket. "Would it be all right if we took a quick look around in her room?"

"If you think it'll help you find who done it, knock your socks off." Crushing out the cigarette butt, she rises and takes us down the hall. "That girl kept a messy room," she says as she pushes open the door.

Paige Rossberger's bedroom is barely large enough for the full-size bed beneath the window. I see a tangle of sheets. A pair of jeans on the

230

floor. Sneakers tossed in the corner. A dresser and mirror are shoved against the wall to my right. There's barely enough space for someone to walk between the furniture and bed.

"Still smells like her," the woman says. "Still feels like she's going to come back. Jesus, that hurts."

I look over my shoulder at her, and for the first time, I see grief in her eyes. "I won't take long, ma'am."

"Take your time."

She's midway down the hall when I think of one more question. "Mrs. Rossberger? Did Paige have a vehicle?"

The woman stops and turns, her head cocked. "Drove an old Toyota. Altima, I think."

"Do you know where the car is?"

"Haven't seen it."

"Make?" I ask. "Model?"

"All's I know is that it's red. Got a dented driver's-side door."

"Do you have any paperwork on the vehicle?" I ask. "Insurance? Title? Registration?"

"She wasn't real big on paperwork."

I make a mental note to search for the vehicle info so I can put out a BOLO.

When Rossberger is gone, I look at Glock. He shakes his head. "Keep your kids close," he says quietly.

"And the rest of the world at arm's length." I

look around the room. "Keep your eyes open for any paperwork on the vehicle."

He nods. "I'll start with the closet."

I motion left. "I'll take the dresser."

I sidle between the bed and chest, step over a lone high heel to get to the dresser. A couple of drugstore perfume bottles sit prettily on the laminate surface. A hairbrush filled with blond hair. I lift the lid on a small box. A beaded necklace. Hoop earrings. Several odd-looking curved pieces of jewelry that are a half inch in length with small rose-gold pearls at each end, possibly for a navel or nose piercing. I replace the lid and move on to the dresser, methodically search each drawer. Underwear and bras. Athletic socks. T-shirts and shorts. Yoga pants. Nothing of interest.

I skirt the bed and go to a night table. I'm hoping to find a cell phone or diary or letter. Anything that might contain a name or phone number or address, but there's nothing there. Paige didn't have much. I open the final drawer. A small candle in a glass votive, its center burned down to nothing. Like the girl, I think, and I curb a wave of what I can only describe as sadness. It's a terrible parallel to the life of the young woman who died long before her time.

It's nearly ten P.M. when I park behind Tomasetti's Tahoe and let myself in through the back door. I'm bone-tired. Beaten down by a lack of sleep, the ugliness of the things I saw today, and frustration. Every step forward has been countered by two steps back and I've hit a wall.

Time to call it a day, Kate. . . .

The kitchen is warm and bright and smells of garlic and bread and some spice I can't quite place. Tomasetti stands at the stove with his back to me, stirring something in a pot, steam billowing. I take in the scene, ridiculously thankful to be home, and I feel some of the darkness pressing down on me melt away.

I haven't talked to him since the wee hours this morning when he left the scene where Paige Rossberger's body was discovered. It seems like a thousand years ago.

"Anyone ever tell you that you look good in an apron?" I tell him.

He glances at me over his shoulder. His face is not one that is easily read, but he looks . . . content. He's wearing an apron that was a gift to me last Christmas and I've yet to wear. Whatever he's cooking smells so good my mouth waters.

"I get that a lot," he says.

"I bet."

"Wine there." He motions to a bottle and two glasses on the counter, the cork lying next to them. "It's from Texas. Sangiovese." He grins. "Drink at your own risk."

"I always do." I set my laptop case next to the

door and cross to the counter, keeping an eye on his body language as I pour into our glasses.

"You get any sleep?" he asks.

"No." I'm not ready to talk about work; I don't want either case to intrude on this moment. So I sidle to the stove, look down at the pot. "Smells good."

"Spaghetti. Homemade sauce. My uncle Sergio's recipe."

"You don't have an uncle Sergio." I hand him a glass. "How's everything?"

He takes a moment to turn down the flame and set the wooden spoon on a folded paper towel. When he faces me, his eyes are clear and deep and . . . at peace. "We found the girls. They're home tonight. With their parents. Four days and he didn't touch them."

The words bring a smile to my face. "Chalk one up for the good guys."

"Yeah." He gives the pot another quick stir. "You try not to get caught up in things, but when kids are involved . . ."

"Hits close to home," I say.

He nods. "This one did."

"There's something to be said about keeping the faith."

"I think there's a gentle admonishment in there somewhere."

I hold on to my smile, but it feels thoughtful. "Back when I was a rookie, one of the old-timers told me something I never forgot. It went something like: 'When a man loses his faith, he loses a piece of his humanity.' "

"Smart guy."

I nod. "Keeping that part of yourself intact takes a lot of effort when you see the things we do, but we can't ever give up hope, especially when our grip is precarious."

"Said the wise woman." Holding my gaze, he raises his glass and we clink them together.

"To happy endings."

Smiling at each other, we sip. The wine is like baked plums and smoke on my tongue and the moment is magical. We stand there for a full minute, saying nothing, comfortable with the silence. With each other. And for the life of me I can't stop looking at him. I can't stop loving what I see. I want to reach out and stop this moment. Keep it forever.

"Any chance this frees you up to assist me?" I ask.

"I'll get my case tied up tomorrow." He sets down the wine, and, using potholders, dumps the steaming pan of pasta into a colander. "So where you at?"

"The land of zero progress."

"Face meet wall."

The investigation enters the space between us and I resent the intrusion. As if in unspoken agreement, we decide to hold it at bay a few moments longer. We'll talk about it on our terms. We won't let it darken this place where we stand.

We heap pasta and sauce onto plates and take them to the table. As we eat, I bring him up to speed on both cases.

"Do you think the two homicides are related?" he asks.

"Two murders inside a few days . . ." I sigh. "I can't see how they're *not* related, but what's the connection? Karn and Rossberger were polar opposites. She was English. He was Amish. They didn't run in the same circles. None of the same contacts. They lived in towns an hour apart. I can't find a single person who knew both of them. No connected threads on social media."

He sips wine, sets down the glass. "Tell me about Karn."

"He was from a good family. Well-liked. Hard worker. No record. Not so much as a parking ticket. According to everyone I talked to, he was the epitome of a good kid. Until yesterday, anyway." I tell him about my conversation with Christina Weaver.

"That's an interesting development. Do you believe her?"

"I do. She was just fifteen years old when it happened. She didn't want to talk. Didn't want to come forward. If I hadn't pushed, if her mother hadn't brought her to the station, I never would have been the wiser."

"Certainly puts a dent in Karn's good-kid reputation, doesn't it?"

"Opens some doors as far as a motive for murder, too."

Tomasetti cuts a slice of bread from the loaf and hands it to me. "You checked males who are close to Weaver," he says. "Boyfriend. Father. Uncle. Grandfather."

"The only person who knows what happened to her is her mother."

"Any chance she—"

"No."

"That level of violence with a fifteen-year-old girl." He says the words slowly, thinking aloud. "What if it wasn't an isolated incident, but a pattern?"

I sip wine, surprised to find that my earlier exhaustion is gone, my mind beginning to spool. "If that kind of behavior was a pattern in a town the size of Painters Mill, it seems like I would have caught wind of it."

"Twenty-one is young. He was just getting started."

"Maybe." My mind has already surged ahead to another possibility. "Also worth noting that he was Amish. That's relevant because even if someone in the community knew what Karn had done, there's a good chance they wouldn't come forward."

"Why not?"

"When you're Amish," I say, "and you screw up or commit some perceived sin, it isn't arrest you have to worry about, it's God and your community. If you stand before the congregation and confess your sin, you are forgiven."

"So there's no need for the cops," he says sardonically.

"It doesn't always happen that way, of course, but it's feasible."

"Taking that mindset into account, there's a better chance that a woman or girl who's been victimized wouldn't come forward." He swirls the wine in his glass. "If Karn was a predator and the behavior was a pattern, maybe one of his victims decided to mete out a little revenge."

"Crossbow doesn't seem like a weapon of choice for a female."

"Maybe it was a boyfriend. A brother. Or father."

"It's a viable theory, but no one else has come forward." I sigh. "Damn it."

He considers for a moment, then looks at me, his gaze searching mine. "Maybe Karn's lousy behavior with women is the missing link."

It takes me a moment to grasp his point. When I do, I feel a piece of the puzzle click into place. "Rossberger was a prostitute."

"Karn hooked up with her somehow. Brought her to Painters Mill. Paid her for sex."

I ponder the dynamics of that, the players

238

involved, and I realize it could fit. "How is it that they both ended up dead? Separate locations. Different ways."

"Taking into account what happened between Karn and the Weaver girl. Maybe he got rough with her. Lost his temper. Took things too far."

I stare at him, a shock wave moving through me. "Are you saying Karn murdered Rossberger?"

"I know it's a leap, but I'm just putting a theory out there for thought."

The premise is so far removed from the way I'd been thinking about the case, I can barely get my head around it. My mind runs with it anyway. "Okay, let's say they were together. He got rough with her." I look down at the table, then at Tomasetti. "Rossberger's mother told me her daughter didn't put up with any crap."

"Maybe she didn't like it, didn't like him, and she told him to piss off."

"He lost his temper and killed her." I shake my head. "It feels like too much of a jump. And how is it that Karn ended up dead?"

He lifts a shoulder, lets it drop. "Maybe she had a boyfriend. Or pimp. He found out what happened. And he did away with Karn."

I nod, but my thoughts are in turmoil because while we might be on to something, the theory is far from proven. "Might be a good time for me to speak with the people closest to him again."

"Like who?"

"His fiancée. Best friend. Parents." I think about that a second. "Rossberger's mother, too."

We've finished eating. Our wineglasses are empty. My head is pleasantly fuzzy. But I'm also exhausted.

I look at Tomasetti. "Did anyone ever tell you you're good at this?"

"Making spaghetti?"

"That, too." Rising, I go to him, bend, and brush my mouth against his cheek. "Thank you for being such a good sounding board."

"There are those rare moments in which I earn my keep."

"One of these days some lucky girl is going to snatch you up." I reach for our plates.

He sets his hand over mine and stops me. "That'll wait."

Rising, he takes my hands in his and pulls me to him. "What do you say we put these two cases to rest for a few hours?"

"Tomasetti, that's the best suggestion I've heard all day."

CHAPTER 18

The things we learn in our formative years stay with us. Right or wrong, the lessons of our youth shape our adult view of the world. Having been raised Amish, I was taught to believe the best about people. Most of the time that philosophy serves me well. I still believe that the majority of people are fundamentally good. As a cop, though, I'm keenly aware that many are not.

It's a little before eight A.M. and I'm sitting in the Explorer in the parking lot of Mast Tiny Homes, waiting for Wayne Graber to show up for work. Despite having spent some quality time with Tomasetti last night, I didn't get much sleep. After a few hours of tossing and turning, I downed half a pot of coffee, showered, and headed to the station. By seven thirty, I was on the road to Millersburg.

Graber pulls in a few minutes before eight and heads into the main workshop. I give him ten minutes and I follow him inside. The workshop is large and noisy, with half a dozen men running saws and nail guns. The air smells of fresh-cut wood and oil stain. I spot Graber standing outside a break room, drinking coffee out of a paper cup, talking to another man. I feel curious eyes on my back as I head that way.

"Wayne?"

He swings around, his expression surprised. "Chief Burkholder."

The man he was speaking with gives me a quick nod and moves away.

"I know this isn't a good time." I extend my hand for a shake to let him know this is a friendly visit. "Just a few quick follow-up questions."

"I can spare a few minutes." He picks up a five-gallon can of paint and a bucket full of tools—a roller with a handle, brushes, plastic sheeting, a tray, and a bundle of stir paddles—and nods toward the rear door. "I'm already clocked in, so if you don't mind, can we talk while I work?"

"Sure." I motion toward the tools. "Looks like you're staining again today."

"These guys make the homes as fast as I can paint and stain them."

We go through the door to the gravel court-yard behind the workshop. He walks between two cabins and stops in front of a third structure that's bare wood.

I make a show of admiring it. "Now that's nice looking."

"It's custom," he tells me. "Sort of a play on the modern farmhouse style, only smaller scale."

"Is there a second level?" I ask.

"Loft."

"Paint or stain?"

"This one will be painted." He pries off the lid of the can. "Any luck finding out who killed Aden?"

"Still working on it," I say. "I wanted to get your impression of his relationship with Emily Byler. I know they were planning to be married. Did they get along?"

"Sure. They were tight." He pours paint into the tray. "He was crazy about her and I'm pretty sure the feeling was mutual."

"That's what I'm hearing," I say. "Did Aden see anyone else before Emily?"

"He talked to a few girls. Nothing serious."

"What about while he was courting Emily?" I ask. "I mean, casually?"

"Aden was good-looking, of age, and unmarried." He stops what he's doing and looks at me as if he's just figured out where I'm going with this line of questioning. "I don't really know what you want me to say, Chief Burkholder. I mean, he was my best friend. It doesn't seem right to speak badly of him when he's not here to defend himself."

"Wayne, this isn't about Aden's private life," I say. "This is about finding the person responsible for his death."

He picks up the roller and rolls it into the paint. As he works, I see his mind churning. Trying to figure out how to answer. The best angle to take. After a moment, he sighs. "You want me to tell you that my best friend was two-timing his fiancée. Is that what you want?"

"All I want is the truth." I wait a beat. "Was he?"

He frowns at me. "Emily was young. She wouldn't . . . you know." He fumbles the word, breaks off the sentence. "They weren't screwing around, okay? I mean, she's Amish and they're all about waiting until marriage."

"Okay. Fair enough."

"So Aden liked sex. He liked women. A lot. So he went out on occasion. That's all I got to say about that because I don't know what he did behind closed doors."

"Do any of these women have names?"

"No idea. I mean, I didn't know them. He usually met them at some bar. A place where the Amish wouldn't see him. I mean, he didn't want Emily to know, right?" He laughs. "And it wouldn't exactly go over if the bishop found out he was two-timing his fiancée."

"How many women?"

He emits a good-natured groan. "Aden's dead and you're going to make me stab the guy in the back?"

"I'm asking you a question that needs to be asked," I say. "There's no pleasure in it. I don't have an agenda. All I want is the truth."

He shakes his head. "Too many. Okay?"

"Where did he meet them?" I ask.

"The Brass Rail," he snaps. "That's all I know."

I pull the photo of Paige Rossberger from my pocket, unfold it, and show it to him. "Was he ever with her?"

Curious about the photo, he cranes his neck, takes a long look. "I never saw her at the house. Never saw her at the Rail." He raises his eyes to mine. "She's the one that got killed, isn't she?"

"Yes."

His gaze intensifies, as if realizing I mean business. "Why are you asking me about her? What does she have to do with Aden?"

Ignoring the question, I hand him my card, but he doesn't take it. He looks away, concentrates on rolling the paint.

"If you knew something that might help me find the killer," I say, "you'd tell me, right?"

"You know I would."

Turning, I start across the courtyard. I'm midway to the workshop when he calls out my name.

I turn back, raise my brows, wait.

"Those loose girls didn't mean anything to him," he says. "It was all about the sex. He loved Em. It would break her heart if she found out he was fooling around on her. I don't want people remembering him that way."

"Thanks for your time," I tell him.

And I walk away.

• • •

When a case stalls, a good investigator knows it's time to start thinking outside the box. Sometimes, you find the most useful information in the most unlikely of places. In the course of any investigation, that's a gift to an investigator. I've known Jimmie Baines, the bartender at the Brass Rail, for twenty years, give or take. Not well, of course; not on a personal level. But I know his reputation. He sees a lot and knows how to keep his mouth shut, so people talk to him. He's tended bar there since before I was old enough to legally buy a drink. In fact, he served me my first official gin and tonic when I was seventeen years old. He has his finger on the pulse of the small population of Painters Mill's underbelly, and he's wily enough to know how to use his talents to stay on the good side of the local cops.

It's ten A.M. when I walk into the station. It's usually quiet this time of day, a good time to catch up on paperwork or phone calls. But with two homicides spooling into high gear, the station is a madhouse. Lois stands at the reception desk, headset clamped over her head, eyes wild. She points at me when I enter, but she can't get away from her call and I have no idea what she wants so I keep moving. In the hall, I pour coffee and then go to the two common cubicles and find Mona, staring at her phone.

"You still on?" I ask, knowing she worked last night and never left.

She startles, sets down her phone. "Yes, ma'am."

"Get me a ten-twenty-seven on Jimmie Baines." I spell the last name.

She swings back to the computer, taps a key.

"Run him through LEADS," I add.

She cranes her neck forward, her fingers flying over the keyboard. "What'd he do?" she asks.

"Nothing, I hope. I just need to talk to him and since we're cops it'll be nice to know if he's wanted for anything before we show up at his door."

She recites a local address and I put it to memory.

"You busy?" I ask.

She grins.

Jimmie Baines lives on a three-acre tract a few miles outside of Painters Mill proper. I pull into a gravel drive and park just off a rusty metal building. The overhead door is halfway down and crooked as if it's come off its track. The house is an older bungalow with a wood deck in front that isn't quite level.

Next to me, Mona recites her findings from various police databases. "Fifty-six years old. Divorced. OVI back in 1997. Disorderly conduct arrest in 1998. Charges dropped. Possession of a controlled substance in 1999. Charges dropped.

Domestic back in 2001." She scrolls. "Looks like he's kept his nose clean since."

"Let's have a chat with Mr. Keeps His Nose Clean and see if he remembers anything interesting about Aden Karn."

We get out and take a beaten-down dirt path to the front of the house. I'm cognizant of the wood planks creaking beneath my feet as I take the steps to the deck. Opening the storm door, I knock.

He doesn't keep us waiting. The door swings open and I find myself looking at a partially clad Jimmie Baines—and more than I ever wanted to see of him. His left cheek is creased, his hair sticking up on one side. Even his goatee is mussed. He's wearing a black muscle shirt with a big gold chain hanging down. Farmer's tan on muscular arms. I can't tell if his pants are shorts, pajamas, or underwear, so I keep my eyes trained on his face.

"Well, this is a surprise." He squints at me, too cool to be discomfited. "What time is it?"

I look at my watch. "Ten thirty."

"Didn't get out of the bar until four," he says.

"Sorry to bother you so early."

He makes no move to open the door; he just stands there looking loose and relaxed, so I add, "I'm working on the Aden Karn case, Jimmie. I have a few questions, if you have a minute. May we come inside?"

I see him mentally tally the condition of his house—trying to remember if he left anything he'd rather I not see in plain sight. It takes him half a minute to decide. "I think that would be all right." He slants a sideways look at Mona.

"Hey, Jimmie." She smiles.

One side of his mouth lifts as he recognizes her and I realize she's frequented the Brass Rail and been served drinks by him.

He takes us to a small living room furnished with a sofa, a chair, and a TV the size of a truck. He motions us to the sofa, then goes to the chair, lifts a pair of jeans off the arm, turns his back to us, and slips them on. "Sorry," he mutters.

Mona and I avert our gazes. I feel her cast a grin in my direction, but I don't look at her.

"So what do you want to know?"

I turn, and even though I don't lower my eyes, I can see he's still zipping up, not the least bit embarrassed.

"You know who Aden Karn is?" I ask.

"I know who he is." When his pants are buttoned and zipped, he takes the chair. "I know he's the one got killed."

I take the sofa, lean forward, put my elbows on my knees. "You heard anything about that?"

"Not really. People are surprised mostly."

"How well did you know him?"

"Just seen him in the bar. Last six months or so, he was a regular. Drank a lot of Heineken.

Liked to dance. Play pool. Smoke cigarettes out back."

"You ever see him with anyone?"

"He came in once or twice with his pals from work. You know, that construction crew."

"Anyone else?"

"Came in with some Amish dudes a few times. I mean, they weren't dressed like pilgrims, but you can tell they're Amish." He touches his hair, gives a half smile. "Fuckin' Dutch boy haircuts crack me up."

"You ever see him with a woman?"

"I seen him with plenty of women. Dude never came in with one, but he never left alone."

Wayne Graber's reluctance to talk about it scrolls through the back of my mind. "English women?"

"A different one every time."

"You ever have any problems with him? Arguments? Or fights?"

The bartender's eyes sharpen on mine. "I never saw anything inside. I mean, I'm behind the bar and stay pretty busy. Most of the guys who come in are well-behaved. Especially the Amish."

I can tell by the way his eyes skitter away that there's something there. He's not trying to hide it, but he wants me to work for it. "What about outside?" I ask, knowing that's where some of the problems occur because I've responded to a fight call once or twice myself.

"You're not asking me to break the bartender's code of silence, are you?"

Next to me, Mona clears her throat.

I hold his gaze, wait.

Jimmie looks away, considering, then nods. "Karn drank too much, and he couldn't handle his booze. Got shit-faced on a regular basis. Whatever female he was with usually drank too much, too. Most of the time, it was harmless stuff. Young people acting a fool. A spilled drink. Smoking in the bathroom. A little pelvis grinding on the dance floor." He sighs. "A few weeks ago, I heard things got carried away out in the parking lot."

"How so?"

"He took a girl out there. To his buddy's car, you know. And they started going at it in the back seat."

Next to me, Mona leans closer.

"You mean they were having sex?" I ask.

"Might've started out that way; I don't know. But they ended up getting into a knock-down, drag-out fight. She must have said no or changed her mind, because Karn got pissed." He grimaces. "Real pissed. We're talking Dr. Jekyll and Mr. Hyde. Next thing I know this chick rushes into the bar, shirt ripped half off. She's drunk and crying, face all smeared. She was marked up, too."

"What kind of marks?"

He shrugs. "Scratches from what I could see. From him pawing at her."

"Did he hit her?"

"I asked. She said no, but her face was marked up."

"Black eye? Cut lip?"

"Didn't see either of those things. She got hostile when I pushed, so I backed off."

"So he assaulted her?" Mona asks.

Jimmie shifts his gaze to her. "I didn't see it happen and no one would say, but judging from the way she looked, I'd say he roughed her up good."

"Did you talk to Karn?" I ask.

Another grimace, this one darker. "Look, I know that kid's gone and I ain't one to talk poorly of the dead. But when he drank, all that boy-next-door bullshit went out the window. I been around the block a few times and I got a lot of tolerance for a lot of shit. I see it go down and I look the other way. The one thing I won't abide is a man putting his hands on a woman. So, yeah, I went out to the parking lot and I had a little talk with that son of a bitch."

"And how did that go?" I ask.

"He calmed down real fuckin' quick." His eyes flick left to the hallway that leads to the rear of the house.

I follow his stare to a baseball bat leaning against the wall. It's been carved with what looks like a gargoyle head on the business end.

"Do you know this woman's name?" I ask.

"I asked around. One of the waitresses said her name is Mandi Yoder."

The name pings in my memory as I write it down. A few months ago, one of my officers took a call when an Amish woman, walking alongside Highway 62 after dark, was struck by a vehicle. She suffered only minor injuries and was transported to the hospital. Only later did we learn that the incident was a possible suicide attempt.

"Amish?" I ask.

"She wasn't dressed Amish, but she had that look about her."

"Age?"

"Too young to be alone in a car with that sack of shit Karn."

I've heard Jimmie described as having a "scary stare." When the situation gets tense, he doesn't blink. He doesn't look away. Or back down to anyone. If someone told me a set of eyes could tear someone's heart out of their chest, I'd think of Jimmie.

"Karn catch any flak for that?" I ask.

"Not that I heard."

"He get into fights with anyone else?" I ask. "Any other women?"

"Not that I heard, but the Rail's a big place, especially the parking lot. We're all about our clientele at the Rail, if you know what I mean. We keep it dark out there for a reason."

• • •

"Jimmie has a different take on Karn, doesn't he?" Mona says as we walk to the Explorer.

"Bartenders see people at their worst," I say as I open the door and slide behind the wheel. "They're like cops that way."

As I back out of the driveway, I recap my conversation with Christina Weaver.

"Holy cow." Mona shakes her head as if the information won't quite settle. "That's the last thing I expected to hear about Karn." She looks at me. "You believe Weaver?"

"I do."

Her brows knit. "So if Karn was a mean drunk and abusive toward women . . ." Mona is still mulling what she's learned about Karn, trying to figure out how it fits into the big picture. "Might be a motive in there somewhere."

"I think it's worth checking."

She nods. "You put your hands on someone's sister or girlfriend, someone might get pissed off and decide to do something about it."

I glance over at her. "Call Lois. Ask her to run Yoder through LEADS. See if she has any outstanding warrants. See if she can come up with an address."

She's already reaching for her cell phone.

Mandi Yoder lives in a four-unit apartment building in Painters Mill, two blocks from the

254

slaughterhouse. It's a two-story brick structure with peeling white paint and an ornate door some creative soul has painted a pretty shade of turquoise. Mona and I take a cracked sidewalk to the main entrance door, which isn't quite closed. I push it open enough for us to slide through and step into a small vestibule. There are two apartments downstairs, neither of which matches the number I have, so we take the curved staircase to the second level.

The landing is uncomfortably hot and smells of cigarette smoke, week-old meat loaf, and feces.

"Someone forgot to take out the trash," Mona mutters.

"Or clean the litter box."

I've just raised my hand to knock when the door swings open. Mandi Yoder startles at the sight of us, but falls quickly into a tough persona. She's so tall I have to look up to meet her gaze. She's rail thin with heavily tattooed forearms. A cigarette hanging out of her mouth. She eyes me with a combination of surprise and disdain.

"Can I help you?" she asks.

I have my badge at the ready. "Mandi Yoder?"

"Yep."

"I need to ask you some questions about an investigation I'm working on," I say.

"Actually, I'm on my way to work, so—"

"This will only take a few minutes."

She looks down her nose at me and then Mona,

as if trying to decide which of us to slug first. "Whatever." She turns on her heel and walks back into her apartment. "You have two minutes, so make it quick."

We follow her into a messy living room with tall ceilings and scuffed walls. Shabby furniture. A bong is tucked into the lower shelf of an end table. Down the hall, a radio blasts out an old Rush tune. The smell of a litter box that hasn't been cleaned hangs in the air.

She doesn't invite us to sit, so we stand next to a coffee table piled with unopened mail, most of which look like past-due bills.

"You're on *rumspringa*?" I begin.

"In case you haven't noticed, I'm no longer Amish." She taps a brow piercing. "They don't much care for gay people so here I am."

I nod. "I'm investigating the murder of Aden Karn."

"Heard about what happened."

"I was told you knew him."

"Someone told you wrong."

"But you'd met him?" I ask. "Spent some time with him?"

"I met him once or twice. In passing. I wouldn't call that spending time, would you?"

"I understand there was an incident at the Brass Rail between you and Karn."

"I don't recall anything like that."

"It happened a couple of months ago," I tell her. "In the rear parking lot."

She laughs. "Please tell me you don't think I killed him."

"I heard he put his hands on you. Got rough."

"You heard wrong. I barely knew the guy. End of story."

"Mandi, we just want to know what happened," I tell her. "You're not in any trouble."

"That's good since I haven't done anything wrong."

"You were in Aden's car that night," Mona puts in. "You argued."

She lets out a lengthy sigh, not taking any of this as seriously as she should. "That frickin' Jimmie Baines is a cokehead. Believe me, I know. You can tell him I said that."

"It would be tremendously helpful if you just told us what happened," I say.

She rolls her eyes with drama. "That's the thing. Nothing happened. There was no incident. No one was involved in anything. And Jimmie Baines is full of shit." She enunciates the words as if she's speaking to a two-year-old, then leans close to me, and whispers, "Would it help if I said it in *Deitsch*? I hear you couldn't cut being Amish either."

"Was there anyone else there that evening who might talk to us?" I ask.

Frowning, she studies us as if we're a couple

of skinny mongrels begging for food. Then she points at the door. "Out."

"Mandi—" I begin.

She cuts me off. "Hit the road."

I reach into my pocket, pull out my card, and take a moment to write my cell number on the back. "Call me if you change your mind about talking."

"Whatever." She takes the card, flips it like a playing card onto the floor. "I have to get to work. Now get out or I'm going to file a complaint."

Back in the Explorer, Mona and I sit there a moment, not speaking.

"I don't think it would be much of a stretch to say we hit a dead end with Yoder," she says after a moment.

I start the engine. "Yeah, I don't think she's going to come around."

She heaves a sigh. "What now, Chief?"

I glance over at her. "When's the last time you slept?"

"Um . . ."

"Go home and grab a few hours and a shower. When you're back, get with Pickles. I want you guys to expand our search for retailers who've sold crossbows. Include Wooster in the search. If you can find any outlying sporting goods locations, include them, too. It'll take some doing, but it's . . . something."

CHAPTER 19

I used to subscribe to the belief that a person's loved ones are the people who know them best. It wasn't until I had some life experience under my belt that I learned the premise couldn't be further from the truth. Sometimes a person's loved ones are the last to know—or the last to acknowledge—a fault or weakness. That's especially true when you're Amish.

Aden Karn was laid to rest this morning. The funeral was held at the Byler farm, mainly because the barn is big enough to accommodate a large group. I didn't attend; a funeral is a time that belongs to loved ones and family and I gave them that because they are due. I did, however, park on the shoulder at the end of the lane and watch the procession of buggies pull in. The Amish turned out by the hundreds.

While I eschewed the funeral, I did attend the burial service at the *graabhof*, or cemetery. I stuck to the periphery of the gathering, doing my best not to intrude. I observed the mourners from afar, looking for any unusual behavior—excessive crying or someone making a scene—conspicuous absences, or the presence of a stranger. But there was nothing unusual. Angela and Lester Karn stood graveside, their expressions downcast and stoic. Emily Byler, clad in black and fighting tears, stood with her parents. Wayne Graber was one of the pallbearers. Even the young men from the gas station showed, dressed in their best Amish attire. I'm loath to approach the Karns on the day they laid their son to rest, but the questions burning inside me will not wait.

It's afternoon when I pull into the parking slot outside The Gentle Cobbler. I'm not surprised to find them working. Some seek the sense of normalcy that comes with the mundane. The comfort of ritual. The foundation of work that is such a big part of Amish life.

A CLOSED sign hangs on the window, but the lights are on. As I cross the sidewalk to the door, I see someone moving around inside. I knock on the glass and wait. Sure enough, Lester Karn comes to the door. His face is grim, his eyes hard when he opens it. He seems to have aged ten years in the last few days. His shoulders are hunched. His chest sunken. His cheeks hollowed beneath his beard. He is the picture of grief.

"I know this has been a tough day." I look past him and see Angela behind the counter, looking at me over the top of the cash register. "I'll keep it short."

Bowing his head in acquiescence, Lester ushers me into the store.

The smells of leather, coffee, and shoe polish hang comfortably in the air as I follow him to the counter. Angela's fingers ting against the keys of the cash register as she prepares it for the day's sales. "God gives us the strength for any hill we have to climb," she says to no one in particular.

"I was at the *graabhof* earlier," I say quietly in *Deitsch*. "It was a good service."

"*Er hot en iwwerflissich leve gfaahre*," Angela says. He lived an abundant life.

"The deacon said there were about three hundred Amish there," Lester says flatly.

"The Amish turn out," I say. "Always."

"Everyone loved him so." Angela moves like a ghost as she comes around the counter. "You have news for us, Kate Burkholder? You know who took him from us?"

"Just a few follow-up questions." I pull out my notebook and pen. "Do any of Aden's friends own a crossbow?"

Lester's brows knit as he seems to consider. "Not that I know of."

I make eye contact with both of them, keenly aware of their pain, and that they're not going to like some of the questions I'm about to ask. "I've talked to a lot of people in the last few days. People who knew or had dealt with Aden. Some of the things I heard raised some questions."

He cocks his head, his eyes like razors on mine. "What kind of questions?"

I lock eyes with him. "Mr. and Mrs. Karn, I'm going to ask you some questions that aren't going

261

to be easy to hear or to answer. I'm going to ask you not to read anything into them. I'm following up on some information that I received. Please bear with me."

The couple exchange uneasy looks, but I push on. "Did Aden have a temper?"

Angela chokes out a sound that's akin to a laugh. "What's that got to do with anything?"

I look at Lester and repeat the question.

The Amish man shakes his head. "No."

"Did he ever strike anyone? Or get into a fight?"

Out of the corner of my eye, I see Angela put her hand over her mouth.

"Of course not," Lester says quickly. "That's not our way."

"Did he have any problems or arguments with any of his girlfriends?"

" 'Girlfriends'?" Angela blinks. "You mean Emily?"

"Any female," I clarify. "Girls or women."

"No," Lester says.

"Were you ever concerned about the way he perceived women?" I ask. "Or the way he treated them?"

"I don't understand these questions," Angela says, her voice rising. "Aden was a good boy. What exactly are you getting at?"

I ignore the question. "Did Aden get along well with Emily?"

"Of course he did," the Amish woman tells me. "He was going to marry her."

"Did he have any other girlfriends?" I ask.

"No!" Angela hisses.

"Did he see any girls before he started going out with Emily? Or while he was on *rumspringa*?"

The woman stares at me, blinking. "No."

I pause, give them a moment to digest the direction of my questions. "Did he ever exhibit any problems with impulse control?" The question doesn't translate well from the English mindset to the Amish way of thinking, but I struggle through. "As a boy or an adult?"

"*Sell is nix as baeffzes.*" Angela looks helplessly at her husband. That's nothing but trifling talk.

"Chief Burkholder, what does this have to do with our son's death?" Lester asks.

"It sounds like you're trying to blame him for what happened," Angela says, her voice rising.

"No, I'm not." I stop speaking, holding her gaze. "I'm following up on some information—"

"What information?" the Amish woman snaps. "From whom?"

"If Aden made a mistake or overstepped in some way," I say. "If he behaved badly, he may have angered someone."

Lester's eyes widen. "The killer?" he whispers.

I nod. "I'm not interested in what Aden did. I'm interested in who he may have angered. If that person exists, I need to find them." I look from Lester to Angela. "If there's anything you can tell me, even if it's something you don't want to discuss, please, I need your help."

"He was a good boy." Angela raises her hand as if to defend herself from a physical attack. "How dare you come here and disgrace our son. How dare you. How *dare* you."

She steps backward, stumbles. Lester and I reach for her simultaneously, but she shakes off both of us. "I will not let you stain his memory."

I look at Lester, and the Amish man shakes his head.

Angela isn't finished. "No wonder you left the *Amisch*. You aren't one of us. You weren't wanted, were you, Kate Burkholder? No one wants a *maulgrischt*." Pretend Christian. She jabs her hand at the door. "Leave us now. Don't come back."

I look at Lester, but he drops his gaze. "If you change your mind, you know where to find me."

"We've nothing to say to you," she hisses.

I start toward the door, go through, shut it quietly behind me. I'm midway to the Explorer, kicking myself for approaching them on the day of the funeral, when I hear the bell on the door behind me.

"Chief Burkholder!"

I turn to see Lester stride toward me. I stop, wait for him. For the span of several seconds, we stand there in the warm afternoon sun. He struggles to maintain his composure, but his face is a mosaic of misery. "She's upset."

"I don't blame her," I tell him. "I know this isn't easy."

He looks away, shoves his hands into his pockets. "Aden was still living with us when he started his *rumspringa*. There was a time or two when he came home in the wee hours of the morning. Alcohol on his breath. Sin in his eyes." He takes a deep breath, looks down the street. "He had a temper."

I nod.

"My wife . . ." He whispers the words as if he's run out of breath. "She was doing laundry once. And she found blood."

"On his clothes?"

He's silent for so long that I look at him. He's still staring off into space. "First time, she didn't mention it. Second time . . . she came to me."

"His blood?" I ask. "Someone else's?"

Another lengthy pause. This time, he looks around, at anything but me, as if trying to find some mental or emotional refuge. His mouth trembles. "It was on his . . . underthings. He wore the English kind, you know. White. And there was blood."

A dozen innocent explanations buzz my brain. A cut finger. A blister on a thumb. A lost bandage. "Did you ask him about it?"

He shakes his head. "No."

"Did you—"

"No!" He cuts me off. "I've said all I'm going to say, Kate Burkholder. That is going to have to be enough. No more questions. Not about Aden. Not about anything. And if you can manage, we'd prefer if you didn't come back."

CHAPTER 20

"One step forward, two goddamn steps back."
Sheriff Mike Rasmussen stands against the wall,
his arms folded at his chest, looking tapped out
and ready to call it a day.

It's ten P.M. and I'm sitting at the table in the
storage-closet-turned-meeting-room Mona has
fondly dubbed "the war room." Tomasetti is
sitting across from me, fingers pecking on the
tablet in front of him. The rest of my officers and
a patrol investigator with the Ohio State Highway Patrol left an hour ago after a frustratingly
unproductive briefing. The whiteboard on the
wall is tattooed with snatches of information
that's been scrawled, erased, and re-scrawled,
the blue marker smeared across its face like a
bruise.

In the last hour, the three of us have gone
through the file on the homicide of Aden Karn
twice, accomplishing little, and arguing a lot.
Now, Paige Rossberger's file is open in front of
me; the table is papered with reports and photographs, official forms, and handwritten notes.
In the hours we've been here, all of it has run
together into a mass of data overload.

"I don't see a connection." Rasmussen sighs.
"There's no link between the victims. Karn was

Amish. A farm kid from Painters Mill. Ross-berger was English. A grocery clerk and part-time hooker from Massillon. I don't think these two homicides are related."

"Too much of a coincidence not to be," Tomasetti mutters.

"Gotta be something there," I add.

Rasmussen tosses us an annoyed expression. "According to the geniuses that have graced this room this evening, we're fresh out of ideas."

I look down at the cup of coffee in front of me that's long since gone cold. I didn't want to leave without finding something—anything—that might move the investigations forward.

Shoving the mug aside, I pick up my notes from the day Glock and I interviewed June Rossberger. The words are blurred.

No ties to Painters Mill
Fired from job
Possibly still working the street
Not answering cell—calls or text—
responds to texts
No boyfriend
No close friends/associates
No known enemies
Vehicle missing—red Altima—BOLO!!
"If I had to guess, I'd say it was one of her men."
"Only dates safe guys."

I drop the papers with enough flourish to draw the attention of both men.

"Paige Rossberger's mother told me her daughter only dated 'safe' guys," I say.

Rasmussen sighs. "I'm just not buying into the Amish-kid-calls-hooker theory."

"It's viable," Tomasetti puts in.

"Paige Rossberger was careful about who she hooked up with." I look from man to man. "She would have considered Karn safe. He was Amish. A twenty-one-year-old farm kid. He called her for a date. And she came."

"Loose connection." But some of Rasmussen's skepticism falls away. "If you want to run with that theory, you're going to have to back it up with something."

I don't have anything solid, but I run with it if only to see where it goes, if there's something there besides a brick wall. "According to his roommate, Karn's girlfriend refused to have sex with him until after they were married. But Karn liked women, liked sex, didn't want to wait. Let's say he made contact with Rossberger."

"He didn't own a car," Rasmussen points out.

"She did," I counter. "The red Altima, by the way, which is still missing. Let's say she drove from Massillon to Painters Mill and they met up." I remind them of the sex toys I found in Karn's closet. "According to Wayne Graber, Karn was sexually active with other women, even though

269

he was engaged. So, it's feasible that they met up."

"Scenarios?" says Tomasetti.

Rasmussen goes first. "Where did they meet?"

"Karn's place," I say. "Wayne Graber told me Karn had brought women there on occasion."

"Would be easy to check registration with the Willowdell Motel, too," Tomasetti puts in.

I make a note to follow up. "I'll do it."

"Sex toys and hookers is kind of risqué for an Amish kid, isn't it?" Rasmussen mutters.

"Fits with the profile we've built on Karn." Tomasetti keeps pushing forward. "*When* did they meet up?"

I flip the page of the legal pad. "I'll see if I can get my hands on Karn's work schedule. Talk to his roommate and see if I can come up with a timeline of when he might've been free. Compare all of that to the time of death from the coroner."

The meeting has become an open brainstorming session. Verbal free association. No direction or self-censoring. It's a technique used to unearth new ideas or take an investigation in a different direction. Put forth theories no matter how unlikely. Discard what you don't use. Dig into what's worth digging into.

Tomasetti picks it up from there. "Rossberger was killed first. She was sexually assaulted. Strangled. Asphyxiated."

"This is where the theory falls apart." Ras-

270

mussen takes off his glasses and rubs his eyes. "It's a fucking leap. Karn doesn't even have a record."

I remind him of my conversation with Christina Weaver. "She's credible, Mike. I couldn't get the whole story from her, but the incident was extremely violent. Her mother had to take her to the doctor. That's all they would say."

The sheriff digests the information, his mouth looking as though he's bitten into something rancid. "Jesus."

"I think Mr. All-American Boy had a dark side," Tomasetti says. "He meets up with Rossberger. Takes her somewhere private, rapes and murders her. Wraps her body in plastic and dumps it."

The sheriff throws up his hands. "Okay, so we add a dead guy to our suspect list?"

Tomasetti laughs, but it's a cynical sound. "And of course, it leaves us with a big, fat glaring question."

"Who killed Karn?" I mutter.

"I think the pimp or boyfriend angle might work," Rasmussen says.

I plow ahead. "Let's say the boyfriend followed her. Realized she had sex with another guy. He stalked her. Accosted her. Murdered her. Dumped her body. The next day, he takes care of Karn."

"Again, all of that would have required some degree of privacy," Rasmussen points out.

Tomasetti steps in. "There are several deserted

properties in the area. Abandoned barns. Plenty of woods."

"What about security cams?" I ask. "Game cams? Any businesses or homes we can check?"

"I'll get some deputies on it first light." Rasmussen punches something into his cell. "We get anything on Rossberger's cell phone?"

"We expedited a warrant to the provider," Tomasetti tells him. "We're still waiting. I'll light a fire first thing in the morning."

"What about her vehicle?" I ask.

"We got an active BOLO," Rasmussen says. "State Highway Patrol is on alert. As it is, we got nothing."

"You get anything from Karn's neighbors?" Rasmussen asks.

"We canvassed the area around the crime scene where Karn was killed," I tell him. "But we haven't talked to his neighbors about seeing a female or a red vehicle. I'll get on it first thing in the morning."

The sheriff looks at his watch. "I don't think we're going to figure it out tonight. I couldn't think my way out of a damn box at the moment. Let's sleep on it. Hit it again tomorrow." He lifts his jacket off the back of the chair nearest him. "I'm going to bed."

CHAPTER 21

I have no idea if my theory about Aden Karn is anywhere close to reality or if I'm completely off base. I don't have so much as a single link and I have exactly zero in terms of hard evidence. Rasmussen is of the belief that Rossberger had an as-of-yet-unidentified boyfriend who found out she was prostituting herself, flew into a rage, and murdered her and, later, killed the man who paid her for sex. While we do have multiple theories to explore, we're no closer to having a suspect.

If Christina Weaver's story is true, there's no doubt Karn had a dark side. Did that dark side play a role in his death? A cop should never blame the victim for any crime committed against them. It's wrong on every level, professionally unethical, and personally corrupt. That said, an investigator must have the temerity to take a hard look at a victim who participated in high-risk behaviors or lived a reckless lifestyle, because those two things can raise the odds of someone becoming the victim of a crime.

This morning, that's exactly what I'm doing. I sent Mona to the Willowdell Motel to take a look at the check-in register, to see if Karn or Rossberger paid for a room in the days before the murder. Glock is talking to the neighbors near Karn's residence in the hope someone saw Rossberger's car or a woman fitting her description. I dispatched Skid to Buckeye Construction to confirm the hours that Karn worked and to find out if he took any time off or left early. I don't expect any earth-shattering information to come of any of it, but at least we're not twiddling our thumbs.

It's midmorning by the time I pull into the lane of the Byler farm. I find Clara and her husband, Andy, sitting at the picnic table, a sweating pitcher of what looks like lemonade between them.

"*Guder mariye*," I call out as I approach. Good morning.

"Hi, Chief Burkholder," Clara says wearily.

I reach the table. "I heard it was a good service yesterday."

"We think so," she says.

"A comfort to be sure." Andy cocks his head. "You have news for us?"

"Actually, I was hoping to speak to Emily for a few minutes. Is she around?"

"She's inside. Lying down, I think." The Amish woman hits me with a stern look. "It's been a trying few days to say the least. Might be best just to let her have some peace for a day or two."

I look down at the ground, then raise my gaze to hers. "I know this is a difficult time. For all of you. I wouldn't be here if it wasn't important."

Andy starts to say something; I see the protest in his eyes, but his wife sets her hand on his shoulder and rises. *"Kumma inseid."* Come inside. "I'll take you to her."

I follow her up the porch steps and into an overheated kitchen that smells as if it's been cooked in all morning. Clara motions me into a chair at the table. I watch her continue into the living room and then the hall. She stops at the first door, pushes it open, and peers inside. "Chief Burkholder is here to see you," she says in *Deitsch*.

A lengthy silence and then comes the whispered reply from Emily. "What does she want?"

"Just a few questions, I reckon. Says it's important. You get yourself together and come on out now. You hear?"

Clara makes eye contact with me as she enters the kitchen. *"Sis unvergleichlich hees dohin."* It's terribly hot in here. She goes to the gas-powered refrigerator and pulls out a plastic pitcher. "I got some mint tea left over."

"Dank," I tell her.

The woman sets two glasses on the table, fills them with tea, and exits through the back door.

I've just taken my first sip when Emily enters the kitchen. She's wearing a black dress that's wrinkled, a black bonnet over her *kapp*, tights, and practical black shoes. Though she and Aden Karn weren't yet married, she'll likely continue to wear black for several months, while she's in mourning. There's an untidiness about her appearance that signals something is amiss. A few strands of hair have come loose to hang down in her face. Tights bagging at her ankles. Worse, her eyes have a hollow look that wasn't there last time I spoke to her.

"I know this has been a terrible few days for you," I begin. "I'll keep it short."

"It's okay," she replies in a monotone voice.

Moving as if in a trance, she goes to the cabinet next to the sink and pulls out a glass, fills it with tap water, and then brings it to the table and sits. She hasn't noticed the tea her mother already set out. It's as if she isn't quite there.

For an instant, I consider delaying talking to her out of concern, but I think of where I am in terms of the case and set my sympathy aside.

"Did you find out who did it?" Emily asks after a moment.

"Still working on it."

"How could someone do something like that?" she whispers. "I still can't believe he's gone. Such an awful thing. I don't understand."

"I don't know." I shrug. "Someone who's very troubled and angry."

She looks at the two glasses in front of her as if trying to remember why they're there.

"Do you know of anyone who might've been angry with Aden?" I ask.

"There is no one." I can tell by the way she shakes her head that she's going to give me more of the same I've heard about Karn a hundred times before. "Everyone loved Aden. He was sweet. Made people laugh. He helped them when they needed it."

I think of Christina Weaver, the scene Jimmie Baines described in the parking lot of the Brass Rail, and I feel a surge of impatience, take a moment to frame my question in a way that won't upset her. "I've been talking to a lot of people who knew Aden," I say. "Some of those people are under the impression that he had a temper."

"That's just crazy talk," she says. "He hardly ever got mad. Had the patience of a saint." Despite the certitude in her voice, her gaze skitters away from mine.

Something there, a little voice whispers.

"Did you and Aden ever get into an argument about anything?" I ask. "Or have any kind of disagreement?"

"Never."

"It sounds as if you had a very harmonious relationship."

"We did," she says, her voice softening. "He was a good man. Would have been a good husband. And a good father, too."

Taking my time, I pick up my glass and sip. "Did Aden court any other girls before you?"

"He might've gone to a frolic or two." Her eyes

snap to mine. "But there was never another girl he was serious about."

"Was he always faithful to you, Emily?"

She recoils, offended. "Faithful? Of course he was. Why on earth would you ask such a thing?"

"He was on *rumspringa*," I remind her. "Sometimes there was alcohol around. People make mistakes—"

"I was the only one for him," she snaps. "He told me so."

Before leaving the station, I printed out a stock photo of a red Altima sedan the same year as Paige Rossberger's. I also pulled a couple of photos of her from one of her social media accounts on the outside chance someone will recognize her.

I show her the photo of the car first. "Have you ever seen this vehicle parked out at Aden's house?"

Her eyes flick to the photo, then away. "No."

I shuffle the paper so that Paige Rossberger's photo comes into view. "What about this woman?"

She glowers at the photo. For the first time I notice sweat on her cheeks and upper lip. "Who is she?"

"Her name is Paige. She was killed, too. I'm trying to find out what happened to her."

"What does this have to do with Aden?"

"I'm trying to figure that out, too."

She looks at the photo again, then at me.

"You're trying to make him out to be a bad person," she hisses.

"I'm asking questions that need to be asked," I say.

I wait, but she sits stone-still, arms crossed at her waist, staring down at the glass in front of her.

"Are you sure Aden was always kind to you?" I press.

Abruptly, she scoots her chair back and rises. "I don't want to talk to you anymore."

Slowly, I rise. Keeping my voice level and calm, I continue. "If something happened, or you know something, please talk to me."

But Emily is beyond hearing. She's reached her breaking point and the resounding crack of it fills the room.

When her eyes fall upon mine again, they're wild with confusion and grief and what I can only describe as rage. "You've no right to come here and talk about him that way," she cries. "Speaking ill of the dead. Leave me alone!"

She looks around wildly, snatches up a glass of tea, and hurls it at me.

I sidestep, but I'm not fast enough. The glass strikes my shoulder. Cold splashes my face and spreads down my shirt. The glass hits the floor behind me and shatters.

"Go away!" she screams. *"Go away!"*

Raising my hands, I step back and sidle toward the door. "All right."

"Evil woman! Don't ever come back!" she screams. "Get out! *Get out!*"

I reach for the doorknob just as it flies open.

Clara steps into the kitchen, her eyes widening at the sight of her daughter. "Goodness gracious!" Her gaze sweeps from Emily to me and the dark stain of tea on my shirt, to the glass on the floor.

"It's okay," I tell her. "She's upset and I was just leaving."

The Amish woman jabs a finger at her daughter. "*Hoch dich anne*," she says firmly. Sit down.

"She's *fagunna*!" Emily uses the *Deitsch* term for "desiring another's ill fortune." "She's saying awful things about Aden!"

"You just settle yourself down." The Amish woman turns to me, her expression angry but controlled. "We buried her beau yesterday, Chief Burkholder. I think she's had enough questions for one day."

I hold her gaze for an instant, then turn my attention back to Emily. "If you want to talk, call me anytime. Day or night. I'll listen."

Without waiting for a reply, I go through the door.

Wayne Graber gets off work at five, so I wait until early evening to talk to him. I find his car parked beneath the carport. As I crunch across the gravel, a flock of crows caw from the cornfield beyond.

"Chief Burkholder?"

I look toward the door beneath the garage portico to see Graber coming through, a beer in hand, his hair damp from a shower. "Is everything all right?" he asks.

"Everything's fine." I reach him and we shake hands.

"You're working late again," he says.

"I didn't want to bother you at work." An awkward silence and then I add, "I have a couple of follow-up questions if you have a moment."

"Sure. What's up?"

I pull out the photo of the vehicle. "I'm wondering if you've ever seen this vehicle."

He leans closer to the photo, seems to examine it carefully. "Looks like a 2012 or thereabouts."

"Twenty thirteen," I tell him.

"I don't think I've ever seen it."

"What about here at the house?" I ask.

"Jeez, I don't think so." He gives me a quizzical look. "Whose is it?"

Instead of answering, I pull out the photos of Paige Rossberger. "What about this woman? Have you ever seen her? Spoken to her?"

He stiffens at the sight of the photo. "That's the girl who was killed."

"Yes."

"Why do you keep asking me about her? What does she have to do with Aden?"

"We believe there may be a link."

"What kind of link?"

I say nothing.

He tightens his mouth. "You're not going to try and pin what happened to her on Aden, are you?"

"We're not trying to pin anything on anyone. I just want to know if she was ever here. If her car was ever here." I shove the picture closer to him, urging him to take a more careful look. "Are you sure?"

"I'm sure." This time, he doesn't look at the photo. "Trying to lay some random girl's murder on Aden is a shitty thing to do. Just because you can't figure out—"

"That random girl was twenty-six years old," I snap. "She had a family. A life. People who loved her."

He looks away, unapologetic, says nothing.

Taking my time, I put the photo back in my pocket. "In the last week before his death, was there a night when Aden didn't come home? Or a time when you couldn't reach him?"

"He didn't have a phone, so it's not like we texted or anything like that." He shakes his head. "I don't think he spent a night out. I really don't."

"When's the last time he had a female visitor here at the house?"

"Last one . . ." He looks up as if trying to recall. "A couple of weeks ago? I don't know. I didn't even meet her. I just remember seeing her

282

walk from his room to the bathroom when I was getting ready to go to work."

"You sure you're not trying to cover for your friend?"

He frowns. "I've told you everything I know."

I stare at him until he looks away. In the periphery of my thoughts, I'm aware of the crows cawing in the cornfield. Time ticking away. That I've reached one more dead end.

"Sooner or later, I'm going to find out who killed Aden Karn," I say. "I'm going to find out who killed Paige Rossberger, too. And I'm going to figure out how all of this fits together."

"Why are you telling me that?"

"Because when I do, you had better hope that every word that came out of your mouth is the truth because if it isn't, I'm going to come for you, too. Do you understand?"

Shaking his head, he sighs. "I got it."

"Have a nice day," I tell him, and I walk away.

CHAPTER 22

I wake with a start from a hazy and disturbing dream. My heart beats a hard tattoo against my ribs. From the dream? Or something else? Beside me, Tomasetti breathes softly. Rolling, I reach for my cell on the night table, check the time. Three sixteen A.M. I've been asleep for two hours. I lie in the warmth of the bed, listening, trying to pinpoint what woke me. I'm aware of the patter of rain against the window. The distant rumble of thunder. I'm about to doze off when the sound of pounding sends me bolt upright.

Next to me Tomasetti sits up and we look at each other. "You expecting someone?" he asks.

"Not this early."

He rolls from bed, slides open the nightstand drawer, and snatches up his Kimber. I get up, yank my sweatpants off the back of the chair, and snag my .38 off the night table.

Tomasetti is already down the hall, his silhouette moving silently into the living room. It's too dark to see much. I'm ten feet behind him when I spot the light slanting through the window near the front door.

"Someone there," he whispers.

"With a flashlight." I sidle to the window and, standing slightly to one side, I use the nose of the .38 to move the curtain aside. Surprise ripples through me at the sight of a man holding a lantern. Flat-brimmed hat. *Amish*, I realize, and I feel a kick of recognition. The figure next to him is clad in a dark-colored dress. Black winter bonnet.

"You know them?" Tomasetti asks.

"I think it's Andy Byler."

Tomasetti flicks on the porch light and, standing slightly to one side, he opens the door and peers out. "Mr. Byler?"

The Amish man turns a grave face to Tomasetti. "We need to see Kate Burkholder."

I come up beside Tomasetti. Emily and her father are soaked to the skin. Evidently, they traveled via buggy all the way from Painters Mill.

"Mr. Byler. Emily. Come in." I step back and open the door wider. "Is everything all right?"

The Amish man shakes his head. "No."

Emily stares down at the ground. Water dripping from the hem of her dress. Her chin.

"Let's get you dried off." I leave the three of them standing in the living room and retrieve towels from the linen closet. Back in the living room, I hand one to Emily and then to her father.

"Bad night to be on the road," I say to Andy.

The Amish man nods at his daughter and for the first time I realize the wet and cold are the least of his worries. He's distraught. He won't look at me. Won't look directly at his daughter.

"She needs to talk to you," he says. "It won't wait until morning."

Curiosity boils in my gut as I turn my attention to Emily. The girl stares at the floor. Holding the bath towel at her side, not using it. Shock, I think, and I glance at her father. He meets my gaze and then slants a look at his daughter. "Dry yourself off, Em, and then you and Chief Burkholder can talk. You can say what you need to say."

The girl raises her head and looks at her father, but doesn't seem to actually see him or even recognize him. She shifts her gaze to me and only then do I realize she is the picture of misery. Hollow eyes. Soaked and shivering but not seeming to notice or care.

Gently, I take the towel from her, blot her cheeks, and then run the fluffy terry cloth down the fabric covering her arms, finally draping it over her shoulders.

"I'll make coffee," I tell them. "Come into the kitchen."

Andy shakes his head. "No," he says. "This is between you and her. I'll wait outside, in the buggy."

I glance at Tomasetti. He catches my gaze and motions the Amish man to the sofa. "It's chilly and wet out there, Mr. Byler. Have a seat here with me and we'll have some of that coffee. How do you take yours? Black? Milk and sugar?"

The Amish man seems to relax marginally and nods. "Black is fine."

My mind scrolls through a number of possible reasons for the middle-of-the-night visit as I guide Emily to the kitchen and put her in a chair. Our farm is an hour's buggy drive from Painters Mill. In the dark and pouring rain, a distance that's not quite safe. I take a few minutes to brew coffee, making small talk that isn't responded to. When the coffee is perked, I carry two cups to the men in the living room. Then I return to the kitchen, pour mugs for Emily and me, and I sit at the table, opposite her.

I push one of the mugs at her. "It's nice and hot," I tell her. "Go ahead and have a sip. It'll help take off the chill."

The girl picks up the cup, sets it down without drinking.

"This must be important for you and your *datt* to travel all this way so late at night and in the rain," I say.

For the span of a full minute, neither of us speaks; then the girl looks at me. "I asked God what I should do and He said to tell the truth."

"The truth is always a good policy," I tell her.

"Sometimes the truth is so awful you can't say it." Her hand shakes when she picks up the mug, so she grips it with both palms, raises it to her lips and drinks. "I wanted it to go away, but it won't."

"Is this is about Aden?" I ask.

She nods. "He was . . . everything to me. I thought he was . . ." She looks down at the tabletop, nods. "I thought he was good. I mean, he *was* good, but . . ." She squeezes her eyes closed for a moment and tears begin to stream down her cheeks. "Sometimes he wasn't."

"It's just you and me, Emily," I say gently. "Whatever you have to say, I'm here. I'll listen."

She stares down at the tabletop. I'm aware of rain tapping on the window above the sink. The low voices of Tomasetti and Andy from the living room. The tick of the coffeemaker as it cools.

"I couldn't even believe it when he wanted to court me. I'm not much to look at." A smile plays at the corners of her mouth. "He was so nice. And such a gentleman. Even Mamm and Datt said so." A sigh shudders out of her. "We didn't . . . you know, do anything for the longest time. Even when we were alone, you know. He was the first I'd ever kissed."

"I understand."

"Everything was perfect. He was perfect. We were going to get married and have children. Then . . . a couple months ago he came over in the buggy and took me out for a hot dog and root beer."

I wait, aware of a tightness in my chest. I've felt that sensation enough to know it's in response to the anticipation of hearing something I don't want in my head.

"We had fun. Afterward, we drank a beer and he took me out to that old gas station."

"Vernon Fisher's place?" I ask.

She nods. "I didn't want to go. All those crude boys. I don't like them. I don't like the way they look at me. The way they make fun. Like they're nice. Only they're not." She shrugs. "But Aden said it was okay. He said we wouldn't stay too long. So we went."

She lifts the mug and drinks. Not because she wants it, but because she doesn't want to say what comes next. . . .

I wait her out.

"All the boys were there and they had this bottle of tequila. They were passing it around. I didn't want any, but I didn't want them to think I was . . . a kid, you know?"

I nod, silent, but I can feel the hairs at the back of my neck starting to tingle. I have an idea where this is going. And it is a place I don't want to go. A place I wish she'd never ventured.

"It was fun at first. I mean, there was music. I felt so grown-up. My head was spinning. And Aden was laughing." She smiles again. "I thought I was having fun. I thought it was going to be okay."

I nod.

"Then he . . . he kissed me," she whispers.

"Right in front of everyone. And all those boys were . . . watching. They were smoking cigarettes and passing around that bottle. Aden kept saying that love is as important as being married. He said that God was love and He would be okay with it because we weren't yet baptized. And he took me into that back room where that mattress is and we . . . you know."

She breaks off, looks down at the tabletop as if she's going to be sick, and she struggles on. "It should have been beautiful. I mean, it was. At first. Yes, I knew it was a sin and I had guilt because we weren't married. I knew all of those things but I couldn't stop. I loved him so much."

Her brows furrow. "But everything was so . . . confused. Because of the alcohol, you know. I drank too much. And we were lying there and the next thing I knew there was someone else in the room with us. It was dark and I couldn't see who it was. I didn't know what was happening, but I knew Aden would take care of me." She closes her eyes tightly, as if doing so will keep the memory at bay. "The man got into bed with us. I tried to leave, but my clothes weren't there. And Aden . . . he said it would be okay. I lost sight of him and I got scared. I began to cry. . . . And then they all came in. And they . . ." She chokes out a sound that's part sob, part gasp. "I can't . . ."

For a moment, the only sound comes from her

rapid breaths. Then I ask, "Emily, did they rape you?"

"Aden said that wasn't what it was," she says quickly. "He said I *wanted* to do it. He said it was my fault because I tempted them. I drank too much and I asked for it. Chief Burkholder, I don't remember so much of it." She squeezes her eyes closed and begins to cry again. "And I'm so ashamed. I wanted to die."

I pick up my cup and sip, giving her a moment, giving myself a moment. I feel rage, but I know it will do nothing but get in the way.

Rising, I go to the counter, pull open a drawer, and remove a notepad. "Do you know the names of the men who were there that night?"

"No." She shifts her gaze to the window, at the darkness and rain beyond, but she's not quick enough to hide the flicker of the lie in her eyes.

"How many of them came into the room?"

"I don't know. It was too dark to see." She squeezes her eyes closed. "Everything was spinning."

I feel nauseated and I think about the murder of Aden Karn and I wonder if—or how—this incident plays into it.

"Did you tell anyone what happened?" I ask.

She raises her eyes to mine. "What would I say? That I went there to sin and had sin committed against me? It was my fault."

"It wasn't your fault," I tell her.

The bitterness of her laugh tells me she doesn't believe me. That she will never believe me. "It doesn't even matter. Aden is gone. Everything is . . . ruined. I don't see how God can forgive me for what I did. I don't see how I can forgive myself."

"God forgives all of us our sins if we ask Him." I'm certainly no expert on the subject, but I say the words because I need to, because she needs to hear them.

She says nothing.

"Did this happen just one time?" I ask.

She squeezes her eyes closed, shakes her head. I sense the shame coming off her in waves. The self-loathing. The blame. "There were a few times when . . . I went to the gas station with him. I can't explain it because sometimes I didn't drink any tequila, and yet I got that crazy feeling in my head. You know, like I was dizzy and . . . then I was in that room with them and I just don't remember."

I curb a surge of fury. "Did Aden or anyone else ever give you any pills? Or ask you to smoke something? Marijuana? Or cigarettes? Anything like that?"

"No."

I take my mug to the counter. I'm aware of the anger thrashing inside me, and I remind myself to keep a handle on it.

After pouring another cup of coffee, I reclaim

my seat. "It took guts for you to come here tonight and tell me the truth. You were very brave. Thank you."

"I don't feel very brave," she mutters. "I feel . . . dirty and . . . more awful than I've ever felt in my life."

"No one has the right to do that to you or anyone else. It's called sexual assault and it's against the law."

The girl looks down at the tabletop, saying nothing.

"Emily, you did the right thing," I tell her. "Now it's my turn to do the right thing. In order to do that, I need the names of the men who hurt you."

Gasping, she raises her head, stares at me, eyes wide with panic. "I don't know who came into the room."

"Are you sure about that?"

"I don't want anyone to know," she whispers. "Please. I didn't want to come here. Datt made me. That's why I didn't tell anyone. I don't want anyone to know!"

I'm too angry to look into her eyes, so I glance down at the mug and take a drink of coffee I don't want.

"Chief Burkholder, if the Amish find out . . . it'll ruin my life more than it already is. Please. I just want to go on like it never happened."

As a formerly Amish woman, I understand

more than I want to. As a cop, I know if I don't get her to open up, the men who assaulted her will get away with what they did. In the state of Ohio, once a sexual assault is reported to the police, it becomes a crime against the state and the victim has no say in the matter.

"Why did you come here tonight?" I ask her.

"Datt made me."

"You came here because it was the right thing to do."

"I just want to forget about it and go on with my life," she pleads.

I consider that a moment. "How did your *datt* find out?"

A too-long pause and then, "I had a nightmare earlier. Woke them up. Mamm came into my room. I told her I wanted to go to God now, and I think that scared her. She begged me to tell her what was bothering me and I did. I think she must have told Datt because he came into my room later and said I had to come here and talk to you."

I think about what must have been going through Andy Byler's head as his wife relayed to him his daughter had been gang-raped. While the Amish are pacifists and do not condone or participate in violence in any way, they're also human. I think about what happened to Aden Karn and I wonder how many fathers have crossed a line to protect their children. How many fathers have countered violence with violence?

I can't force this young woman to do anything she doesn't want to do, including giving me the names of the men responsible. Even if I refer this crime to the prosecutor, without names his office can't pursue charges. I have no DNA. No evidence. If she doesn't cooperate, I don't even have a victim.

"If I were to set up a meeting with a prosecutor, would you speak with him?" I ask.

"I don't want to talk to anyone about this ever again. I just want to forget it and try to move on."

I think about the situation in terms of the murders of Aden Karn and Paige Rossberger and I know this has to be somehow related. Another devastating link in a chain of many.

"Emily, when I showed you the photos and asked if you recognized the vehicle or the woman, were you telling me the truth?"

"Of course I was. I've never seen her before."

"Were there ever any other women at the gas station when you were there?" I ask. "English women? Amish women?"

Her brows come together as if she's trying to remember, but she shakes her head. "I never saw any other girls, but I was only there three or four times. And I was never awake when we left."

It's five A.M. and I'm sitting at the kitchen table, an empty mug in front of me. Dark thoughts keep me company.

"I'd give you a penny for your thoughts, but I'm not sure I want to know."

I glance up to see Tomasetti enter. He's freshly showered and dressed—in a suit and tie, of course—and makes a beeline for the still-brewing coffee.

"Anyone ever tell you that you look nice in that suit?" I try to smile, but it's not a good fit so I let it fall.

"You should see me in my boxers." He looks at me over his shoulder as he pours. He's smiling, but I see clearly that he's aware of my state of mind. That he doesn't like it. He knows me well.

He brings the carafe to the table and fills my mug. "Must have been a tough conversation."

"I don't even know where to start," I say.

He returns the carafe to its nest, then takes the chair across from me. I keep my eyes on the mug. I know if I look at him, he'll see what's written all over me. I'm too angry. Too . . . emotional. None of those things are ever a good look for a cop.

"I couldn't get much out of Byler," he tells me. "So I'm sort of in the dark here."

I recap my conversation with Emily Byler. "They drugged her and they gang-raped her. Not once, but several times. A seventeen-year-old Amish girl. And now, all she wants is for no one to know."

He looks away, mutters a curse beneath his

breath. "So Karn farmed her out to his friends."

"She was innocent. A kid. Pliable. In love with him. He was the first male to pay attention to her. She *trusted* him." I think of all the things he took from her, the things she won't be able to get back, and I find myself thinking that if Aden Karn wasn't dead, I'd want to kill him myself.

Back off, Kate. . . .

"He betrayed her in the worst possible way," I say.

"The names of the men involved would have been nice to have," he says.

"She'll never tell. She wants to forget it ever happened. Tomasetti, there's a big part of me that understands that." I slap my hand against the tabletop. "She's holding on by a thread."

"I guess the question now is what are you going to do about it?"

"I don't know. Damn it. Something, for God's sake."

He stares at me, holding my gaze so that I can't look away. "I know you too well to be concerned about you doing something you shouldn't."

"If there was ever a time when that would be warranted . . ." I blow out a breath, release some of the high-wire tension inside me. "The entirety of this case, I thought Karn was a wholesome Amish kid whose life was cut short. I wanted to find the bastard responsible and I wanted to hang him up by his balls."

"Then you find out Aden Karn was a morally corrupt son of a bitch."

There's a moment of quiet.

"This development adds an interesting dimension to the case," he says slowly. "It may open some new avenues in terms of motive, anyway."

I was so angry, so emotional, that my brain hadn't yet gone there. Alas, the danger of what can happen when a cop feels too much. "Someone, who ostensibly cared about Emily Byler, found out that Karn and his sleazy friends raped her. And they killed him for it."

My mind grinds through that a moment. "We need to find out if there were any other girls or women who didn't come forward."

"What about Andy Byler?"

I shake my head. "He just found out tonight."

"Let's take a closer look at Rossberger's associates. See if we can find a boyfriend or male friend. Father. Someone who found out what happened and sought revenge."

We fall silent. The only sound comes from the drip of rain off the roof outside.

I lift my cup, look at him over the rim. "Have you ever worked a case and thought maybe the victim deserved what he got?"

"Karn isn't the first morally bankrupt victim whose death you've investigated."

"He's one of the most vile." I look away, find

myself looking at the floor where Emily had stood. I see the mud from her shoes.

"I know you well enough to know you'll do your job whether you like or respect or detest your victim."

"I don't want to be that hardened cop. The one who doesn't feel anything. The one who doesn't care. The one who looks at everyone as if they're a criminal. But, Tomasetti, this case . . . It's got me by the throat."

"You're not hardened, Kate. You're not cynical. You're pissed. Because you care. There's a difference." With a half smile he adds, "Cynicism is my job, remember?"

When I don't respond, he adds, "This isn't the first time you've put your victim on a pedestal. Remember: You don't fight for them because of who *they* are. You fight for them because of who *you* are."

I blow out another breath, send some of the anger out with it. "Thank you for saying that."

He reaches across the table and takes my hand in his. "You going to be okay with all of this?"

"Yeah."

When he smiles, I feel some of the weight lifted off my shoulders and not for the first time I'm reminded of everything he's brought to my life, and why I love him so unconditionally.

"Thank you for talking me off the ledge," I tell him.

"It's nothing a decent bartender couldn't have done." He shrugs. "They solve most of the world's problems, you know."

"If you ever retire, some bar owner is going to snap you up."

For a moment, we smile at each other. Then he gets to his feet and pulls me up to face him. "Too bad we can't play hooky today," he murmurs.

"No way we can pull that off."

He leans into me, slides his arms around my waist, and presses his mouth to mine. "On the other hand." He looks down at me. "It's not yet five thirty in the morning."

"Which means I need to get going."

"Or it might mean we have an hour or so to kill before our cell phones start ringing."

"You're already dressed." I straighten his tie, flick the knot with my forefinger. "You're wearing your good suit today."

"Fuck the suit," he says, and sweeps me into his arms.

CHAPTER 23

I'm sitting in the Explorer in front of Vernon Fisher's gas station, windows down, watching the sun rise and listening to a cardinal chip from atop the maple tree a few yards away. I'm thinking about Aden Karn and Emily Byler, the masks people wear, and how those masks contrast with the personas they present to the rest of the world. I've always believed I have good instincts when it comes to seeing any darkness that lurks in the hearts of men. I'm loath to admit it, but I'd been wrong about Karn—and blind to a slew of possibilities in terms of motive.

Not a good look, Kate.

The crunch of tires on gravel pulls me from my thoughts. I glance left to see Vernon Fisher pull up next to me in an old Chevy pickup truck I've never seen before. His window is down, music blaring, and he's glaring at me, a cigarette hanging from his mouth. Not happy to see me parked in his driveway so early in the morning, a fact that gives me a disproportionate rise of pleasure.

Frowning, he jams the truck into park, tosses the cigarette to the ground, and gets out.

I meet him at his vehicle. "Get a new truck?"

"Bought it this morning for fifteen hundred bucks."

"Nice." I run my hand over the fender. "You must be an early riser."

"Ain't been to sleep yet, so . . ." He shrugs. "This about Aden?"

I tug the photo of Paige Rossberger and the red Altima from my pocket, unfold them, and show him the picture of the woman. "Have you ever seen her?"

He gives the photo a cursory look and shakes his head. "Who is she?"

I shuffle the photo of the Altima so that it's on top. "What about this vehicle?"

Another perfunctory look. "Nope."

"Are you sure? You didn't take a very good look. Take your time. Take a good long look. This is an important moment for you."

He narrows his eyes, not sure of my meaning. He doesn't look at the photo. "No offense, Chief Burkholder, but I looked at those photos. I answered your questions. I'd appreciate it if you'd let me go inside and get some sleep."

I'm aware of the cardinal chipping away. The truck engine ticking as the engine cools. The sun warm on my back. I think about Emily Byler, and I feel that dragon of rage snap its tail.

"I understand you've had a few parties here at the station," I say, keeping my voice conversational.

"That isn't against the law, is it?"

"No, it's not." I look at the gas station, pretend

302

to study the façade. "Kind of an interesting venue for a party. How many have you had out here?"

He tosses me a look that's part perplexed, but mostly annoyed. "We might've had a few. What does that have to do with anything?"

"We?" I assume my own perplexed expression. "Who else?"

"Just me and a few buddies. You've seen them out here."

Emily's voice comes at me from the recesses of my mind . . . *And then they all came in.*

"Maybe I should talk to them, too," I say. "What are their names?"

"I reckon you'll have to figure that out on your own." One side of his mouth hikes into a smile, a chess player realizing he's about to checkmate. "I haven't been playing the music too loud, have I?" He looks around, Mr. Innocent, indicating there isn't a neighbor in sight.

"Silly of me not to notice something so obvious." I add an amicable tone to my voice. "By the way, you do know the age of consent in Ohio is sixteen, right?"

"I'm not sure why you'd mention that," he says. "I haven't had any young girls out here. I don't do that shit."

I hold my temper at bay. "Rape and sexual-battery laws in Ohio cover a lot of different scenarios." I shrug, a teacher explaining a complicated algebra problem to a student who doesn't quite get it. "I mean, a person can be charged with rape if they coerce an individual into drinking or taking drugs so that the victim is impaired and unable to resist sexual advances. Did you know that?"

The good-old-boy pretenses fall away. "I thought this was about Aden."

"It is."

He stares at me, all semblance of good humor and cockiness giving way to nerves—and thinly concealed temper. Out of the corner of my eye, I see his hands clench into fists, and I'm keenly aware of my radio mike pinned to my lapel, my .38 strapped to my hip. That I'd like nothing better than to punch his fucking lights out.

"The law is fascinating," I hear myself say. "Did you know that rape is a first-degree felony?"

He stares at me, eyes level and set, his nostrils flaring.

"Also." I say the word with emphasis. "Did you know there's a mandatory prison term for certain conduct, like drugging the victim? And if force or coercion was used, the offender faces life imprisonment." I shake my head. "*Life*. Can you imagine?"

"I don't know why you're telling me that."

"Judging by the look on your face, you know exactly why I'm telling you this."

"You've no cause to speak to me like that." He

glances over his shoulder at the gas station. "I have to go."

"Please do. Get some rest. In fact, you'd better get as much sleep as you can because in the coming days and weeks and months, you're going to need it." I raise my hand, touch the tip of his nose with my index finger. "I'm relentless, Vernon. One wrong move, and I'm going to be all over your shit. Do you understand?"

Looking shaken, he steps away from me, looks me up and down as if he's expecting a physical attack. I hold my ground, stare hard at him.

"You're not allowed touch me like that. You can't threaten a citizen," he snarls. "Just because you can't figure out what happened to Karn doesn't mean you can come here and take it out on me."

"Maybe you should file a complaint."

"Maybe I will."

"Better yet, why don't you take your best shot right now?" I motion toward his hands, which are still clenched into fists. "Look at you. All that rage. All that scary teeth grinding. And you don't have the balls to do anything about it."

"Fuck you." He turns and starts toward the gas station.

I hold my ground, my heart pounding, and I watch as he reaches the office door, jams the key into the lock. "Vernon?" I call out.

He glares at me over his shoulder.

"Just so you know . . . the criminal statute of limitations on rape and sexual battery in Ohio is twenty-five years. Think about that while you're trying to sleep."

Muttering something unintelligible beneath his breath, he yanks open the door and disappears inside.

A cop does not take time off during a homicide investigation. Not one day. Not even a few hours. There's too much to do. Too much going on. Always the concern that something will break when you're not there. The investigation becomes your life and everything else is reduced to white noise. When Tomasetti showed up at the station and asked me to go for a drive, I almost refused. But there was something in the way he looked at me when he asked, and I sensed the importance of his request.

I didn't know our destination. He kept the conversation light during the hour-long drive from Painters Mill to Cleveland. He's thoughtful, pensive, preoccupied, and I let him be. Only now, as he makes the turn into the cemetery entrance, do I realize the significance of what we're about to do.

I don't have an aversion to cemeteries. I see them as peaceful, reflective places. Amish cemeteries are utilitarian and, of course, plain. They're part of the landscape, a cornfield or pasture that was donated by a family generations ago and transformed to a place to bury the dead. Amish cemeteries are the kind of place you drive past every day and you think about someone who's buried there. Someone you loved or knew or knew of. Maybe you miss them for an instant or you feel the tinge of that old ache. If enough time has passed, you don't think of their death; you think of their life. If you're lucky, for just a moment, you feel close to them. Sometimes, you feel close to God.

Populated with hundreds of century-old oaks, maples, and elm trees, Calvary Cemetery is a far cry from the quaint Amish cemeteries of Holmes County. It's a solemn and regal setting with over three hundred thousand graves, some dating back to the 1800s.

Tomasetti doesn't need a map or signs to find what he's looking for. He's been here hundreds of times in the past seven years. As we wend along the neat asphalt road and idle past dozens of stunning monuments, headstones of every shape, size, and scope, and trees with leaves that shimmer like new copper in the late-afternoon sunlight, he reaches for my hand.

He stops the Tahoe in a quiet section, the headstones dappled with sunlight, the granite specks glinting and winking.

"It's pretty here," I tell him. "Quiet."

"I didn't notice for the longest time." Finally,

he looks at me. "In three days, we'll be married."

Despite the solemnity of the moment, I feel a smile emerge. Holding his gaze, I squeeze his hand. "It's about time, don't you think?"

"Past time." A smile plays at the corners of his mouth and then he looks through the windshield at the graves. "I thought this would be a good time for us to come here. For me to tell you about them."

He releases my hand and gets out. He rounds the front of the Tahoe to open my door, but I'm out by the time he reaches me. We walk side by side to a large slant headstone with TOMASETTI engraved across the top. It's a pretty stone, cut from blue-gray granite and sitting atop an equally pretty foundation. There's a heart at the top, to the left of the name. Praying hands to the right. Lower, three names have been etched into the surface. NANCY JEAN, LOVING WIFE AND MOTHER. DONNA MARIE AND KELLY ANN, BELOVED DAUGHTERS. JOHN.

"I feel like I should know how often you come here," I say. "But I don't."

He shrugs. "I used to visit every month or so." He motions to a bench several yards away. "Spent the night on that bench once or twice, early on. I think it's been about six months since I was here last."

Healing, I think.

I nod, look at the stone, not sure what to say

next, sensing this time is for him. For *them*. And my time to just . . . be.

"Kelly would have been sixteen. Donna seventeen." He shakes his head. "Hard to believe it's been seven years. Sometimes it seems like a hundred. Some days . . . like it happened yesterday and I'm getting the call all over again."

Two years before we met, his wife and children were murdered by a career criminal during a vicious home invasion. Shortly afterward, Tomasetti left the Cleveland Division of Police and began his career with BCI. We met when he was assigned to assist me in the course of a terrible case in Painters Mill. Though two years had passed since he'd lost his wife and children, he was floundering, personally and professionally, and he was far from coping. He was drinking too much and mixing alcohol with prescription drugs. On the fast track to self-destruction or death—whichever came first. I hadn't been doing much better and yet somehow, in the midst of all that turmoil, we managed to start a relationship.

"You've come a long way in the last few years," I say.

"Had some help." Grinning at me, he squeezes my hand.

He looks at the stone and sobers. "They were good kids. Just . . . little girls. They wore pink. They liked to swim and play teacher. Nancy was a good woman. A good mom. She was a good wife and I loved her." He looks at me and for the first time in a long time, he lets me see the depth of his grief.

"I was unfaithful to her once," he says after a moment. "I never told you. I was . . . ashamed. But I slept with a cop I was working with. It nearly cost me my marriage."

I look at the stone, the etched name of the woman he'd loved. "Hopefully, you spent some time in the doghouse."

"Oh, yeah." He gives a self-deprecating laugh. "Took some time but we worked it out."

"Just so you know . . . you're one of the most loyal people I've ever known."

"Not always," he admits. "Lucky for me, I'm capable of learning from my mistakes."

An uncomfortable silence ensues. I get the impression he's struggling to tell me something else, so I give him the time to work through it.

"I worked a lot," he says. "I drank too much. Didn't spend enough time with my children. I didn't appreciate them as much as I should have."

"We don't live our lives thinking our loved ones are going to be snatched away," I tell him.

Lifting my hand, he brings it to his mouth and kisses my knuckles. "I wasn't a very good husband. I wasn't as good a father as I should have been."

"So you say."

"Just giving you fair warning." He gives me a good-natured frown. "So you know what you're getting into."

"I know exactly what I'm getting into," I tell him. "And I know everything I need to know about you."

He starts to say something, but I raise my hand and press my finger to his lips. "Despite all those flaws, I love you."

Blinking, he looks away, his jaw tight and working, stoic.

"It was good for me to come here," I say. "To meet them."

"I'm glad you came."

After a moment, I look down at the memorial. "What do you say we swing by the florist and bring back some flowers before we head home?"

He doesn't smile, but I see the warmth in his eyes. "I think that's a fine idea."

Hand in hand, we walk back to the Tahoe.

I spend the rest of the afternoon locked in my office, rereading every scrap of paper and digital record I've amassed on the murders of Paige Rossberger and Aden Karn so far. I study the autopsy reports and photos, picking apart every detail, every word, looking for something—anything—I missed, looking for things that simply aren't there. I scrutinize every interview. I look at photos of the victims, the crime scenes, and everything that's come back from the lab so far.

Striking out there, I study the map I've pinned to the wall and I go to it. I circle the crime scenes in red marker, every other relevant location in blue. Lester and Angela Karn's shop. The Byler farm. June Rossberger's home in Massillon. Aden Karn's home. The pickup point at the Lutheran church. The gas station where Vernon Fisher lives. Even the Brass Rail Saloon. I connect the dots, try to come up with routes and timelines, by vehicle or horse and buggy.

All of it leads directly to nothing.

Back at my desk, I spool up the videos I took of the scene on Hansbarger Road and the bridge where Rossberger's body was discovered, and I watch them again. All the while frustration grinds at the back of my brain.

Nothing there, Kate.

At four P.M. a tap on my door draws me from my focus. Margaret, my newest dispatcher, stands in the hall outside my office, headset clamped over her ears. "You look like you could use some good news," she says a little too cheerily.

She's over twenty years my senior—and I was raised to respect my elders regardless of my position as chief—so I swallow the surly response on my tongue. "That could quite possibly be the understatement of the year."

"Call came in on the tip line, Chief. I think you're going to want to hear this one."

So far, we've received a total of twelve calls on our "tip line." Four were obvious pranks. One a wrong number. One blaming the incident on a UFO sighted out by the old drive-in theater. The rest were viable and checked out, but not helpful in terms of the case. We don't have the budget for an official tip line with a unique number, so we use the main number with an extension that sends callers to voicemail where they are assigned a unique identifying number to ensure their anonymity. From there, they're instructed to leave a message and urged to call back with any additional information and to check in later to see if they have cash coming from the reward.

"I'm all ears." I lean back in my chair, my attempt at enthusiasm not quite coming through.

Using my desk phone, she punches the Speaker button, then dials the number, taps in a four-digit code, and sinks into the visitor chair.

The speaker crackles and hisses and then a voice sounds.

"I'm uh . . ." The male caller clears his throat. *"I'm calling about the Aden Karn thing. Look, I don't want to get involved, but you need to check the young Amish dude has the gas station. Fisher, I think his name is. I ain't saying he done it, but I seen him out there to Hansbarger with a crossbow a couple weeks ago. Almost like he was practicing or something. Anyway . . . that's all I got to say."*

An elongated hiss follows and then the click of the caller disconnecting.

I sit up straighter, look at Margaret. She stares back at me with a slightly smug I-told-you-so expression.

"Play it again," I say.

This time I listen for unique characteristics of the caller's voice. There's static on the line and a slight echo. Still, I make a couple of observations. "He's trying to disguise his voice," I murmur.

Across from me, Margaret nods. "Sounds like it."

"Play it again."

She does.

This time I notice the Amish-English accent. It's subtle, but I'm able to discern the upward lilt that softens the vowels. "He's Amish," I say. "Trying to conceal it." Not exactly an earth-shattering revelation. The victim was Amish, after all. Vernon Fisher is Amish. A third of the population of Painters Mill is Amish. Even so, it's something and worth noting.

I glance at Margaret. "Again."

This time, I concentrate on the words themselves. What he's saying, looking for hesitations, indications that he's lying. I get nothing.

"Is there any way we can get our hands on the caller's number?" I ask.

"Well, we set it up to be anonymous, but I'll see what I can figure out."

"Send a copy of the recording to my cell," I say, thinking aloud. "Forward it to Tomasetti and Rasmussen, too. Type up a transcript in case we need it."

"You got it, Chief." She gets to her feet.

I think about the call in terms of specifics. The caller asserted he witnessed Vernon Fisher using a crossbow at the scene two weeks before Aden Karn was killed. When I asked Fisher if he owned or had access to a crossbow, he said he didn't. An anonymous tip is by no means a slam dunk, but it may be enough for me to obtain a warrant.

"Call Judge Siebenthaler," I say. "Tell him I'm on my way over with an affidavit for a search warrant."

She's already heading for the door. "I'll catch him right now, Chief."

"Margaret?" I say.

She stops, turns, and raises her brows, expecting another barrage of commands.

Instead, I smile. "Nice work."

Her mouth twitches. "Roger that," she says, and makes her exit.

CHAPTER 24

I know better than to get my hopes up over an anonymous tip; most of the time they don't pan out. That I'm enthusiastic stands as testament to my level of desperation. And, of course, my dislike for Vernon Fisher. Judge Siebenthaler is no fan of anonymous tips, either. He balked after reading the affidavit I put together. In the end, he'd acquiesced, but narrowed the scope of what I could search for and where I could search for it, and a task that should have taken an hour ended up taking two.

It's nearly seven P.M. now and I'm in the Explorer heading toward Vernon Fisher's gas station. Officer T.J. Banks rides shotgun. Despite having worked through the night and most of the day, he looks fresh and alert as he skims the warrant. "So, we're permitted to search the main building, attached garage, and one outbuilding?" he asks.

I think about my exchange with the judge and nod. "And we're limited to confiscating items that are directly related to a crossbow, crossbow paraphernalia or accessories, and/or hunting."

"So if we find a bloody knife . . ."

"I think we could legally seize it and make the

argument that it's covered under the 'hunting' umbrella."

"A noose . . ."

I slant him a look as I make the turn onto the street where the Karns live.

He grins, then sobers. "Do you expect any trouble from Fisher?"

The serving of a warrant is one of the most dangerous duties a cop performs. No individual likes having their privacy invaded, or their things rifled through by the cops. Add a bottle of tequila and half a dozen intoxicated hooligans and this is exactly the kind of situation that could go south.

"Glock and Tomasetti are going to meet us there," I tell him. "To make sure everyone behaves themselves."

I make the turn into the gas station to find four vehicles parked nose-in against the building, telling me the regulars are already there. The overhead door stands open. Glock's cruiser is parked next to Tomasetti's Tahoe, a generous distance away from the other vehicles. Tomasetti is standing against the door of the Tahoe, talking on his cell, watching me. I pull up behind them and kill the engine. My window is down a few inches and I hear the blare of chain-saw rock emanating from the garage.

"Keep your eyes open," I say to T.J. as I open the door.

"Roger that."

Glock exits his vehicle as I start toward the overhead door. He's already wearing his duty gloves, his eyes scanning.

Tomasetti drops his cell into his pocket and strides toward me. "Looks like the whole gang is here," he says.

"Lucky us," Glock puts in as he falls in beside us.

There's no time for Tomasetti or Glock to read the warrant, so I give them the same instructions I gave T.J. as we walk toward the structure. "This is a limited search. Anything crossbow or hunting related. We have access to the main structure, including the office, back room, restroom, and garage. Also, that outbuilding." I motion right and then glance at Glock. "I think it would be best if we got everyone out of the main building before we begin. Visitors are free to leave if they wish. Detain Fisher. If he prefers to be inside with us while we execute the warrant, he can."

"You got it, Chief."

One of the young men I recall seeing during an earlier visit comes through the overhead door and squints at us as if we're Martians having just landed our spaceship. He's holding a cigarette in one hand, a beer in the other.

"Someone invite the cops?" he says over his shoulder.

Giving him a nod, I move past him, go through the overhead door, spot Vernon Fisher standing inside, a bottle of beer in his hand. He makes eye contact with me and starts toward me. "Three times in one week," he drawls. "I must be doing something right."

I cross to him, hand him the warrant. "This is a search warrant. My officers and I have permission to search these premises. I suggest you read it carefully."

He takes the warrant, looks down at it as if it's covered with biohazard. "If you don't mind my asking, Chief Burkholder, what the hell are you looking for?"

"It's all in the warrant." I flick the document with my index finger. "You can remain inside with us if you prefer, but I'd like everyone who does not reside here to get out."

"In case you haven't noticed, we're a little busy." He adds a note of amusement to his voice, but he can't hide the irritation or contempt in his eyes.

"She be shaking you down, dude!" one of the men calls out.

"Break out the tequila!"

"Body-cavity search!" comes another voice.

A round of raucous laughter ensues.

Fisher looks down at the warrant, eyes darting, as if he thinks he's smart enough to find some error that will send us packing. "This is a bunch of crap." He looks from me to Glock and back at me and frowns. "We're out here minding our own business and you dumbasses want to go through all my shit? That ain't right."

"Read the warrant." I look at T.J., motion toward the door that will take him inside. "Start in the office area."

"Hands off Leandra!" a man holding the bottle of tequila shouts, gesturing with the bottle toward the sex doll.

I make eye contact with Fisher. "Tell your friends to leave or they will be escorted out."

Hissing a curse, Fisher shakes his head. "She wants you guys out."

There are four other men inside as far as I can tell. Two of them start toward the door. Another stands next to the door that leads to the office. The fourth is beneath a car that's up on a lift.

I divide my attention between the two men remaining inside. "That includes you. Leave or I will arrest you," I say. "Do you understand?"

A nasty jeer flies at me, but I ignore it. Slowly, the two men, beers in hand, shuffle toward the parking lot. When they're through the door, Glock trails them, and stops midway between the building and our vehicles where he can keep an eye on everyone present.

Fisher stands just inside the overhead door, arms crossed at his chest, glaring at me. Tomasetti is standing at the door, staring at him in kind.

I look around the garage. An industrial fan mounted on the wall blows a steady stream of oily-smelling air through the shop. There's a big workbench against the wall opposite the overhead door. Above it, a pegboard is covered with a mosaic of tools. A couple of rollaway toolboxes are against the wall to my left. Good-size air compressor with a coil of hose hisses on the floor.

Tomasetti looks at Fisher, then motions to the car that's up on the lift. "Anything we need to know about in that vehicle?"

"I don't have shit to say to you," Fisher tells him.

Tomasetti smiles. "In that case, lower the vehicle," he says. "Now."

Snarling a profanity beneath his breath, Fisher goes to a small control box mounted to the wall and flips a switch. A mechanism clicks and then the jack begins to descend.

I'm a linear thinker, so I slip on my duty gloves and start with the steel shelving unit next to the overhead door with plans to work my way around the room. For several minutes, I methodically work my way from top shelf to bottom, moving aside quarts of oil, various types of filters, gallon jugs of coolant, transmission fluid, and windshield-washer fluid. I check behind and beneath the shelves as I go, and replace everything before moving on to the next unit. It's tedious, dirty work. I keep an eye on T.J. as he works inside the office, going through the desk. Tomasetti is digging through the vehicle that was lowered, working his way through the front glove compartment, center console, beneath the seats, and to the rear.

Fisher opens a beer and chain-smokes as he paces beneath the overhead door. He's irritated with us, but knows there's nothing he can do about it.

When I finish with the shelves, I sidle to the nearest rollaway toolbox. It's bright red, expensive-looking and likely new. One by one, I open the drawers. They're shallow. Filled with an array of wrenches, hammers, compressor hose fittings, and pliers. The lower drawers are deeper and contain a grinder and drill, a case of drill bits, grinder disks. I feel beneath each drawer, check the sides. I'm about to move on to the second, older-looking rollaway, when I realize I didn't check the back. I'm looking over my shoulder, watching a terse exchange between Tomasetti and Fisher, when I reach around. Almost absently, I run my fingers against the smooth steel, surprised when my fingers bump something.

The toolbox is extremely heavy, but it's on casters so I push one side of it around so I can see the back. The floor tilts beneath my feet when I spot the broadhead tips of the crossbow bolts. Two of them, taped to the back of the rollaway with silver duct tape.

I stare at them for a beat, not quite believing my

eyes. To say I hadn't expected to find anything this earth-shattering would be an understatement.

I straighten, stand there a moment, trying to get my head around it. I look at Tomasetti, who's already noticed my response. Even Fisher has stopped pacing.

Tilting my head, I hail T.J. on the radio. "Ten-seven-eight." Through the glass, I see him stop what he's doing and turn to look at me. I nod and he starts toward the door.

I say Tomasetti's name, but he's already striding toward me, his eyes flicking from me to the toolbox.

"What?" Fisher says. "Did you find a fucking wrench or something?"

Tomasetti goes to the rollaway and stretches to look behind it. He's not easily surprised, but I see the flicker of it on his face as he hauls the toolbox away from the wall. The lighting isn't great, so he tugs the mini Maglite from his pocket and sets the beam on the back of the rollaway.

"My my," Tomasetti says.

Without speaking, I tug my cell from my pocket and snap half a dozen photos of the bolts from different angles and distances. I'm aware of Tomasetti fishing nylon gloves from his pocket, working them onto his hands. T.J. comes through the door, looking confused. I glance at Fisher. He's sidled closer. I see his eyes flit to the back of the rollaway. His brows snap together.

"You've got to be shitting me," he says.

The beer he's been holding falls to the concrete. And then he's out the door and running toward the woods.

CHAPTER 25

Fisher tears out of the garage and darts left. Ten yards away, Glock spots him and starts after him, but when one of the other men dashes for a vehicle, Glock changes course and goes after the nearest man instead. And then I'm past them, running full out across the parking area. Fisher is fifty feet ahead, running like a gazelle, feet barely seeming to touch the ground. I hear the crunch of gravel beneath my boots, hear the rush of my breaths, feel the strain of my muscles. Out of the corner of my eye, I see Tomasetti fall in behind me. I don't know where T.J. is. And in that moment, my only thought is to stop Fisher.

I'm midway across the lot, running as fast as I can. Ahead, Fisher enters the woods. There's no path, just an ocean of trees, bramble, and high grass, and he plows into it like a tank.

Shit, I think, and hit my lapel mike. "Ten-eighty." I pant out my location. "Ten-seven-eight." Chase in progress. Need assistance.

"Stop!" I shout at Fisher, knowing it's futile to try to catch him. He's younger than me. Faster. "Police! Stop!"

I burst into the woods. Branches slash at my face and hair. Undergrowth tears at my clothes. I muscle through, hands raised to protect my eyes. I sidle between two good-size trees, catch a glimpse of Fisher fifteen yards ahead, and I push myself into a sprint.

I call out his name. "Stop!"

The trees seem to thrust from the ground as the land slopes sharply upward. I hear Tomasetti behind me as I struggle up the grade. Vaguely, I'm aware of my police radio lighting up as deputies respond. I leap over a fallen log, claw through raspberry bush and saplings. Catch sight of my quarry through the trees, and I change course. I'm no slouch when it comes to running, but the grade is so precipitous I have to use my hands in a couple of places. The terrain is rugged, littered with rocks and deadfall, and within minutes, I'm out of breath, my quads burning as if they're on fire.

A dead branch comes out of nowhere, catches my shirt, yanks it. I hear fabric rip, keep going even though I've lost sight of Fisher. I reach the apex of the hill, look around. The woods are thinner here. I pause, try to catch my breath, spot movement ahead and to my left. I launch myself back into a run. Not as fast. I'm running out of steam, so I try to pace myself. I hear someone behind me. No time to look. The ground slants sharply down. I pick my way around rocks the size of truck tires. I think there's a creek ahead, but my sense of direction is skewed.

The ground drops away beneath me. I turn,

plant my feet sideways to avoid sliding, but I'm not agile enough. My left foot finds purchase on a rock, but the rock gives way and I slide. My left hip strikes the ground hard. I reach for a sapling, but I'm not fast enough and I roll. Once, twice. My feet flailing. Arms reaching. Handholds flying past. Shit. *Shit.* I'm about to roll a third time when the small of my back strikes a tree trunk, stopping me. I twist, scramble to my knees, look around. I'm almost to my feet when I see movement scant feet away. At first, I think Tomasetti has caught up with me. I swivel, spot the pale oval of Fisher's face. Ball cap. Blue shirt. The branch comes out of nowhere. I hear a whoosh! It strikes my left cheekbone. A lightning burst of pain and then I'm reeling backward. My shoulder strikes a sapling. I slide in mud and go down on one knee. I'm keenly aware of my .38 against my hip. Think better of reaching. I set my hand on my baton. Something in my eye, a dark blur, messing with my vision.

Fisher stands three feet away, chest heaving, face red and covered with sweat. "I didn't do anything!" he screams.

I yank out my baton as I scramble to my feet. "Do not move!" I shout.

Hissing a curse, he swings again. I turn away, but the branch slams into my shoulder. Pain zings down my arm, but I'm too pissed to feel it.

I lunge at him, swing the baton, find purchase. Fisher squeals.

"Drop the branch!" I shout. "Get on the ground! Facedown!"

The next thing I know Tomasetti rushes past me and slams into him. His shoulder rams into Fisher's chest. I hear the breath leave Fisher's lungs. He flies backward, arms flailing, and lands on his backside.

Tomasetti comes down on top of him. Knees spread. Body weight full on. "Facedown!" he roars. "On the ground! Arms behind your back!"

Fisher twists, brings up the length of wood, swings. But Tomasetti grabs the branch, twists it from the other man's hands, and tosses it aside. He grasps Fisher's arm and twists. "Get on your belly!" he shouts.

The other man howls and his body goes still. "Okay! I'm done!" Fisher stretches out his free hand. "I'm down!"

I blink something out of my left eye, swipe at it with my hand, see blood on my glove as I tug handcuffs from the compartment on my equipment belt.

"I got him." I kneel next to Tomasetti, grasp Fisher's wrist, snap open the cuffs.

"You okay, Chief?"

"Yep."

I'm not sure how bad the damage to my face is, but it hurts. I can feel the blood dripping down my temple. I don't let myself think about it as I snap the cuffs into place. Fisher puts up a token struggle, more residual adrenaline than actual fight, but I crank the bracelets down tight.

When the cuffs are in place, I rise and we haul Fisher to his feet. For the span of a full minute, the only sound comes from the three of us huffing and puffing.

"Why the hell did you run?" Tomasetti asks.

"You fuckers planted that shit." Fisher shakes his head and looks down at the ground. "That bitch, Burkholder, threatened me. Said she was going to get me."

I sense Tomasetti's eyes on me, but I don't look at him. After a moment, he runs his hands over the other man's jeans and shirt, checking for weapons, turning his pockets inside out. "You got any weapons on you?" he asks.

"I got nothing," Fisher mutters.

Frowning, Tomasetti finishes patting him down. "He's clean."

T.J. bursts from the trees, slows upon spotting us. His expression relaxes as he takes in the scene. "Everyone okay?"

"We're fine."

He's breathing hard, but not as labored as the rest of us, and it makes me feel a little . . . old. He raises a gloved hand and opens it. "Found this thirty yards back."

I go to him, look down at what appears to be a wad of cellophane. On closer inspection, I discern the white powder and rocks inside.

I look at Fisher. "What is it?"

He grimaces. "That ain't mine."

"In light of the bolts we found in your garage"—I send a pointed look at the wad of cellophane—"you realize whatever's in the bag is the least of your problems, don't you?"

"Not to mention slugging the chief of police," Tomasetti puts in.

Fisher meets my gaze. His face is sweaty and red, his hair sticking to his forehead. "Those bolts are not mine. I have no idea where they came from or who put them there. But they do not belong to me."

"How did they end up taped to the back of your toolbox in your garage?" I ask.

"I don't know. The only thing I can figure is someone put them there."

"Like who?"

"Like you," he snarls. "I guess you found a way to make good on those threats, huh?"

"You're under arrest," I tell him.

"What for?" he cries. "I told you. Those bolts aren't mine."

"So you say." I nod at T.J., who has a "cage" in the back seat of his cruiser. "You want to transport him?"

"My pleasure, Chief." He crosses to me, hands

330

me the bag of dope, then grasps Fisher's biceps. "Let's go, dude. Watch your step."

I remove an evidence bag from a compartment on my belt and drop the cellophane inside.

"Probably coke or meth," Tomasetti says. "I've got a field test kit in the Tahoe."

"Thank you."

When they're out of sight, he crosses to me, tugs a handkerchief from his pocket, and hands it to me. "He got you pretty good with that branch."

I take the kerchief, press it against the cut on my browbone, try not to wince. "Please tell me I don't need stitches."

"Butterfly bandage will probably do." He glances over to make sure T.J. is out of sight, then reaches up and brushes his knuckles against my face. "Some ice might help."

I sigh. "I'm not going to have a black eye for our wedding, am I?"

"Maybe." A smile touches his mouth. "But you look good in blue."

It's not exactly a tender moment, but I find myself smiling and for the span of several heartbeats, we smile at each other. I feel that familiar flutter of breathlessness in my chest and despite the dark events of the past week, a burst of pure happiness breaks through. In that moment, I'm not Kate Burkholder the chief of police. I'm Kate Burkholder the woman who is about to marry the man I love.

I look down at the bag in my hand, pull myself back down to earth. "What do you think about Fisher?" I ask.

"I think he's a solid suspect. Those bolts are certainly damning." He shrugs. "Multiple people said he had a thing for Emily Byler."

"Criminals aren't exactly the brightest bulbs in the pack."

"We'll know a lot more after we get him into the interview room."

"Be nice to tie this up," I say.

"Chief of police might just have time to get married." He puts his arm around my waist, and we start toward the hill that will take us back to the gas station.

It's ten P.M. and I'm sitting in a windowless interview room at the Holmes County Sheriff's Department, trying not to acknowledge the headache pounding my skull. The scuffed-up table in front of me is secured to the floor with bolts and surrounded with four plastic chairs. Next to me, Tomasetti leans back in his chair, scrolling through his phone. Sheriff Mike Rasmussen manspreads in the corner, studying a page of his leather-bound notebook. The only sound comes from the buzz of the light overhead. A video camera watches us from the ceiling.

"CSU did a presumptive Hexagon OBTI test on both bolts." Tomasetti doesn't look up from his phone as he speaks. "Both tested positive for human blood."

My mind jumps to the next logical question. "Was there enough residue to extract DNA?"

"Bolts were sent to the lab," he says. "DNA will probably take a week or so, depending on how backed up the lab is. I'll jam it through if I can."

"Gonna match," Rasmussen predicts.

"I sent a photo of the broadhead to Doc Coblentz earlier," I tell them. "Preliminarily, he believes the incised wounds on Karn's body could be from those bolts." I consider a moment and add, "I'm no expert, but even a cursory visual comparison of the shape of the broadhead to the wounds looks spot-on. Same number of points. Size seems about right."

"Forensic pathologist should be able to confirm," Tomasetti adds. "We might be able to get that as early as tomorrow."

I look at Tomasetti. "Did you guys process the scene?"

"Just finished up. Sent several items to the lab." He swipes left. "Box cutter. Duct tape. Bedsheets from the back room."

I think about Paige Rossberger. "Plastic sheeting?"

He nods. "There was a partial roll in a storage closet. We may or may not be able to match it."

"Maybe we can match the details of the cut," I say.

"We should know in the next day or so."

A sharp rap sounds on the door a moment before it swings open. A Holmes County sheriff's deputy escorts Vernon Fisher into the interview room. His hands are cuffed behind his back. He's clad in wrinkled blue coveralls and thong sandals, and his usual cockiness has given way to a downcast persona. The smirk has been replaced with a morose expression that tells me he knows he's in serious trouble. From where I'm sitting, I can smell the stink of nervous sweat.

I make eye contact him and motion to the chair across from me. "How's your evening going so far, Vernon?"

He gives me a withering look. I try not to smile, but I'm not sure if I succeeded.

The deputy fishes a key from his utility belt, unlocks one cuff, and motions Fisher into the chair. When he obliges, the deputy secures the cuff to a security ring in the center of the table, cranks it down tight, and leaves the room.

Fisher eyes the three of us, his gaze reflecting a combination of resentment and despair.

"Do you know why you're here?" I ask.

He shifts his stare to mine. "The only thing I know is that you got the wrong guy and you're going to try to hang me for something I didn't do."

"This is your chance to set us straight." I reach into my pocket and pull out the card containing the Miranda rights and I read them to him. "Do you understand your rights?"

"I understand all that just fine. All's I got to say to you is this: I've never seen those bolts before in my life."

Taking my time, hoping he doesn't ask for an attorney because that would instantly shut down all questioning, I glance down at my notes. "Vernon, I need you to tell me how those two bolts got taped to the toolbox."

"I have absolutely no idea."

"Do the bolts belong to you?"

"No. I don't use broadheads. Never have. Never will."

"Do you own a crossbow?"

He hesitates, looks around as if seeking a window or door through which to escape. "Look, I got an old combination bow."

"When I asked you before if you owned a crossbow," I say, "you said you didn't."

"I know it looks bad, but I figured you didn't *need* to know because it wasn't an issue. I hadn't done anything wrong. I wasn't anywhere near where Karn got killed." Grimacing, he looks down at the tabletop. "I know you don't believe me, but I swear to God those bolts are not mine."

It's not the first time I've heard an impassioned denial; to be honest, it's not the tenth or even the hundredth time. Every criminal who's been

335

arrested for a crime lies about it. I know that's cynical, but it's true.

"Tell me about the crossbow," I say.

"I haven't used it for years. Not since I went deer hunting with my cousin. Didn't even get a deer that year."

"Where's the crossbow now?" I ask.

"I think it's at my parents' house. Covered with dust. My *mamm* didn't want it in the house so she gave it to Datt and he put it in the barn."

Tomasetti sighs. "Did you murder Aden Karn?" He asks, the bad cop, asking the big question.

Fisher straightens, moving his legs and arms as if gripped by a sudden restlessness. The cuff jangles against the table ring. "No."

"Where were you the morning he was killed?" I ask.

"I told you. I was in bed. Asleep."

"With Leandra," Tomasetti mutters.

Fisher burns him with a glare. "I was there, damn it."

I take him through a dozen questions that have already been asked, sticking to friendly territory, loosening him up. He fires off the same answers. No hesitation. His demeanor indignant and resolute.

"You and Karn were arguing about the truck you bought from him."

"I was in the right," he says. "After Karn was

killed, Wayne made good on it and gave me back my six hundred bucks. Ask him."

"Did you ever threaten to kill Karn?" I ask.

He startles, rattling the cuff again. "That's a bullshit question."

"Set me straight," I say.

"It was a figure of speech, for chrissake! I was pissed! I mean, about the stupid truck. He ripped me off. You can't hold that against me."

"So answer the question," I say. "Did you threaten to kill him?"

"Yes, but I didn't mean it literally!"

I make a note in my pad, flip the page. "Tell me about your relationship with Emily Byler."

An emotion I can't quite pinpoint flashes, but he tucks it away quickly. "I don't have a relationship with her. I barely know her."

"That's not what I heard."

"You heard wrong."

"Have you ever had sex with her?"

He shifts in the chair. "Not that I recall." He has the gall to stutter.

"Are you saying it's possible you did, indeed, have sex with her and you don't remember? Is that what you're telling me?"

He shifts in the chair. "I'm just saying . . . things get kind of crazy out at the gas station sometimes. I mean, everyone's partying. There's a lot of drinking. People get wild, but no one gets hurt."

Only they do. "You had a thing for Emily."

"No, I didn't."

"You were attracted to her."

"No."

"Were you jealous of her relationship with Aden Karn?"

"No."

I flick my pen against the notepad. "So far, you've lied to me about the crossbow. You lied to me about the bolts. You lied to me about threatening Karn. I think you're lying to me about Emily Byler, too."

"She belonged to Aden." Quickly, he clarifies the statement. "I mean, she was his girl."

"That didn't matter when you were drunk, though, did it? When Aden was drunk?"

He looks at me as if he can't believe I'd say such a thing. Wondering how I know . . .

"No."

"You were obsessed with her. And when you saw them together, you were jealous. Aden was the only thing standing in the way of your having her."

"That's not true!"

"That's why you pumped her full of alcohol. Why you got Aden drunk. That's why you let things get out of control. So you could have what you wanted."

I'm aware of Mike Rasmussen staring at me. Not sure what I'm doing or where I'm going with

338

this. He's wondering how I know what I know. How I'm going to make the connection between Emily Byler and the murder of Aden Karn.

"That has nothing to do with what happened to Aden." He hisses the words between clenched teeth.

"You raped his girlfriend," I say. "How does that not involve Aden?"

I see his teeth grind an instant before he lunges. His chair flies back. The cuff yanks against the security ring. He punches at me with his free hand. I lurch backward, dodge what would have been a nasty blow.

"Hey!" Rasmussen jumps to his feet.

Tomasetti is already around the table. He grasps Fisher's free hand, twists his arm, brings it up behind his back. "Sit the hell down."

The sheriff uprights the chair, jams it beneath Fisher. Tomasetti shoves him into it.

"That's bullshit!" Fisher roars. "Yeah, we got a little crazy a couple of times. She was into it. I'm telling you, she didn't do anything she didn't want—" He bites off the sentence as if realizing he's already said too much.

"Was Paige Rossberger into it?" I ask.

"I don't know her!"

"Was she into it when you put your hands around her throat and squeezed?" I snap. "Was she into it when you put that bag over her head and cut off her air?"

"I never met her. I swear."

"DNA never lies," I tell him.

Breathing hard, Fisher looks at Rasmussen and Tomasetti as if expecting them to come to his rescue. "You're trying to pin a bunch of shit on me that I know nothing about!"

I look at Tomasetti. "We've got a lot to work with here, don't we?"

"District attorney is going to have a field day," he returns.

"It's really too bad Leandra can't alibi him," I say.

Fisher looks at us as if he can't believe what we're saying. "I did not murder Karn!" he shouts. "I don't care what that bitch told you! She's fuckin' lying!"

The door swings open. A deputy steps in, his eyes scanning the room. "Everything okay?"

"Get me out of here!" Fisher cries. "I want my lawyer."

CHAPTER 26

It's late when Tomasetti and I arrive home. I'm standing at the kitchen counter, pouring rye into tumblers, when he comes through the door. I glance over my shoulder as he hangs his jacket on the coatrack. Then he's behind me, his arms around me, and I feel his mouth against my neck.

"You hate rye," he whispers.

"After today, I think I may have developed a taste for it."

"I guess the good news is, we may just have our guy."

I turn to him, put one of the tumblers into his hand.

He takes it, sips, looks at me over the rim, and gives me a half frown. "How about if I re-butterfly that cut for you?"

I sip, resist the urge to shiver as the rye burns its way down my throat. "Midnight snack first?"

"Back in the old days we would have forgone the food—"

"And the bandage—"

"And just finished the damn bottle of rye," he says.

"And solved the case in the process." I smile, but I'm only half kidding.

Neither of us had time to eat earlier, so we take

a few minutes to put together a plate of cheese, crackers, and grapes. Tomasetti fills two glasses with ice water, and we meet at the kitchen table.

We clink our tumblers together and for a few minutes concentrate on the food. But I sense our thoughts zinging. Tomasetti never hesitates to speak his mind. Tonight, he's contemplative.

"You pushed Fisher pretty hard," he says after a moment.

"He deserved it." I take another sip of rye, thankful for the burn this time, and the pleasant buzz pressing into my brain.

His gaze latches on to mine. "You don't think he did it."

"I don't like Vernon Fisher. I think he's a rapist and a smug little son of a bitch." I sigh. "Tomasetti, I don't think he murdered Aden Karn or Paige Rossberger."

"Do you have someone else in mind?"

"I wish I did."

He considers a moment. "The crossbow bolts are pretty damning, especially if they contain Karn's DNA."

"I know. And I can't ignore that. I won't. But it would have been incredibly stupid for Fisher to hide those bolts at his residence when he could have shot them into the woods, burned them, or even buried them."

"You think someone planted them?"

"All I'm saying is that this was way too easy."

342

I look down at my tumbler of rye, think about refilling it. "That's not to mention the fact that all of this came to fruition on the basis of an anonymous tip."

His gaze sharpens on mine. "Any chance you can get any info on the caller?"

"Our phone system isn't exactly cutting-edge. Believe it or not, that might work to our advantage in this case. We might be able to ascertain where the call originated. Margaret is working on it. Even then, the information may or may not be helpful."

"I don't have to tell you Rasmussen wants to run with Fisher."

"Considering the amount of evidence against him, and everything we know about him, I think we should." I wrap my hands around the glass, twirl the amber liquid inside. "But I don't think we should close the investigation just yet. Does that make me crazy?"

"Crazy like a fox, maybe. There's something to be said for a cop following her gut."

"That's kind of noncommittal," I say. "You're not a noncommittal kind of guy."

"I like Fisher for this, Kate."

"Do you think he murdered Paige Rossberger?"

He considers a moment. "You have all those young males out there, drinking every night, probably doing drugs, looking for trouble. According to Emily Byler, things get out of

343

control on a regular basis. So one night, one of them calls a hooker. She shows up. There's a disagreement. An argument ensues. Things get physical." He grimaces. "It wouldn't be the first time a woman in a vulnerable position paid the price."

"I think someone planted those bolts. Someone not opposed to seeing Fisher fry."

"Then you should follow your gut. Fisher is in custody; he's not going anywhere. I sure as hell don't have any sympathy for the guy."

"It just feels a little too . . . tidy." I reach for the bottle of rye and splash another two fingers into my glass. "I hope I'm wrong. I'm pretty good at that sometimes."

Setting down his tumbler, Tomasetti takes both of my hands in his, waits until I look at him. "You've got good instincts, Kate. Follow them. Look at every piece. Shake it up. Mix it up. Turn it inside out. Do what you need to do because if you're not one hundred percent convinced we've got the right guy, it's going to eat at you."

"I guess you know me pretty well."

"Just between us, I *like* you pretty well, too." Rising, he pulls me to my feet.

I smile at him and for an instant I feel like a fool because my vision blurs with tears. "You don't agree with me and yet you're telling me to pursue what I believe is right."

"That sort of goes with the I-like-you part."

I go to him, fall against him, put my arms around his shoulders. "I don't make it easy, do I?"

"Well . . ."

Playfully, I punch his shoulder. "In three days, we'll be married."

"You're not getting cold feet again, are you?"

"Not a chance." I lay my head against his shoulder, loving the feel of him, the smell of him, the warmth of his body against mine. The knowledge that we are one.

"You don't think we're going to screw this up, do you?" I whisper.

"We got this," he says. "Piece of cake."

It's difficult to focus on life—even momentous once-in-a-lifetime events—when someone else's life has been taken. But for the living, life goes on. I spent the night caught in a fitful slumber, trying to reconcile my misgivings about the arrest of Vernon Fisher. First thing this morning, the BCI lab confirmed that the duct tape found at Fisher's residence was from the same roll of tape used to bind Paige Rossberger's body. By all appearances, Fisher murdered her during a night of sex and drugs. Whether someone else was involved remains to be determined.

When it comes to the motive for Karn's murder, I can only speculate. Once Fisher crossed the indelible line into homicide, did a switch flip in his head? Did anger over the truck and his obsession with Emily Byler send him to Hansbarger Road, where he ended the life of the man standing in the way of everything he wanted?

There's no doubt Fisher is a viable suspect. He had motive, means, and opportunity. We have indisputable circumstantial and physical evidence against him. The duct tape. The crossbow bolts found at his residence. In the coming days, the lab will likely link the DNA inside Page Rossberger's body to Fisher, proving he either raped her or had sexual relations with her. All of it combined is a virtual arsenal of evidence any prosecutor would give his right arm for.

So why do I feel as if we got it all wrong?

"Because you're getting married in two days and you're a nervous wreck," I mutter as I make the turn into the lane of my brother's farm.

Thoughts of the case melt into the background as I enter the world of my youth. Memories press into me, old friends who haven't always been fair or easy to like. Thoughts of my childhood recur, deep enough to hurt, and not for the first time I'm swept away by a sense of nostalgia. The remembrance of what it was like to be an Amish girl, innocent and carefree. The knowledge that I was part of something larger than me. That my family would always be the foundation of my world. Back then, I was comforted by the parameters set forth by the community. I didn't see those rules as something to be fought against, but to be followed without question.

The leaves of the apple trees in the orchard flutter like burnished copper. The maple tree in the side yard—the one I helped my *datt* plant—ushers me to my childhood home as I make the final turn and curve around to the back of the house. Though it's barely nine A.M., four buggies are parked in the gravel area adjacent to the chicken coop. I recognize one of the buggies as belonging to my sister, and only then does it strike me that the Amish are already preparing for the wedding. *My wedding.*

Holy cow.

A hard blow of anxiety punches me in the chest, and I can't help but wonder: How did this day arrive so quickly? It's a silly musing, of course. Our wedding has been planned and delayed for over a year now. How is it that I feel so . . . unprepared?

My sister, Sarah, has left several phone messages for me in the last week—from the Amish phone shanty, of course. I've been so tied up in the case, I didn't make time to stop by the house to see her. This morning, with the case winding down, I'm scrambling to remedy my inattentiveness.

I park behind a buggy and start toward the farmhouse at a brisk clip. I'm midway there when the back door swings open. My brother, Jacob, and another Amish man I don't recognize wrestle a long wooden bench through the door, shoes scuffing the concrete, the backrest scraping the jamb.

"I've got the door." I rush up the steps to the porch and hold it open while they struggle through. "*Guder mariye*," I say. Good morning.

Both men wear blue work shirts, suspenders, and straw summer hats. Jacob makes eye contact with me as he passes. His face is ruddy with exertion and shiny with sweat. "*Nau es is veyich zeit.*" Now it's about time. But he softens the words with a grin.

I smile back.

The other man is older, with a long salt-and-pepper beard, his smile revealing two missing eyeteeth. "*Die broodah is die faasnacht kummt hinnerno*," he says between grunts. Your brother is slow as molasses in January.

Jacob grumbles a good-natured response and they continue toward the barn. I stand there a moment and watch until they disappear inside, and I realize they're adding seating to the barn for the ceremony. Preparations for which I've been AWOL and they started without me. Ignoring the flutter of unease in my gut, I go through the door. I hear the women before I see them. The chatter of female conversation in *Deitsch*. A murmured joke. The occasional laugh. The rattle and tap of

348

kitchen work executed by deft, capable hands.

The kitchen is a study in controlled chaos. My sister-in-law, Irene, stands at the counter, rolling dough quickly and efficiently, her back straightening and bending as she works. My sister, Sarah, stands next to her, pressing dough into a glass pie pan. A few feet away, a woman I went to school with slices apples with a paring knife. A large older woman mans the counter, peeling McIntosh apples at high speed.

"If you didn't talk so much," she drawls in *Deitsch*, "you might just get those apples sliced before they turn brown."

The good-natured scolding is followed by a chorus of laughter.

I'm so dumbfounded by this early show of support that for a moment I can't find my voice. Instead, I stand in the doorway, taking in the scene, trying to figure out exactly how I fit into it.

A dozen boxes of mason jars are stacked against the wall. A bushel basket of apples sits on the floor at the feet of the woman peeling. Another bushel basket of celery has been shoved against the cabinet.

Amish weddings are a huge affair, as social as they are religious and steeped in tradition. Even in a town as small as Painters Mill, most weddings are attended by three or four hundred. Growing up, I attended dozens. As a girl, it was all about the pie and volleyball and playing with my peers. As I grew older, I was awed by the mystery and wonder of what it meant. Later, as a teen, I felt certain that part of being Amish would never be for me.

Of course, my wedding will be a far cry from a typical Amish wedding. There will be no service beforehand; Bishop Troyer will not perform the ceremony. Some Amish will not attend, simply because I'm not a member of the church and they don't consider me part of the community. But I know that just as many Amish will come. They'll help with preparations, the men moving furniture and clearing the house for what will likely be a hundred or more attendees. The women will deal with the details and preparing food.

"Katie!"

I startle at the sound of my sister's voice. I look up to see Sarah looking at me over her shoulder, her hands busy with the dough. And then all eyes are upon me, and suddenly I feel excruciatingly self-conscious and out of place. I'm in uniform this morning, my .38 strapped to my hip, and it's never been so glaringly obvious that I'm not part of this. I'm not one of them.

"You're busy," I say, and immediately wish I could take the words back.

Sarah tilts her head. "We're making pies is all. Apple."

"We might have those pies before the wedding if Anna could slice a little faster," says the older woman.

One of the women snickers. Another coughs into a kerchief. I'm pretty sure I hear a chuckle from the woman slicing the apples.

"Can I help?" I barely recognize my own voice and clear my throat. "I'm a pretty good slicer."

"We got this, Katie," says Sarah.

"*Sitz dich anne un bleib e weil.*" Irene, my sister-in-law, wipes her hands on her apron and pulls out a chair. You just sit yourself down and stay awhile.

Before I can comply, she crosses to me and takes my hand, guides me to the chair. "This is Lovina," she says, motioning to the large woman. "And you remember Anna." She motions with her eyes to the woman slicing apples. "They're here to help with the food."

"Sarah's been doing most of the work," Irene says.

"Got the chickens and celery lined up a while back," Naomi puts in.

"Don't forget all those mason jars," Anna adds.

"Pies'll be finished today," Irene says breezily.

It occurs to me that the wedding is the day after tomorrow and I feel that beast of panic gallop through me.

Giving a final finger-press to the dough, Sarah wipes her hands on a towel and grins at me. "I don't believe I've ever seen Katie Burkholder without something to say."

"Ain't that the truth." Chuckling, Irene goes to the gas-powered fridge and pulls out a plastic pitcher of what looks like tea. She snags a glass out of the cabinet, pours, and places it in front of me. "Got some mint in it. Good for a nervous stomach."

I see the mouths of the other two women twitch as I sink into the chair. Only then do I realize my legs are weak.

Sarah pours tea for herself, too, snags a lined pad of paper from the counter, and brings both to the table. "Your dress is all ready, by the way. You can take it with you if you'd like."

"Thank you," I tell her. "I will."

"If you have a few minutes, I wanted to talk to you about food."

"I'm sorry I haven't been in touch," I say. "I've been tied up with the case . . ."

Waving off my concerns, Sarah falls into the chair with a sigh, as if she's been on her feet too long. "Well, you got that awful killing solved. Everyone's been talking about it. Praying, too. For all of them."

"I wasn't the least bit surprised when that Fisher boy didn't join the church," Anna says.

"Been trouble since he was two years old," Naomi adds.

"His *mamm* is just beside herself," Irene tells

me. "She's over in Berlin, you know. We're going to take a casserole to the family after the wedding."

Using an old-fashioned No. 2 pencil, Sarah scribbles on the pad; then her eyes find mine. "We've got roast chicken with bread stuffing, mashed potatoes, gravy, and creamed celery. Pies for dessert, of course. Apple and cherry." She offers a knowing smile. "Apples are from our own orchard."

"I think that's perfect," I say.

"We're going to hold the ceremony in the barn. That's where we put everyone when we have worship here. More room, you know. Cooler there, too, since we'll be baking."

"Of course."

"The eck table is in the living room. Jacob and William will bring a couple of extra tables down from upstairs, too." The eck table is where the bride and groom sit for their meal with their "side sitters," or bridesmaids and groomsmen, in this case my siblings and their spouses.

She motions toward the box of canning jars on the floor. "We'll set up tables for eating in the yard. Plain white tablecloths. And mason jars with celery stalks for the centerpieces. Oh, I almost forgot, Ella Mae Miller is going to make one of her cakes."

The sound of my sister's voice, the background conversation, the clang of dishes, fades to babel.

I stare across the table at her, remembering how close we'd once been, wishing we could somehow break down the barriers between us and get it back, and for the first time since I left Painters Mill when I was eighteen years old, I feel as if that one small wish is possible.

I rise so quickly, my chair screeches against the floor. Vaguely, I'm aware of the room going silent. The clang of cookware and dishes quieting. I feel all eyes on me. Without looking at anyone, I leave the kitchen and walk into the living room. The eck table is in the corner. The only adornment is a mason jar with a few stalks of celery, the leaves still intact and tucked into the jar as if someone put it there just to see how it might look.

A surge of emotion seesaws in my chest. I close my eyes against tears, silently curse myself for letting them encroach. Needing something to do, I go to the table, pick up the mason jar, set it down. Lowering my head, I set my hands on the table and lean, feel those first dangerous tears squeeze between my lashes.

"Katie?"

My sister's tentative voice sounds behind me. Knowing I'm busted, that I won't be able to conceal or stop what I don't want her to see, I raise my head, swipe at the tears, and then I turn to face her.

"You're all right?" she asks, her voice gentle.

I see concern in her eyes. A tinge of confusion.

"I'm fine." I choke out a laugh because it's a lie and we both know it. I take another swipe at the tears.

"You're not happy with what we've done?" She offers a smile. "We can change it. However you'd like. The food. The table—"

"It's not that," I cut in. "It's . . ." Stupidly, I let the sentence dangle. Because I'm not sure how to finish. I'm not sure I can.

"You're nervous, no?"

Now it's my turn to laugh. "Sarah, I've been living with him for two years."

"Oh . . . well." She drops her gaze, then raises her eyes back to mine. "Then what?"

"It's . . . this," I stammer, motion toward the table, the kitchen doorway where the women have gone silent. "I'm . . . overwhelmed. I didn't expect any of this. And I'm thankful."

She blinks. "Oh."

"I didn't expect to . . . feel so much."

"Good feelings, though, no?"

I nod. "I haven't been Amish for almost twenty years. I haven't been much of a sister or sister-in-law. I'm not sure I deserve everything you've done. And yet here you are. All of you. Putting together a wedding not everyone approves of or even cares about. It means something."

"Well." Crossing to me, she takes my hand in hers and smiles. "You know how the Amish are when it comes to weddings. Give us a reason to socialize and eat, and we're all over it." She pats my hand. "Now, come on into the kitchen, finish your iced tea, and let me finish those pies. We've got celery next and I think that's going to take all afternoon."

CHAPTER 27

It's after five P.M. and I'm in my cubbyhole office at the station, making a final run through the myriad paperwork, reports, photos, and videos from the Karn and Rossberger murders. Earlier this afternoon, Sheriff Rasmussen referred both cases to the Holmes County prosecutor, who will likely charge Vernon Fisher with two counts of aggravated murder. I should be pleased; Fisher is behind bars. If convicted by a jury of his peers, he'll be off the street the rest of his life.

Despite the little voice inside my head telling me I did my job, that I should chalk one up for the good guys, let it go, and get married, the case sits in the pit of my stomach like a rock.

I should have left for home hours ago. I have a thousand things to do before the wedding. And yet here I sit feeling out of sorts because I'm about to walk away from two cases that feel unfinished and . . . *wrong*.

"Chief?"

I glance up to see my second-shift dispatcher, Jodie, standing at the doorway of my office. "I've got Doc Coblentz on line two. Are you still here?"

"Always here for the doc." I punch the blinking light on my desk phone. "Hey, Doc."

"I figured you'd be gone by now," he begins. "Don't you have a wedding to get to?"

"Day after tomorrow," I tell him. "What's up?"

"I wanted to let you know, I heard back from the forensic pathologist at the BCI lab."

I'm in the process of shutting down my laptop, folding the top down, giving him only part of my attention. "DNA?"

"That's forthcoming." He pauses. "Remember me telling you about the oily substance we found in and around both incised wounds on Aden Karn's body?"

"I do." I stop what I'm doing and give him my full attention. "I've since learned that some hunters and archery enthusiasts use wax or oil on their bolts in the theory that it improves the accuracy and increases the speed of the bolt as it travels."

"I'm sure that's true. And frankly, Kate, I'm not sure any of what I'm about to tell you is important in terms of the case, but I wanted you to know the lab work revealed some interesting details about this particular substance."

"How so?"

"Well, it's not the type of wax or oil that's normally used for an archery-related bolt. The substance is, in fact, a mix of water, glycerin, propylene glycol, cellulose gum, tetrahydroxy-propyl—"

"Doc, my eyes are glazing over. What is that?"

"It's an intimate lubricant."

I'm no prude, but I'm so dumbstruck that for a moment I'm not sure how to respond. "You mean for sex?"

"Exactly. Water based. Safe for latex and polyurethane condoms."

"Seems like an unusual ingredient to use for a crossbow bolt." Even as I say the words something sparks in the back of my mind.

"I've no idea if it's relevant in any way," he tells me, "but I thought you should know. I'll put it in the final report."

"I appreciate the phone call." I'm about to hang up when he speaks.

"Chief?"

"Doc?"

A brief hesitation and then, "See you at the wedding."

My heart jigs in my chest and I feel a big, dumb smile spread across my face. "See you there."

I'm still smiling when I hang up and turn back to the file. Even as I begin to page through—*just one more time*—the doc's words play in the backwaters of my mind.

. . . intimate lubricant.

Water based.

Safe for latex and polyurethane condoms.

At some point in the course of this investigation, I happened upon "personal lubricant." I've seen it or heard someone talking about it. But where?

The questions scratch at the back of my brain as I page through the file. Dozens of reports and forms I've seen a hundred times before stare back at me. I open the subfolder containing the photos. The crime scene. Autopsy photos. Aden Karn's body. The final photo I come to is the one I took of the box in Karn's bedroom closet. Inside, I see the sex toys—and a tube of intimate lubricant. A ting sounds as my brain makes the connection. At the time, I'd considered it a personal item with no connection to the case. Now, I'm not so sure.

Personal lubricant is not such an unusual item to have. Human beings are sexual creatures. But for the very same substance to be found on a murder victim and the two bolts that killed him is too much of a coincidence. I think about Karn's relationship with Fisher, and I try to imagine how Fisher might've gotten his hands on that tube. Even if he did, how did it get back to Karn's bedroom closet?

Likely, some of the young men who spent time at the gas station brought women there and engaged in sex. I think about Emily Byler and Paige Rossberger and I realize there were probably a slew of other women whose names I'll never know. That's not to mention the sex doll. Did Karn take his box of sex toys and lubricant to the gas station for a night of sex? Did the tube of lubricant get passed around? Did Fisher find it, realize it would make a decent wax for his bolts, and take it? But if that's the case, how did the tube find its way back to the box in Karn's closet? The questions take me full circle.

Of course, there could be *two* containers of personal lubricant floating around. But when we searched the gas station, no one mentioned finding lubricant. Not that my officers were specifically *looking* for it. Regardless, it's probably a good idea to obtain another search warrant for the gas station and have another look. While I'm dotting my i's and crossing my t's, I should probably swing by Karn's former residence and pick up the tube in the box, if only to check for fingerprints.

"Jodie?" I call out.

The dispatcher comes to my office door. "Yeah, Chief?"

"Who's on duty this evening?"

"Mona."

"Give her a call and ask her to meet me over at Wayne Graber's place, will you?"

"Right now?"

"Yep."

Jodie shows at the doorway of my office, looking worried. "I hope I'm not overstepping, Chief, but aren't you supposed to go home? I mean, you're getting married . . . aren't you?"

I smile. "Just a quick stop on my way home. Tell Mona it'll only take a few minutes."

"Roger that." She swipes her forehead with drama, feigning relief. "See you at the wedding, Chief."

I call Rasmussen on my way to Wayne Graber's place and recap my conversation with Doc Coblentz.

"*Sex lube?*" he says. "Seriously?"

"I don't know if it's the same tube. But if Fisher used the lubricant I found in Karn's closet for the bolt that killed Karn, his prints should be on the tube," I say.

"Even if he did use the lube for the bolt, how did that tube end up back in Karn's closet?"

"I don't know, Mike. I haven't worked that out yet." I consider a moment. "Maybe the tube got passed around during a night of sex at the gas station. After Karn was killed, maybe Fisher went into Karn's place and got rid of it, thinking it would never become an issue."

"Why didn't he just throw it away?" Rasmussen sighs. "Look, Kate, I know you're not completely on board with Fisher, but—"

"If we find his prints on that tube, Mike, I'm in." I pause. "Will you do me a favor?"

"Since you're about to get married . . ."

I smile. "Will you send a deputy out to the gas station to see if there's a tube of personal lubricant there perchance? Make sure we're okay on the date of the warrant."

"You got it." He clears his throat. "I'll see you at the wedding."

The late-afternoon sun shimmers like gold dust on the field corn as I make the turn into the driveway of the house where Karn had lived. Wayne Graber's muscle car is parked just off the garage portico. Mona's vehicle is nowhere in sight, telling me she hasn't yet arrived.

I bend my head to my lapel mike as I exit the Explorer. "Ten-twenty-three," I say, letting Jodie know I've arrived on scene.

"Roger that, Chief."

"Mona," I say, "what's your ETA?"

"I'm on Hogpath heading your way," she tells me. "ETA eight minutes."

"Copy that." I enter the garage portico, go directly to the door, and knock. A black cat slinks around the side of a garbage can and rubs against my leg. I'm kneeling to pet the cat when the door swings open. I look up to see Wayne Graber standing at the door, looking at me.

"I see Kitty Bell has you charmed," he says by way of greeting.

I straighten. "She's friendly."

"Especially if she thinks you're going to feed her." He bends to the cat, picks it up, and rubs its scruff. "Hey, girl." He's still wearing his work clothes. Flannel shirt and trousers. Scuffed boots. Budweiser in hand. Cap pulled over his hair.

"I heard about Vernon Fisher," he says. "Can't hardly believe it."

"He'll be formally arraigned tomorrow."

"I guess you never really know about people, huh?"

"Sometimes."

He pushes his cap up. "Can I help you with something?"

"I'm following up on some information I received from the coroner's office," I tell him, keeping the purpose of my visit vague. "I'd like to take another look at Aden's bedroom if that's all right with you."

"What are you looking for?"

"There was a box," I say. "In his closet. It'll just take me a minute."

"Uh . . ." He looks down at the cat, uses two fingers to rub the back of its neck.

When he makes no move to invite me inside, I add, "I can come back with a warrant if you prefer," I say. "No problem."

"No sense in you going to all that trouble. I ain't even been back there. I guess I've been putting off packing up his stuff for his *mamm* and *datt*." Holding the cat in one arm, he pushes the door open and goes inside. "Come on in. Take whatever you need. I'll just stay out of your way."

I follow him into the living room. The TV is tuned to a 1990s sitcom. A fast-food burger and fries sit atop an old-fashioned TV tray. "Sorry to interrupt your dinner," I tell him as I start toward the hall. "I won't be long."

"No problem." He stops in the middle of the living room. "Chief Burkholder?"

I turn to him and raise my brows.

"I just wanted to say . . ." He fumbles the words and, looking ungainly, shoves his hands into his pockets. "I knew Vernon was an asshole, but I never . . . I never thought he was capable of killing anyone."

I stare at him a moment, taking in the awkwardness, the lack of eye contact and I nod. "I think a lot of people were surprised. That's how it goes sometimes."

He looks at the TV and doesn't say anything else, so I continue down the hall, my mind already on the box in the closet. Wondering how I'm going to reach the top shelf. In the back of my mind, I'm pondering whether it's even worth confiscating at this point.

I push open the door to Karn's bedroom. The lighting is dim, so I flick the light switch, but it doesn't come on. I go to the window, open the curtain. A glance outside tells me Mona hasn't yet arrived. Vaguely, I'm aware of the TV in the living room. The laugh track and voices. I cross to the closet, open the door. There's no stool or chair to step on, so I lift a wire hanger from the rod, bend it, and use it to slide the box toward me.

"Come on," I mutter beneath my breath.

The box comes into view. I'm reaching for it when the scuff of a shoe against the floor spins me around. I catch a glimpse of Graber. Lips peeled back. Teeth exposed and clenched. Fist drawn back. I raise my hands, duck right, but I'm not fast enough. His fist plows into my nose. I fly backward, hit the wall, land on my butt.

I twist, reach for my .38, thumb off the strap. Before I can yank the gun from its holster, a second blow lands at the crown of my head. A pile driver pounding a post home. Stars scatter in front of my eyes. Graber lunges at me. I'm on the floor, my back against the wall. A split second to react. I bring up both legs, slam my feet against his knees, try to hyperextend them.

He roars a curse, stumbles back. I draw the .38, bring it up. My position is awkward; my elbow hits the wall, skewing my aim. "Stop!" I shout. "Police! *Stop!*"

Finger inside the guard. I squeeze off a shot just as he kicks the .38. A bullet tears a hole in the ceiling, but I manage to hold on to my weapon. I scramble right, try to get into a better position, line up for another shot.

"Stop!" I scream.

The blow comes out of nowhere, a train ramming my forehead. My head snaps back. My vision narrows and dims. Hazily, I'm aware of Graber kicking the gun from my hand. I hear it clatter to the floor. Leaning down to me, he rips the radio mike from my lapel, flings it aside.

"Why the fuck did you come back?" he bellows. "Why couldn't you just stay the hell away? Karn is dead. You got Fisher. *Why?*"

I blink, try to clear my head.

He's agitated. Looking out the window. Panic branded into his features. Not sure what to do next. For the first time I notice the shoulder sling, and the crossbow at his side. Deadly and complex looking. A tidal wave of fear washes over me.

"You weren't supposed to come back!" he screams. "We were done! Fuck!"

My vision clears. I stare at him, taking physical inventory. I'm dazed, but not injured. I don't let my gaze slide toward the bed, but I know my .38 is beneath it. In the periphery of my vision, I spot my radio on the floor a few feet away.

"Wayne, you're not a suspect," I say. "Don't do anything stupid."

"This is your fault," he snarls. "What the hell am I supposed to do with you now?"

"Just walk away," I say. "There's still time to fix this."

"Shut up!" Spittle flies from his mouth. "I need to think!"

My mind clicks back into place. I look at him, try to put myself in his shoes. "I know what Karn was," I say.

I see the words impact him. Like an invisible

fist, punching him hard enough to stun. "What did you say?"

"I know he was a sexual predator. I know what he did."

He looks at me, blinking, not quite trusting his eyes, his ears. "Everyone thought he was a saint," he says. "All that boy-next-door charm. Mr. Fucking Perfect. They had no idea what he turned into when he took off the mask."

My eyes have adjusted to the thin light. I can just make out the outline of my pistol beneath the bed. I'm not sure I can reach it from this side. Graber stands between me and the radio.

"I know he hurt people," I say quietly.

"Hurt them?" A horrible laugh pours from his throat. "He didn't just *hurt* them. He . . ." His voice breaks. "The guy was a monster. There was something wrong with him. Some part of his brain was just . . . gone."

Keep him talking, Kate. Buy some time. Mona is on the way.

"Tell me what he did," I say.

"He'd go on the prowl. Pick up a woman in a bar. Or some dumbshit kid who wanted to party. He'd take them out to the gas station. Get them drunk or high or both, and when they were passed out, he . . . Made me sick." He spits the words out as if they're razor blades. "Did Emily that way. Sweet, innocent Em. Can you believe that?"

"You were there?" I ask.

"I took her home that first night. She was . . . in an awful way." He chokes back a sob, swipes at tears. "They all climbed on her at the same time."

"Who else?"

"The sons of bitches at the gas station. It was a game to them. Find a woman. Pump her full of booze. Then they'd take turns with her. They were a bunch of animals."

"What about Paige Rossberger?" I ask.

Graber's expression darkens. "Karn had had her out there before. Gave her a hundred bucks. For sex. She trusted him, I guess." His mouth twists. "She liked to party. So he took her out there. Got her high. Everyone . . . did her. After they left . . ." His voice trails and for a moment he looks as if he might throw up. "She was just . . . lying there, passed out on that old cot, and Karn went over to her and started messing with her. She came to, cussed him out, pissed him off, so he gets this . . . plastic bag and he . . . puts it over her head. She hit him, kicked him, so he fucking tied her up, and he kept putting that bag over her head. *Playing* with her. By then she was . . . going nuts. Scared, you know. So he put tape on her mouth."

Tears creep down his cheeks. This time, he doesn't seem to notice. "I knew he was going to take it too far. I told him to stop. He wouldn't listen. He was like . . . getting off on it. Couldn't stop. And then she started . . . turning blue. She stopped moving . . ."

With half an ear, I listen for Mona's cruiser in the driveway. As he speaks, I let my eyes glide to my pistol. I might be able to jam my arm and shoulder beneath the bed and reach it. Put him down before he can get the crossbow into position . . .

"Karn brought out the devil in people." The timbre of his voice softens, deepens. "He liked it when the others joined in. He tried to get me to . . ." He shakes his head. "If you didn't join in, you watched. If he got inside your head, though . . ." He grimaces. "He could make you want. Make you lust."

He stares at me and in that moment I know he isn't without guilt. He was there, after all. How else could he recount what happened?

Engage him. Keep him talking. . . .

"You stopped him," I say.

"I guess I did."

"Wayne, why didn't you go to the police?"

"They were all against me," he said. "All of them. Fisher. The rest. They said they'd tell the cops *I* was the one who killed her."

"So you took matters into your own hands," I say.

"I knew he wouldn't stop. He liked it too much. I couldn't deal with it. I mean, he was going to take me down with him."

370

His expression changes, as if he's remembering I'm not an ally and he still has to deal with me. He knows he's already crossed the point of no return.

I keep talking. "You knew his routine. You met him out on Hansbarger Road. And you stopped him."

"I'm not going to talk about that."

"He was a killer," I say softly. "You had a reason for what you did."

"I'm not going to jail for it." He jabs his thumb toward the door. "Every one of those guys who had a go at that hooker will walk into that courtroom and tell them I was the one done her. It's their word against mine."

"If you turn state's evidence, the prosecutor will work with you, Wayne. It's not too late to stop this."

"Don't bullshit me." He steps closer and reaches for the crossbow. "I know I'm done. Best I can do now is run. Thanks to you."

A burst of energy courses through me. As he leans over me, I draw back and drive my fist into his crotch. A guttural sound grinds from his throat. Clutching his groin, he goes to one knee. I'm ready and kick him away with my right foot.

He reels sideways. I scramble left, dive toward the space beneath the bed. His hand slams down on my back. His fingers latch on to my waistband. I make a wild grab for the pistol, but he yanks me back. I twist, draw back, punch him in the mouth hard enough to cut my knuckles. His face is red, cheeks suffused with blood and slick with sweat. Mouth open, a string of drool hanging down. Murderous eyes on mine.

"You bitch!"

I twist, scramble to my feet, lurch toward my radio.

Graber lunges at me, makes a grab. I abandon the radio, rush the door, go through. Slam it. No lock. *Shit.* Then I'm down the hall. In the living room. I glance through the window. *Where's Mona?* The pound of feet behind me.

I dart toward the front door, twist the knob, find it locked. Horror flashes at the sight of the double-cylinder dead bolt. I think about throwing myself through the window and running to the Explorer. But I don't know if Graber has my gun. No time to debate.

I pivot right, burst into the kitchen. I lunge to the back door, yank it open. Then I'm across the porch, take the steps in a single leap. I'm in the backyard. Outbuilding to my right. Aboveground pool on my left. Cornfield straight ahead.

"You fucking bitch!"

Graber's voice. A few yards behind me. I tear across the yard. Arms pumping. Boots pounding. I plunge into the cornfield. A blur of yellow stalks. I sprint down the row, cut right, plow across six rows, keep going. I need to

372

circle around, get to the Explorer, my radio and shotgun. Warn Mona that he's armed.

The stalks are six feet tall, making it difficult to see. Leaf blades slash at my face as I run. I look behind me, but there's no sign of Graber. I listen for movement, but the blood racing through my veins roars like a jet engine. I cut over two more rows, go left.

"You know I can outrun you!"

Despite the sweat pouring down my back, gooseflesh rises on my arms. He sounds crazed. Out of control.

I struggle to keep my bearings as I run. Concentrate on putting distance between me and Graber, but at the same time I'm getting farther from the Explorer. My best hope is to loop around and get behind him.

I pour on the speed. Cut over a dozen rows. I stop and listen. A stalk snaps nearby. Graber is in good physical condition. Younger. Faster. He can probably outdistance me. I need my radio. A weapon.

I slow my pace, change direction, start back toward the house and my Explorer. I try to stay silent, listening, but the dry stalks crackle. I cut over two more rows. Break into a jog, keep going. Ahead, I see the chimney of the house. The top of the tree in the yard. Two hundred feet to go. Almost there.

Over the pounding of my heart, I hear the

crunch of tires on gravel. Mona, I realize. Relief courses through me. I quicken my pace, eyes scanning left and right. I'm pretty sure Graber is behind me now. Several rows over. The house is a straight shot, dead ahead.

I sidle between two stalks and stop, listen. No sign of Graber. I look over my shoulder. Adrenaline explodes in my chest at the sight of him, the crossbow leveled at me.

"There you are," he says.

I hear the *toing!* of the bow being fired.

CHAPTER 28

The world stops. A hard punch of terror. A sound escapes me as I spin. Pain slashes my left shoulder. The guitar-string whine of the bolt as it whizzes past. Then I'm running full out. Adrenaline pushing me. Arms outstretched.

"Mona!" I scream. "Graber! He's armed!"

I pray she can hear me.

I plunge to the row on my left. Continue at breakneck speed. I don't have to look to know Graber is reloading. A crossbow isn't as fast as a rifle. But fast enough that I won't be able to put enough distance between us to avoid being shot again.

Out of the corner of my eye, I see blood on my biceps. Pain throbs, but somehow, I don't really feel it. A stalk cracks behind me. No time to look. I dodge left, plunge ahead. Running blind. Too fast. Don't misstep. Don't fall.

"He's armed!" I shout.

I burst from the cornfield, in the backyard, running as fast as I can. I hear Graber behind me. Too close. I zigzag to make myself a more difficult target, but I'm not doing a good job of it. I feel the bull's-eye on my back, like a neon light. Panic an inch away.

The *toing!* of the crossbow sounds. The bolt

whirrs to my left, strikes the house. I veer right. Praying he can't reload before I go around the corner of the house.

"Mona!" I scream. "Wayne Graber! He's armed!"

Toing!

I reach the corner, dodge left. Scant seconds of cover. I fly toward the front of the house, tear around the corner. Mona's cruiser ahead. She's standing near the front door, beneath the portico, eyes on me. Speaking into her radio.

"Graber is armed!" I shout. "Behind me!"

I jam my hand into my pocket, fumble the key fob. Tunnel vision on the Explorer. Shotgun in the rear. Two seconds to reach it.

Toing!

Heat tears into my side. A branding iron against my ribs. Intense pain knocks me sideways. Not going to make it to my vehicle, but Mona is armed. My only hope. I pivot left, enter the portico. She's rushing toward me, hand over her weapon, eyes fixed on a point behind me.

"Crossbow!" I scream. "Shots fired!"

As if in slow motion, I see her draw her .38. I see her mouth moving, but I don't hear her voice. I glance left, see Graber flip out another bolt. His face is a mask of rage. A predator in the throes of a kill.

Mona raises her weapon. "Halt!" she screams. "Stop!"

Toing!

I hear the zing of the bolt fly past. Graber slows, grabs another from his pack.

"He's reloading!" I shout.

Mona has assumed a shooter's stance. Good form. Feet spread. Finger inside the guard. Eyes on her target. In that instant, a thousand years seem to pass.

Frozen, I realize.

A curse flies as I sprint toward her. "Get down!"

I plow into Mona, fling my arms around her hips, shove her backward, toward cover. I take her to the ground. Then I'm on top of her, clamber to my knees. Keenly aware of Graber thirty feet away. No cover between us.

I snatch Mona's .38 from her hands. Fumble it. I bring it up and fire blind. *Bam. Bam. Bam. Bam.*

Graber's legs buckle. He goes down. The cross-bow clatters to the ground next to him. Clutching his abdomen, he yowls like a panicked cat.

I scramble to my feet. Vaguely, I'm aware of Mona doing the same. "Radio," I snap.

"Shots fired!" She chokes out the address. "Shots fired! Ten-thirty-nine!" Lights and siren. "Ten-fifty-two!" Ambulance needed.

Her voice falls away as I approach Graber. He's lying on his back, legs kicking out, heels digging in to gravel. Hands spread over his abdomen, blood seeping between his fingers. I'm aware of sirens in the distance as I kick the crossbow aside. I'm shaking violently, my hands and legs. I see blood on his shirt, more on his thigh. The slow pound of dread in my gut because I didn't want this to happen.

His eyes are open and he's looking at me. Mouth moving, but no words coming.

"Do not move," I hear myself say.

Groaning, he lifts his leg, bending it at the knee, dragging his heel through the gravel. "You fucking . . . shot me."

"Be still." I kneel, pull the handcuffs from my belt. "There's an ambulance on the way."

"Chief?"

I glance over my shoulder to see Mona approach. She's pale and shaking. "You okay?"

"I'm fine." I capture Graber's wrist with one of the cuffs. "Give me a hand."

He groans when we roll him over. I cuff his other hand and leave him on his side.

"Um . . . Chief." Mona motions to my uniform shirt. "You're bleeding like crazy."

The amount of blood on my shirt shocks me. For the first time, I acknowledge the pain streaking down my side, the burn in my arm. "Got me twice, I think." A quiver of uncertainty runs through me even as I say the words.

"Maybe you ought to lie down," she says.

"I'm okay," I say. When she only continues to look at me, her expression worried, I add, "I'm fine."

She tilts her head to her shoulder mike. "Ten-seven-seven on the ten-five-two?" she says, asking for the ETA on the ambulance.

"Two minutes," comes the dispatcher's voice.

"I'm going to get my first aid kit." Jumping to her feet, she jogs to her cruiser and goes to the trunk.

I look down at Graber. He stares back at me, his face pale, chest heaving, a sheen of sweat on his forehead. I'm not sure how many times I fired my weapon or how many times he was hit. A large amount of blood has soaked through his shirt.

"Ambulance is on the way," I tell him.

He raises his head, grimaces, looks around. "I'm not a killer," he rasps.

I say nothing.

"Karn wouldn't have stopped," he whispers. "He would have done it again. Dragged me down with him. I did what I had to do. It was the only way to keep him from hurting anyone else."

"Tell it to the judge," I say.

When I look back down at Graber, his eyes are closed.

It's after one A.M. and I'm sitting in an interview room at the Holmes County Sheriff's Department, trying not to relive the scene at Wayne Graber's place. After the incident, because I was forced to use Mona's weapon, she and I were separated, put

379

into official vehicles, and interviewed first by the chief deputy with the sheriff's office and, later, by an Ohio Bureau of Criminal Investigation special agent. Mona's firearm was appropriated for processing. I made my official statement and for two hours I answered question after question after question. It wasn't until the special agent I was speaking with noticed fresh blood coming through my uniform shirt that he offered to drive me to Pomerene Hospital. I spent a couple of hours in the ER for two bolt injuries. The one on my arm was taken care of with a butterfly bandage. The one that struck my rib required seven stitches to close. Lucky for me, it hit at an angle and bounced off the bone. A fraction of an inch in any direction and I likely would have spent the evening in surgery.

Wayne Graber was transported to Pomerene Hospital with two gunshot wounds. He's listed in critical condition, but is—to my relief— expected to survive. The Holmes County Sheriff's Department will be taking over the investigations into the homicides of Aden Karn and Paige Rossberger. BCI will be conducting the officer-involved critical-incident investigation. Both Mona and I have been placed on paid administrative leave until the investigation is complete.

This isn't the first time I've resorted to the use of a firearm in the course of my job. I'm well versed on the protocol; I know what to expect in the coming days and weeks. That understanding does little to alleviate the emotional weight of having shot someone or the stress of being removed from my position as chief, if only temporarily. Though Graber was a direct threat and likely would have killed me and Mona if I hadn't stopped him, I can't help but wonder if there was another way. If I could have done something differently.

Sheriff Mike Rasmussen sits across from me, his expression grim. An Ohio Bureau of Criminal Investigation special agent sits at the head of the table, fingers pecking on the tablet in front of him. Because of our relationship and upcoming marriage, Tomasetti recused himself from the debriefing and for obvious reasons will not be involved in the case. I haven't spoken to him since this morning, and I have desperately missed his solid presence through all of this.

Mona sits next to me, clutching a pen and staring down at the report form in front of her as if wishing she could take back every word. Despite the fierce expression and the I-got-this persona, she looks anxious, exhausted, and more demoralized than I've ever seen her.

"I think that's about all we're going to accomplish this evening, Chief Burkholder." The special agent looks from me to Mona. "Officer Kurtz."

She hands him the report.

He takes it without thanking her, gathers his papers, tucks all of it into a leather planner, then rises. "I'll be in touch."

Giving a final nod at Rasmussen, he makes his exit.

For the span of a full minute, the only sound comes from the buzz of the light overhead. Looking miserable, Mona pretends to study the tabletop in front of her. I glance down at my cell phone, check for calls, see six from Tomasetti, and I set it down.

Rasmussen gives me a tired smile. "He's out in the hall. In case you're wondering."

Despite the stress of the last hours, I manage to smile back. "I thought he might be."

He clears his throat, looks from me to Mona and back to me. "I think all of us are pretty tapped out. Anything we didn't cover tonight, we can tackle in the morning if that's all right with you."

"Sure."

The sheriff rises, sets his hand on my shoulder, and leaves the room, leaving the door open behind him. Without looking at me, Mona picks up her cell phone, tucks it into its compartment on her belt, and gets to her feet.

I rise, trying not to wince when the stitches pull. "Mona?"

She looks at me and raises her brows.

"You're going to be okay," I tell her.

Unable to hold my stare, she drops her gaze to the tabletop and shakes her head. "I don't see how. I screwed up."

I glance through the door, see Tomasetti standing a few feet away, staring at me. I sweep my gaze to Mona, letting him know I need a few minutes with her, and he nods, understanding.

I close the door, go back to the table, and lower myself back into the chair. "Sit down."

Uncertainty infuses her expression, but she pulls out the chair and sinks into it.

"You want to talk about it?" I ask.

"You mean about the massive elephant sitting in the room with us?" She shakes her head. "I don't think we have a choice."

I wait, watch as she struggles with what she needs to say.

"I froze." She looks down at the tabletop, then forces her gaze back to mine. "I saw Graber coming. I saw the crossbow. I knew what to do. And I just . . . I couldn't. It's like . . . time stopped. For me. I mean, he kept coming. And I couldn't move. Even though I knew he was going to—" She bites off the sentence, chokes out a sound, fights back emotion. *I almost got you killed.*

"And yet here I am," I say.

"No thanks to me."

I haven't yet decided exactly how to handle the situation; I haven't had the chance to think about how to respond. As chief, I have to know she can do her job. It's my responsibility to give her the tools she needs to do it and help her build back her confidence. On a personal level, I want to support her.

"It was a pretty terrifying situation," I tell her. "It happened fast. There was a lot going on. A lot of adrenaline."

"Chief, I froze. After all the training. I should have been able to handle it."

"Maybe," I say. "Maybe you should have been able to perform your duty as a police officer." I feel the sting of the words even as I utter them. Still, I let them hang, like needles sinking into a nerve. "But I think it's also important for you to understand that this afternoon you were faced with the most difficult decision a cop will ever have to make. You had to decide whether to use lethal force. You had two seconds to do it. You were scared. And you don't exactly have a lot of experience under your belt."

"Bottom line is I made the wrong choice. I almost got you killed."

"Mona, I'm not going to deny that you made a mistake. I'm not going to minimize the magnitude of it."

"I feel like the only right thing for me to do is resign." Tears shimmer in her eyes. "Maybe I'm not cut out to be a cop."

"Look, I'm not going to handle you with kid

gloves. You made a mistake today. You're not the first cop to freeze up and you're damn well not the last. It's not the end of your career."

"How can anyone trust me now?" she says. "*I* wouldn't trust me."

I nod, let the statement ride. "When's the last time you slept?" I ask.

"I don't know." Annoyed, she swipes at her eyes. "I don't see what that has to do with—"

"You've been on for twenty-four hours. You're exhausted."

Sighing, she hangs her head.

"All I'm going to say is this isn't the best time for you to be making a major career decision. We're both on administrative leave for a few days. When we're rested and back to work, we'll talk. If you decide you want to stay on as a patrol officer—and I hope you do—let's take a look at your training. Let's put you with another officer for a few weeks. Let's do what we need to do and see how it goes."

She swallows, looking slightly less miserable. "Okay."

"You've been a good cop, Mona. I think you have the potential to be a better cop, and I think you have a bright future with the Painters Mill PD." I set my hand on her shoulder and squeeze gently. "That's all I'm going to say for now. It's been a long day. Let's get some rest and talk about it when we get back to work."

• • •

I find Tomasetti standing in the hall. His eyes sweep over me, then land on mine as I tread slowly toward him. The urge to run to him and throw my arms around his neck is powerful, but there's a deputy nearby, so I settle for the best smile I can manage.

"You know how to give a guy a heart attack, don't you?" he says.

"Someone needs to keep you on your toes."

His gaze drops to the bloodstain on my uniform shirt and he looks away, sighs. "Kate—"

I cut in before he can finish. "I'm okay."

His eyes flick to the door of the interrogation room behind me. "Mona?"

"She's going to be fine."

"Another close one." He's not an emotional man, but I hear a shudder when he blows out a breath. "What am I going to do with you?"

I do smile then. "Tomasetti, if I didn't know better, I might just think you were smitten with the chief of police."

"No doubt about it." He looks down the hall to where two deputies are carrying on a conversation. "Pretty inconvenient that there are so many people around," he says in a low voice.

"That we're standing in a public hall at the Holmes County Sheriff's Department definitely doesn't help."

"What do you say we remedy that?" He

reaches into his pocket for his keys. "Need a ride home?"

"Agent Tomasetti, that's the best offer I've had all day."

Drizzle floats from a misty black sky as we cross the parking lot to his Tahoe. He opens my door, but stops me before I can get in. Gently, he backs me against the side of the vehicle, presses his body against mine, then sets his hands on either side of my face.

"You scared the hell out of me," he says.

"I'm sorry. I tried to call—"

He quiets me with a kiss that quickly deepens to . . . something else. As if of their own accord, my arms go around his neck and I pour everything I have into the kiss, into the moment, into him, and for a second I'm rendered incapable of containing the love I feel for him.

He breaks the kiss, pulls back, and looks down at me as if I've done something to awe him. "If it's not too much to ask, could you forgo the getting shot?"

"I'll do my best. Up my game if I can."

"If it's all the same to you, I'd like to keep you around for a while."

Loving the warm and solid feel of him against me, I touch the side of his face, brush my fingertips over his mouth. "How long exactly?"

"A couple of lifetimes." He grins. "For starters."

"I think that's the plan."

Never taking his eyes from mine, he steps aside and opens the door of the Tahoe. "Let's go home."

CHAPTER 29

Being placed on administrative leave after an officer-involved shooting is a uniquely terrible position for a police officer. For a span of time—usually days, but sometimes weeks—you're ousted from a job that is a huge part of your life. You no longer have interaction with coworkers who are more like family. You have too much time to think about what happened and relive every horrifying moment. Worst of all, you spend that time second-guessing your every decision, your every move.

I understand the protocol. I'm a firm believer that all critical incidents should be thoroughly investigated by an outside, independent agency. None of that makes it any easier to get through.

It's dawn when I let myself into the chicken house at the farm, wire basket in hand to gather eggs. Four of our hens are still in their nesting boxes. The rest are pecking around on the ground. From where I'm standing, I see at least five eggs that were laid overnight.

"You girls have been busy," I say.

The hens cluck in annoyance as I shoo them through the door and into the yard so they can free-range the rest of the day. And, of course, so I can gather eggs without getting my hand pecked.

I'm thinking about the wedding tomorrow morning, trying not to worry about all the things I didn't get done. On another level, I'm also thinking about Mona, considering calling her when my cell phone jangles from the back pocket of my jeans. Setting down the basket, I tug it out, and look at the display. I don't recognize the number, but I hit the Talk button and answer with, "Burkholder."

"I've been thinking about what you said."

It takes me a moment to identify the voice as belonging to Mandi Yoder, the young woman who, according to bartender Jimmie Baines, was assaulted by Aden Karn in the parking lot of the Brass Rail Saloon.

"What can I do for you?" I ask.

"I'm ready to talk."

A pause ensues. I get the impression she's wishing she hadn't called. That she's still on the fence about telling her story. I want to encourage her, but I know if I push too hard, she'll hang up and the opportunity will be lost.

"I'm listening," I say after a moment.

"Aden Karn was a bad dude," she tells me.

Around me, everything goes silent; my every sense is laser focused on the voice on the other end. "Tell me what happened."

The silence goes on for so long that I think she's hung up on me. Then she whispers, "I've been to the gas station. I went there one night with Karn. There were a bunch of guys there. We . . . it was a nightmare."

I hold the phone against my ear, close my eyes against a burst of emotion as the final piece of the puzzle falls into place. The one that will tie up the loose ends and ensure every guilty party is held accountable.

"Do you have any names?" I ask.

"All of them."

I take a deep breath, let it out slowly. "Would you be willing to talk to Sheriff Rasmussen about what happened?"

"I was hoping to talk to you . . ."

"I'm on administrative leave," I tell her.

"I dunno," she says quickly. "Maybe I should just—"

"Mandi, Mike Rasmussen is a good man. He's honest. Fair-minded."

"Will you be there?"

"If I can." I wait a beat. "I'll set everything up. Later today?"

Another sigh hisses over the line. "Okay."

"Thank you."

She hangs up without replying.

CHAPTER 30

My *mamm* had a lot of sayings about a lot of things, including weddings. One of her favorites went something like, *En die ehe kann sei gmacht in Himmel avvah mann is verantwortlich fa da hochzich*, which in English translates to: A marriage may be made in heaven, but man is responsible for the wedding. As a kid, I didn't understand the meaning of the idiom. This morning, I've never understood those words more fully or had more appreciation for them.

I'm in the passenger seat of the Tahoe, trying not to fidget as Tomasetti takes it up the gravel lane toward the house where I grew up. He's wearing a nice black suit this morning. White shirt. Skinny black tie. It's as Plain as he gets. I'm wearing the dress my grandmother made. After the alterations and a little back-and-forth, I have to admit, it's perfect. Black shoes with low heels. Not Amish, but not quite English. Like me.

"The Amish turned out in force," Tomasetti murmurs.

A tremor of nerves moves through me at the sight of dozens of black buggies lined up in neat rows in the paddock Jacob opened up for parking. It's the same paddock our parents used when worship was held here at the farm when I was a kid. Several vehicles are parked in the gravel area near the house. I see Glock's cruiser. Doc Coblentz's Escalade. A Holmes County Sheriff's Department SUV. Three more vehicles belonging to my dispatchers. The sight of Mona's Ford Escape conjures a heartfelt smile.

"I suspect this may be one of the most unconventional weddings most of them have ever attended," I say.

"I'm sure they expect nothing less," Tomasetti says.

Though some of the Amish may sing a hymn or two, there will be no sermon this morning. The ceremony will be delivered by a Mennonite minister and will last only a few minutes. Lunch and the socializing that follows, however, will likely last several hours, which explains the presence of the two young hostlers. They're Amish boys of about twelve or thirteen who are charged with unharnessing the buggy horses, putting them into one of the lower paddocks, and supplying them with hay and water.

As we make the final turn, I realize the farm where I grew up has been transformed. Dozens of tables and chairs have been set up in the side yard—picnic tables, worktables, card tables, and chairs of every size and variety. Vaguely, I recall telling my sister I wanted to have the reception outside, weather permitting, and she came through—Amish-style. A woman in a blue dress sets vases of celery on the tables. Another is carrying a tray of pies to what looks like a dessert table. Two more women are setting up a beverage station—a cooler for water, plastic glasses, coffee, and pitchers of iced tea. It's a spectacle of organized chaos and once again I'm reminded of my *mamm*'s words.

A marriage may be made in heaven, but man is responsible for the wedding.

I was absent for most of the preparations. Tied up with the Karn and Rossberger cases, and not for the first time the enormity of the effort that went into all of this hits home. The meaning of that takes my breath away and I struggle to find my voice. "This is undoubtedly one of the most hands-off weddings in the history of womankind," I hear myself say.

"You were a little busy with a couple of homicides," Tomasetti mutters.

We haven't talked much about the cases. Yesterday, Wayne Graber was officially charged with the murder of Aden Karn, felonious assault for the attack against me, and the attempted murder of a police officer. Mandi Yoder came through and agreed to be interviewed by Sheriff Rasmussen. Thanks to her bombshell testimony, Vernon Fisher now faces a slew of new charges. Four of the other men who spent time at the now-infamous gas station were arrested.

I spent an hour or so with Emily and her

mother. I told them what I could about Karn. I can only hope the truth, however painful, will help with the healing process. I don't believe the girl will ever come forward with her own story, but the door is open if she changes her mind.

"Looks like we're in for one hell of a party." Tomasetti's voice pulls me from my reverie.

The barn door stands open wide. Inside, I see rows of benches and chairs, men and women milling about, making sure everything is in just the right place. I can't help but think of the Amish girl I'd been, sitting on one of those very same benches, feeling like an outsider and utterly certain love would never come my way. The quiver of emotion that follows is so profound, I set my hand against my chest if only to still my heart.

"The Amish know how to put on a wedding," I manage.

Tomasetti parks next to a red PT Cruiser and arches a brow.

"Pastor Tom," I tell him.

"Feels like I should have met him by now," he says.

"I think we're just going to wing it."

"Good thing that's our specialty."

I see him staring at something in the near distance and follow his gaze. An earthquake of emotion trembles through me at the sight of

Bishop Troyer. Using his walker, the old man hobbles toward the barn.

"I'll be damned," Tomasetti murmurs. "Looks like the old guy made it, after all."

I almost can't believe my eyes, and I have to blink back tears. "I hope he knows how much that means to us."

"Maybe we'll get the chance to tell him." He shuts down the engine. "You ready?"

I'm aware of my pulse running too fast. Heat on the back of my neck. My palms are wet and I resist the urge to wipe them on the skirt of my dress.

Smiling, he takes my hand, raises the other, and wipes a tear off my cheek with his thumb. "If I didn't know better, Chief Burkholder, I'd say you're nervous."

" 'Terrified nervous wreck' might be a little more accurate."

"Says the woman who faced down a crazy guy with a crossbow."

"What about you?" I ask.

"Am I nervous?" Taking his time, he leans toward the rearview mirror to straighten his tie. "The only thing I'm nervous about is this tie. Do you think it's right with this shirt?"

The laugh that pours out of me eases the nerves. "Definitely right for an almost-Amish wedding," I say.

"In that case." He lifts my hand and brushes a

kiss across my knuckles. "You know we've got this, right?"

"Piece of cake," I whisper.

He looks through the window to watch two Amish men carry a bench into the barn. "What do you say we put everyone out of their misery and go tie the knot?"

"I say that's the best idea you've had all day," I whisper.

Leaning close, he kisses me, and then we get out of the Tahoe and start toward the barn.

ACKNOWLEDGMENTS

I owe untold thanks to my publishing family at Minotaur Books. First and foremost, I wish to thank my editor, Charles Spicer, who just happens to be the best editor on earth. Many thanks to my wonderful agent, Nancy Yost—I appreciate you and your friendship more than you know. To the rest of the team at Minotaur Books, my gratitude and heartfelt thanks for the support and for doing what you do so very well on my behalf: Jennifer Enderlin. Andrew Martin. Sally Richardson. Sarah Melnyk. Sarah Grill. Hannah Pierdolla. Kerry Nordling. Paul Hochman. Allison Ziegler. Kelley Ragland. David Baldeosingh Rotstein. Marta Fleming. Martin Quinn. Joseph Brosnan. Lisa Davis. My sincerest thanks to all.

Center Point Large Print
600 Brooks Road / PO Box 1
Thorndike, ME 04986-0001 USA

(207) 568-3717

US & Canada:
1 800 929-9108
www.centerpointlargeprint.com

31659061892770

An evil heart

MCN LargeP FIC Castillo **31659061892770**

DUE DATE	MCN	12/23	40.95

PRI